CW00521768

The Scorched Girls

Law of Sandtown, Volume 1

M K Farrar

Published by Castle View Press, 2023.

THE SCORCHED GIRLS

First edition. September 18, 2023.

Written by M K Farrar.

Chapter One

Raye Diante dipped his brush into the large tub of paint, then swept his arm in an arc, splattering the canvas with a red the same shade as blood.

As was his signature style, his painting was of the desert on a large canvas. He guessed some would call it abstract art—in that it wasn't immediately obvious what the image was—but it made sense to him.

He stepped back to take in the whole picture and tugged down the hem of his short-shorts, ensuring his butt cheeks were covered.

Raye didn't class himself as a transvestite or even a drag queen, he simply enjoyed how he felt in what society called women's clothing. His cowboy boots hit mid-calf, exposing what he thought to be a great set of legs. They were bare right up to the frayed bottoms of his washed-out denim Daisy-Duke shorts. His top was equally revealing, showing off his naval and abs, and today his long hair was braided, Viking style, as was the style of his makeup, with black eyeliner ringing his baby-blue eyes. He considered his eyes to be his best feature, which was saying a lot, as he generally thought all his features were pretty damned good.

It was four in the morning, but the small town around him was far from sleeping. After the sun went down was when Sandtown, California, came to life.

It took a special kind of person to live in the middle of the desert during the summer. In the daytime, temperatures rose to more than a hundred degrees, and it was impossible to do much other than sleep under the misting systems that most of the long-termers had installed around their trailer homes.

Raye used the nights to work.

He sold his art to tourists who came to gawp at the place many considered to be the last lawless town in America. It made him chuckle how much people were willing to pay for something that only took him a matter of hours. It wasn't that he didn't put much effort into his work, but he painted in a flurry of energy and excitement, caught up in the moment, so the piece was completed quickly.

The tourists thought it made them cool to take a real part of Sandtown home with them.

Raye took pride in his work, and not every piece made it to the small store he ran off the side of his trailer home. He didn't even need much money, especially since he was clean now. Most of it went to gas or the generator, or food and water, or simply more painting supplies. He didn't want for much.

The nearest grocery store was a Mini-Mart four miles away in a town called Calrock. The residents of Sandtown didn't have the infrastructure to keep substantial quantities of food chilled or frozen for any length of time, so they did runs into town, often picking things up for their friends and neighbors to save too many unnecessary trips. Gas was expensive these days, and though they lived in RVs and campers, they didn't all have separate vehicles as well.

Raye rinsed off his brush and dipped the bristles into the yellow paint pot this time.

Before the paint reached the canvas, he stopped, lifted his chin, and sniffed the air. Above the sharp tang of paint and denatured alcohol, something was burning.

That wasn't unusual in itself. People often had bonfires, sometimes to destroy trash, other times to simply party around. The smoke in the air didn't smell like a bonfire, though. It was different, and his skin prickled with awareness that something wasn't quite right.

Raye lowered the brush and dunked it back in the denatured alcohol to prevent it drying out. He picked up a cloth, wiped his hands, then headed outside.

His neighbor, DeeDee, sat out on a hammock, reading a book by a small lamp and swatting away the numerous bugs attracted by the light. A crocheted rug covered most of her body as protection against the night chill. She was a skinny woman who could be anywhere from forty to sixty. Whenever he'd tried to find out, she'd tapped the side of her nose and said, 'That's only for me to know.'

She noticed him standing there. "You okay, sweetie?"

Raye frowned. "I'm not sure. You smelling that? Something's burning."

DeeDee worked in fashion, altering old items of clothing she picked up—making bags out of old pairs of jeans, or dresses out of oversized t-shirts. Her shop—which was another trailer—was where he'd gotten his short-shorts from. They all had to make a living some way or another. More recently, a few of them had started doing online work, even making YouTube channels about their lives out in Sandtown, but for the most part, the long-termers, known as Sanders, still made their money selling items to tourists or each other.

DeeDee sat up and put her book to one side. "It'll just be them over at The Crowbar, won't it? Partying, as usual."

The club, located on the other side of town, often had live music, provided by the residents of Sandtown. The bands and singers didn't get paid to play—it was simply something they enjoyed. Hella Billy—an ex-biker from Florida—ran The Crowbar and had done so for years.

"Nah, that's more like metal burning," Raye said.

Clutching the blanket around her, DeeDee swung her legs out of the hammock and got to her feet. She craned her neck as though hoping to spot something. "Maybe someone's set fire to one of the old vehicles on the outskirts of town. Teens screwing around. You know what they can be like once they've got a few drinks, or something a bit stronger, into them."

She was probably right, but Raye couldn't shake the feeling that something was off.

"I think I'm gonna check it out," he told her.

She shrugged one shoulder. "Be my guest."

Raye grabbed a light jacket from his trailer and headed along the road in the direction he thought the smoke was coming from. None of the roads in Sandtown had been paved, but they'd all been driven on so much now that the sand and dirt had compacted into a solid surface.

Though most people who lived here year round started their homes in a trailer, most expanded their living space with more permanent structures created out of whatever they could get their hands on. Raye had been in Sandtown for six years now, but before that he'd spent most of his forty years homeless, trying to get by in Los Angeles. Like many of the other Sanders, he'd had issues around alcohol and drugs, something that had been the result of mental health issues since he was a teen. His brother had found this place for him and loaned him the money to buy the trailer which was now his home. Raye didn't know where he'd be without that helping hand.

Most likely dead.

As he walked, he noted the art that was everywhere. It was one of the things he loved about Sandtown. Bright graffiti covered the sides of the trailers and RVs, and pretty much anything else that was standing still long enough for someone to paint. Metal scrap work had been turned into sculptures and art installations created out of them.

Sandtown was a mecca for creative people, but also people who struggled in normal society. Drug and alcohol use were rife, as was crime. People got desperate, and there was no police department here. The inhabitants of Sandtown took care of those who wronged them in their own way.

Raye nodded his hellos and lifted his hand to those residents who acknowledged him passing. He didn't ask any of them about the fire, aware he'd most likely get pulled into a conversation and it would delay him actually finding out if his suspicions were right.

An endless expanse of stars stretched overhead. He thought it was the most beautiful thing in the world. Kind of ironic that the most beautiful thing in the world wasn't actually part of the world, but something beyond it. He'd never known so many stars even existed before he'd moved out here; the light pollution in Los Angeles meant he hadn't been able to see them. Strange how something that was supposed to help you see actually made you more blind to what was really out there.

In the distance, an orange glow lit the desert sky.

That direction was nowhere near the club, or the pile of abandoned vehicles that were basically metal shells now. The glow looked like it was coming from one of the trailers.

"You okay, Raye?" Nelson, an older skinny man who ran the garage, called out to him.

Raye didn't pause his pace but called out, "I think one of the trailers is on fire!"

As a rule, Raye didn't run. He couldn't remember the last time he walked at anything more than a brisk pace, but he found his legs moving faster than they had in a long time. Tension ramped up, and his heart beat faster, his mouth running dry.

He turned a bend, bringing him to one of the areas of town that normally served the snowbirds. Most of the sites were empty this time of year, waiting to be filled by those who only arrived when the cooler months did.

But there was one trailer sitting there. And it was burning.

The orange glow in the trailer's windows wasn't anything like an electric light, and it was far too bright to be that of candles. The way it flickered and moved, like a living thing, jolted something inside him.

"Fire!" Raye yelled, picking up his pace. "There's a fire!"

He racked his brains to try and remember who owned the trailer but drew a blank. Old Fitz used to have this spot, but he'd died going on twelve months ago now. His old body couldn't take the heat anymore, and he'd finally succumbed to it. The site had been standing empty for months after that. It had only been recently that someone else had taken the spot, but for the life of him, Raye couldn't remember who. People were always coming and going from Sandtown. During the summer months, like now, there tended to only be a couple of hundred of the long-termers here, but in the winter months, the numbers swelled to the thousands. It was impossible to keep track of everyone.

The shout of 'fire' had brought others out of their homes, and now he found he wasn't alone. Other residents had joined him, so he'd created a trail of them behind him.

Living somewhere as dry and hot as Sandtown, and being a long way from any fire department, fire could do some serious damage. One of the other long-termers—another artist, but one who worked with metal, called Tye Guess—lost his entire home and workshop not so long ago because he'd left a chunk of glass in a spot that had magnified the sun, and a nearby piece of paperwork had caught fire. They'd been lucky in that it hadn't spread to any nearby properties, but the place had been burned to the ground, and poor Tye had been forced to start over.

More people came running—most of whom he'd known for years. DeeDee had left her hammock and joined them, as had Nelson Buccani, the mechanic. Raye even spotted some of the guys from the club. News of the disturbance had got them on their motorbikes to check it out.

"Who's got a phone?" someone shouted. "Call nine-one-one."

Raye shook his head. "We don't have time for that. The whole place will be gone by the time the fire department arrives."

"Is anyone living there?" DeeDee asked.

"Yeah," Nelson said, "it's that young couple. The ones who arrived a couple of months ago."

"Fuck." Raye looked around, hoping he would see them standing with everyone else. "Are they in there? Has anyone seen them?"

DeeDee's face crumpled with worry. "I don't know. We need some water. Someone gets some buckets."

"Water's not going to do it," Raye said. "We need fire extinguishers."

"I've got one in my trailer," someone shouted and was met with replies of, "Me too."

The small group burst into action, most likely happy to have something productive to do. The fire appeared to be contained down one end of the trailer for the moment, but it wouldn't stay that way for long. If the young couple was still inside, the fire—or more likely the smoke—would kill them.

Not thinking, Raye ran up to the trailer door and grabbed the handle. For a split second, his brain couldn't seem to process if what he was touching was freezing cold or burning hot, but then the pain hit him. He let out a yell and snatched his hand away again. A bright-red line ran across his palm.

Fuck.

He stared at the handle. The door hadn't moved during the brief time he'd grabbed it. Why was that? Had the heat welded the door shut? Or was it locked?

"Hey!" he shouted. "Is anyone in there? You need to get out. There's a fire!"

Would anyone inside even still be alive? He couldn't imagine what the temperature was like inside the trailer.

He yanked off his top and wrapped it around his hand as protection and tried again. The material protected his skin, at least momentarily, before he had to let go. It was long enough for him to know that the door wasn't opening.

"Shit. It won't open." He turned to the others, hoping one of them would come up with an idea about what to do next.

A couple of the men had returned with full-sized fire extinguishers.

"Someone break down the door!" a woman shouted.

"Or smash a window," Nelson suggested.

"Won't that make things worse?" said DeeDee. "I thought you weren't supposed to allow oxygen on a fire."

Nelson stared at her. "How can we make things fucking worse? The whole trailer is burning up."

Someone picked up a large rock—there were plenty lying around—and smashed one of the windows. Smoke billowed out, toxic black plumes into the desert night, and instinctively, Raye ducked. The flames grew larger, but then someone stuck the hose of the fire extinguisher through the hole the smashed glass had left and let out a blast.

Raye didn't think there was any possible way it would work, but amazingly, they at least seemed to be containing the fire.

Had the couple locked it from the inside, and had there been an accident, maybe a candle caught a drape or something and they were too out of it to notice? Smoke killed more people than fire in these situations, though the fire would have done a number on their bodies by now as well.

Or had someone else started the fire and locked the couple in there?

The young woman who lived closest to the burning trailer spoke up.

"I saw them fighting in front of their trailer earlier tonight," Stormi said. "The two of them were screaming at each other. The guy got right up in the girl's face. I was considering intervening, but then she turned around and ran back inside."

All kinds of scenarios ran through Raye's head. Had the man done something to the girl and then started the fire to cover his tracks? Could the fire have been started on purpose?

One thing about the Sanders, when they needed to come together, they did, and they did it well.

"Has anyone got a flashlight?" he asked. "I need to get inside."

Someone handed him one.

Hella Billy, who was well over six feet tall and almost as wide, stepped forward. "Let me."

He had a metal rod that he jammed in the doorframe and used his strength to crack the lock. Something caught, and Billy brought the rod down again, and the door flew open.

More smoke billowed out. It caught in the back of Raye's throat, and he coughed, doubling over. He held the back of his hand to his mouth.

"Don't go in there, Raye," Nelson called to him.

"I have to check. Someone might need help."

Deep down, he knew that if anyone had been inside during the fire, they'd be dead by now, but if he didn't check, it would forever play on his mind that maybe he could have saved someone.

He stumbled up the steps, keeping his head down and his mouth covered. The heat was intense. The metal of the trailer was still hot. His eyes streamed with the toxic smoke, and he did his best not to inhale. They'd managed to keep the worst of the fire confined to the bedroom, but there was still a huge amount of damage.

He turned toward the bedroom. The fire had burned a hole through the top panel of the door, and through the gap, and the smoke, Raye was able to make out the room beyond.

In what remained of the bed, lay the scorched figures of the young couple.

They were well beyond saving.

Chapter Two

"You have got to be fucking kidding me."

Lawrey Winters groaned as she rolled over in bed and grappled for her phone. The ringtone had infiltrated her dream—an enjoyable one, as far as she recalled—but had followed her into wakefulness.

"Yeah?" she answered, her voice thick with sleep.

"Sarge, we've had a call come in about a possible double homicide over in Sandtown."

She sat up, her heart immediately racing.

"Tommy?" she asked.

She'd known Iris Bartlett, the woman on the phone, her entire life, and didn't need to explain who Tommy was. Half the town had witnessed what Lawrey had gone through with the boy.

"Not that I'm aware of. Young couple, apparently."

Lawrey's son lived in Sandtown, which was located about four miles northeast of her hometown of Calrock. He was twenty-six years old now and a full-grown adult, but that didn't stop her worrying about him. They'd had some rough times in the past.

Tommy wasn't in a relationship, at least not one he'd told his mother about, so she hoped that meant the incident didn't involve him. She supposed that wasn't unusual—he didn't tell her about much in his life. She normally only learned about things later, when she was picking up the pieces.

She glanced at her bedside clock. It was after five in the morning.

"I'll be right there."

She hadn't gone to bed until after midnight, sitting up drinking a beer and trying to forget her shitshow of a life by watching Netflix. She'd run into her ex-husband, Patrick, at the store, which was fine in itself—they were still on friendly terms—except that he'd been with his new, thirty-year-old wife. Lawrey didn't like to think she was one to judge, but a fifteen-year age difference seemed like too much to her. She and Patrick had grown up together, had been sweethearts in high school and got married as soon as they'd finished. Tommy had been born not long after, when they were both only nineteen. Everyone said it wouldn't last and, of course, they'd been right. Lawrey's stubborn streak had set in, however, and she'd refused to give up on the relationship, even when the pair of them were barely speaking. It had been Tommy who'd come between them in the end. Patrick couldn't deal with him any longer and had said it was either him or their son. Lawrey didn't hesitate in making that choice.

Lawrey swung her legs out of bed, pulled on the pants and shirt that were over the back of the chair in the corner. She went into the bathroom to relieve herself, washed her face and hands at the sink, and then dragged her wavy, mousy-brown hair into a ponytail. She didn't wear makeup—could barely remember if she even owned any or when the last time was she'd bothered to apply some. She didn't have time for that shit anyway.

She rubbed at her eyes and squinted. Fuck, she felt like she was getting old. Her vision used to be twenty-twenty, but now she was having to hold things at a certain length to read them and struggled to make out signs at a distance, too. She needed to make an appointment and get her eyes tested, but it was another thing to go on the list of things she never seemed to have time for.

The air-conditioning unit made a strange clunking sound, and Lawrey glanced over her shoulder.

"Don't you fucking dare," she warned it.

The last thing she needed was for it to die on her. Temperatures were in the eighties last night, and that was with the sun down. She wouldn't sleep a wink if she didn't have the air.

Lawrey would have liked to take a coffee with her, but she didn't have time for that either. She grabbed her car keys off the side and headed for the front door. Before she'd even made it outside, her cell phone rang once more. She checked the screen.

It was her partner, Abel.

"Hey," she answered. "I'm on my way."

"I am *not* happy about being woken up at this time," he grumbled.

"You think I am?"

"Fucking Sanders causing trouble again. That place should be shut down."

"They normally take care of their own shit, Abel. That we've been called out makes me think something serious has gone down."

"I don't know why I even have to be there. None of them will talk to me anyway. They'll only want to talk to you, and that's only if you catch them in a talking mood."

It was true. The long-termers out in Sandtown didn't like the police. Most of them had a rap sheet as long as her arm, and plenty had experienced something that had made them mistrustful of the cops. The only reason she had an in was because of Tommy. People liked Tommy, despite his issues, and of course Tommy vouched for her.

"You want me to pick you up on the way?" she asked.

"Sure thing, Law."

The sun was breaching the horizon as she left the house. Her hometown of Calrock was a relatively small town with several thousand residents. Within ten minutes, she pulled up outside her partner's house. It was a single-story, wooden structure, with a wraparound porch and a swing seat that Marlene always used to inhabit during the day, but Abel currently occupied. He got to his feet as she stopped the car, his gut straining against the front of his shirt. He was about five years older than her and heading for retirement, and he'd always made no attempt to hide the fact that he couldn't wait. Things had changed for him recently, however, and now the idea of retirement didn't hold the same shine it once had.

Lawrey didn't bother to get out. Abel rounded the vehicle and got into the passenger seat. He let out a large sigh, as though the weight of the world was on his shoulders, which right now, Lawrey knew was true.

"How's Marlene doing?" she asked before she drove off.

"Oh, you know. Not so good. She's sleeping a lot, but I think that's mostly down to the meds."

Marlene was Abel's wife of the past thirty years and had been diagnosed with terminal cancer a couple of months earlier.

"The kids have been great," he continued, "checking in whenever they get the chance. I told you that Suze has moved back in with us now, to help out. We can't leave Marlene on her own for too long these days."

"Yes, you said. That must be hard on Suze as well."

"It is, but she's a good kid."

The 'kid' he referred to was about the same age as Tommy, but Lawrey knew what he meant. Suze had given up her life in the city to come home and take care of her mother in her final days. It wasn't easy for any of them.

She reached over and patted his hand. "Marlene is lucky to have you all."

He sniffed and shook his head. "Nah, we've been the lucky ones. I can't imagine what our lives would have been like without her. This is the absolute least we can do."

Lawrey did her best not to put herself in Marlene's position and failed. What would happen if she got sick like that? Who would take care of her? She had her mother, but the two of them butted heads like a pair of baby goats, and Tommy definitely wouldn't be in any fit state to take care of her. It wasn't something she could ask of her ex either, and she could hardly see the new wife being happy with him moving back in with his childhood sweetheart to nurse her through her final days. She had friends—good friends—but it wouldn't seem right to put something like that on them. That kind of thing was what family were for.

She'd probably look toward her sister, but Maddie had enough on her hands with two teenagers who liked to push the boundaries.

"Let's do this," she said, "so you can get back to your wife."

"Yeah, and before it gets too damned hot."

Lawrey cranked up the air and pulled back out onto the street.

They drove the paved but potholed road to Sandtown. It wasn't difficult to spot where the incident had happened. A trail of gray smoke curled into the sky like a signal.

The fire department, which was located another town south from Calrock, had gotten there before them, as had uniformed police, who had created a cordon around the trailer. The trouble with fires was that they destroyed evidence, and it wasn't only the fire responsible, but the water that was invariably used to put the fire out again. It destroyed fingerprints, footprints, and DNA, and then the water moved everything around so they could never be one hundred percent sure of the position of even the bodies by the time they got forensics in there.

She stopped the car a short distance away and climbed out.

There was more of the trailer remaining than she'd expected. It wasn't quite a blackened shell, but if it had been left much longer, it would have been.

"What the hell happened here?" Abel wondered.

She jumped to the most obvious possibility. "Could be two people were smoking, got too wasted, and set fire to their own trailer while they were passed out. Wouldn't be the first time it had happened."

Abel arched a bushy eyebrow at her. "Wouldn't be the first time someone in Sandtown set fire to a trailer to run someone out of town either."

"True, but they normally wait until the owners of the trailer are out."

The fire had attracted a crowd of residents, who stood by, watching the scene uneasily, speaking in low voices to one another. They wouldn't like seeing the police here. Automatically, Lawrey found herself searching for her son's face, but that wasn't the only thing she was looking for. How often did someone commit a crime like this and stay with the crowd to see the result of their work?

"Get some photos of them," she told Abel. "We don't know who might be watching."

"Will do, Sarge."

They would need to get the bodies to the morgue as soon as possible. Dead bodies and temperatures of over one hundred degrees did not make for a good combination.

A uniformed sergeant who was in charge of the scene noticed them arrive. Darrell Potts hoisted up his pants and strolled over. He thought a lot of himself and moved with a swagger he didn't deserve.

Lawrey had worked with him on plenty of occasions, and she wasn't afraid to admit she didn't like the man. He was one of those cops who thought everyone was below him, and he didn't hold back on his disdain for the people who lived in Sandtown. She wasn't sure if he was intentional about that, given that her son was one of those people, or if he'd simply forgotten.

"What have we got, Darrell?" she asked.

"Fire was noticed shortly after four this morning by the Sandtown residents. They managed to break a window and get it contained with a couple of fire extinguishers until the fire department arrived. Two bodies were then discovered in the bed. Fire looks like it started in the bedroom, but we can't be sure right now."

"Have you called in the arson squad?" she asked.

"Yeah, but they're having to come in from out of town, so they won't be here until this afternoon, at the earliest."

"Damn it."

She bet they could get here sooner, but they'd seen the location of the fire and decided there was no rush. She made a mental note to get on the phone and tell them to hurry it up.

"Any idea who the victims are yet?" she asked.

Darrell glanced back over at the small crowd of residents. "Locals say they're a young couple, names of Stephan and Emily, but we don't have any surnames yet. I'm sure it won't be too hard to figure out."

She agreed. "We can run what remains of the plates and hopefully find some ID inside, too."

"Goddamn, I can't believe it's this hot so early," Darrell said, flapping his hand in front of his face. "Going to be another scorcher."

"That tends to be how it is in the summer when you're in the middle of the desert, Darrell," she pointed out.

He didn't seem to pick up on the sarcasm in her tone. "Yeah, let's get this wrapped up as quickly as possible so we can all get home. I don't want to be out in this heat a moment longer than necessary."

No one cared much about the residents of Sandtown. She knew a lot of the opinion of people in nearby towns was that whatever happened to them, it was most likely because they deserved it. They brought it upon themselves. There was little patience among the local authorities for them, and even less when they were pulled out of their beds in the early hours and sent to investigate all the way out here.

That wasn't how Lawrey felt, however.

"Two people are dead," she said. "You might be uncomfortable, Darrell, but at least you're still breathing. We won't be rushing through this just 'cause you can't handle a little heat."

He raised an eyebrow in her direction. "Seriously, Law? They probably burned themselves up, fucking idiots. Stoned and drunk and left a cigarette lit."

"Until we know that for sure, we'll be treating this investigation no differently than we would if it had been a fire at your neighbor's house. Got it?"

"Yes, ma'am," he said, though his tone was laced with sarcasm.

"Good."

She wouldn't say it out loud, but she wished she could get inside, too. The heat at this time of year was completely draining. She'd happily hibernate through the summer months, if she could, but she was needed.

The desert heat, together with the heat from the still smoldering trailer, was on a whole other level. She didn't much believe in God or the Devil, but she thought if there was a Hell, it was standing in the heat of a still-smoking trailer in the middle of the desert.

Lawrey opened the trunk of her car and took out a couple of sets of protective outerwear. While she didn't want to add another layer of clothing when she was already sweating, they needed to protect the crime scene. This might have been an accident, but until she knew for sure what they were dealing with, she'd treat it as a possible homicide.

"Let's take a look."

She and Abel pulled on the protective outerwear, ducked under the inner cordon, and approached the trailer, where the door already stood open. Darrell had followed behind.

"Residents say they had to break the door down to get in," Darrell said. "Might have been the heat sealed it shut, though."

She moved slowly and cautiously, taking in the details. The specialist arson squad would be the ones who thoroughly investigated the cause and origin of the fire, but since they wouldn't be here for a while, she made sure to scribble in her notebook about whatever details might help. Arson scenes were difficult to investigate.

Before she'd even got inside fully, something on the doorframe caught her attention.

"Check this out," she said.

A broken security chain, snapped in two, hung from the frame.

"That answers one question then, doesn't it," Abel said.

"And what's that?"

"That they must have done this to themselves. If they locked the door and put a security chain on, someone else didn't set fire to the trailer."

She shook her head. "We can't know that for sure. We don't even know where the fire originated from yet. Maybe a window was open, and someone threw a lit match inside while they were sleeping and then they closed it again. Or they set the fire underneath the trailer. Right now, we're assuming the smoke and fire is what killed them, but until we've had the autopsy done, we can't assume that either."

"You think someone might have killed them and then set the fire to cover their tracks?"

"I'm saying we don't know anything for sure yet, so let's keep an open mind."

The water from the fire hoses had done enough to cool down the trailer to allow them to enter. She climbed the few steps that led into the body of the home. She tried not to think too hard about the odor of grilled meat that hung on the air. Though the fire department had put the fire out, the body of the trailer had retained the heat. That, combined with the smell, was cloying.

Everything had been blackened with soot, and they had to tread carefully. The fire could have easily weakened or destroyed any floorboard joists.

"Could we be looking at a meth lab fire?" Abel suggested. "It wouldn't be the first time someone's been found to be cooking in Sandtown. Plenty of trailers burn down that way."

She took in her surroundings. "Possibly, but I don't see any equipment around here. That's not to say it's not drug related, but I'd at least expect to see some beakers or funnels or a Bunsen burner, but there's no evidence of that."

"Maybe someone cleared it out first."

"But then why start the fire?"

"Punishment? Someone might have been encroaching on someone else's turf."

She shook her head slowly. "I don't know, I'm not getting a meth lab fire. This place looks too much like someone's home. That doesn't mean to say this isn't drug related, though. Plenty of the crimes around here are."

One end of the trailer was relatively untouched, other than the smoke damage, but the other was visibly charred. The bedroom door had been shut when the fire started—something that had most likely saved the rest of the trailer from being completely destroyed—though the panels had burned through by the time they'd put the fire out.

Careful not to touch anything, Lawrey climbed through the hole in the door, then straightened. Directly ahead was what remained of the bed.

The bodies of the two victims weren't completely charred, but the damage done was bad enough that they wouldn't be easily recognizable to anyone who didn't know them intimately. They lay, side by side, on a mattress that was also partially destroyed by both the fire and the subsequent water used to extinguish it. It was impossible to tell with the naked eye if there were any other injuries to the bodies. They'd have to wait for the autopsy report to get that kind of information.

What had happened here? Were the victims alive when the fire started? If so, why hadn't they made any attempt to escape? This wasn't the first fire Lawrey had attended, and she doubted it would be the last. Normally, she'd expect to find the bodies in various positions, where they'd attempted to flee the fire. In this one, she'd have thought they'd have at least tried to get to the door. Maybe they wouldn't have been able to open it; it was easy to become disoriented in a fire. But it was unlikely for them to lie there and do nothing.

She said as much to Abel, who had followed her in.

"Maybe the smoke got them first," he suggested. "Carbon monoxide poisoning knocked them unconscious, and then the fire started later."

"It's possible, but there's something about how the bodies are laid out. How do you sleep, Abel?"

"In whatever position I can get most comfortable in," he replied.

"I sleep on my side."

Both victims' limbs had curled in, drawing up toward their chests. It was caused by the heat and common in burn victims. Even so, it was clear they were both lying on their backs.

"If the smoke had got to them, or they suffered from carbon monoxide poisoning, do you think they would have both been lying side by side in bed like that? Neither of them lying on their fronts or side, or curled up against the other one? If they'd been coughing, maybe one would have even been hanging partly off the bed?" She walked around the other side of the mattress to study the male victim.

"Do you know what this reminds me of," she said, glancing over at her partner.

"What?" Abel asked.

"They look like two people who've been placed in their coffins."

Chapter Three

L awrey was relieved to be out of the trailer.

The stench of smoke clung to her skin and hair, combining with the sour tang of sweat. Already, the sun was fully up, bright and hot, and she found herself squinting against it and raising her arm to shelter her eyes.

She stripped off the protective outerwear, happy to be rid of it.

"I don't think we're looking at an accident," she told Darrell, who'd hung around outside the whole time. "We're going to need to hurry up that arson squad. What about the medical examiner?"

"They've all been called, but I can't do much more than that. Why do you think this wasn't an accident?"

She filled him in on her observations.

He narrowed his eyes. "You think this is a homicide because of the way they're positioned on the bed?"

"A suspected homicide."

She glanced over at the crowd of Sandtown residents. It had thinned slightly since she'd first arrived, but there were still plenty of people around. She recognized a number of them, since this wasn't her first visit or investigation in Sandtown. Only a month earlier, she'd been involved in one of the town's few children going missing. It hadn't been pleasant, though the eight-year-old boy had been found eventually. The boy had gotten hold of a bottle of liquor and taken it to a pit near the canal, where he'd fallen down and hadn't been able to get out again. Getting into that kind of situation when the weather was this hot was a potentially lifechanging situation. They'd been lucky to have found him or it would have been a tragic ending. Unfortunately, due to his intoxication and the bottle found beside him, CPS had to be involved. No one liked that, but in Sandtown their involvement was even less welcome. The people who lived here didn't believe the state should stick their noses into their business, but when a child was potentially in danger, they had to do something.

She brought her thoughts back to the current investigation.

"Learning the identities of the victims needs to be a priority," she said. "They most likely have families somewhere who'll need to be notified of their deaths."

It was the worst part of her job, having to tell families that their loved ones would never be coming home again. It broke her heart a little every time, but it needed to be done. Better that they knew and were able to put their loved ones to rest with a proper funeral than never knowing what had happened to them.

"Who first found the bodies?" she asked Darrell.

"A *man* by the name of Raye Diante." The sergeant's opinion of the kind of person Raye was rang clear in his tone.

Lawrey nodded. "I know Raye. Any other witnesses we need to talk to in more depth?"

"I've no idea." Darrell swept his hand toward the waiting crowd. "Go knock yourself out, though I don't know what you'll get out of them. Bunch of stoners and wasters. They probably don't even know what day it is, never mind be able to give us any information about what happened here.

Wouldn't surprise me if one of them was responsible. Wouldn't be the first time one of them has set fire to someone else's trailer."

Asshole.

Of course, Sandtown had more than its fair share of problematic people, but not all of them should be written off that way.

Lawrey caught sight of her son standing among the other residents. He'd inherited his father's height and leanness but had her mousy-brown hair and blue eyes. Their gazes met, and she tweaked her lips in a smile for him. He didn't smile back but lifted his chin in a nod.

She wished she could give him a hug, but they didn't have that kind of relationship. They were in a good place now—better than they had been for many years—but that didn't mean things were easy between them.

Sometimes she wondered how much of the way Tommy turned out had to do with her. She had no doubt that she was the way she was because of her upbringing, but had the way she'd hardened herself to life, in order to protect her own heart, also meant she'd hardened herself to her own son? But then she looked at her sister and saw the great relationship she had with her kids, and that made her question things all over again.

Of course, her sister hadn't gone through the same as her.

No one knew why their father had preferred Lawrey over her sister. Her mother blamed herself for what happened, and Lawrey blamed her in a way, too. How had she not noticed? How had she not seen?

It was the reason Lawrey had decided to train as a cop, as soon as Tommy got old enough to start school. She knew it was a way of trying to take back control of her life. Her ex accused her of wanting to play the hero, but what was wrong with that? If she could save just one little girl from going through *that*, then her life might actually mean something.

Lawrey went in search of Raye.

She spotted him sitting on an upturned crate. Raye was normally the life and soul of a party, friendly and happy, and eager to chat, but right now he appeared to be a shell of himself. His hands trembled, as he had them clutched between his bony bare knees, and one of his cowboy-booted feet bounced up and down.

"Hey, Raye," she said as she approached. "You got a minute to talk about what happened?"

"Yeah, Law. Though I'm not sure what I can tell you."

"I hear you were the one who first found the couple."

She liked Raye. He was mild-mannered, and he'd worked really hard to get clean.

"Yeah, I got to the trailer first, but I'd been shouting about the fire, so lots of others were there, too."

"Were you the one who broke down the door, and so broke the security chain?"

He gave a small laugh. "No, have you seen me? I couldn't break anything down. That was Hella Billy."

She knew the name. "Hella Billy who runs The Crowbar?"

"That's right." Raye twisted his neck left and right. "He was here a short time ago but must have gone back to the club."

"Don't worry, I'll catch up with him. Can you run me through what happened before you noticed the fire?"

He blew out a breath. "I don't know what to tell you. I was painting, and I smelled smoke. I knew right away that it was something serious. I left my place to look for it and saw the light of the fire quick enough. I shouted that there was a fire, and then I tried to open the door in case someone needed my help." He held out his hand to reveal a large blister surrounded by a red mark across his palm. "Of course, stupid me didn't think about the handle being hot."

"You should get that checked out."

He opened and closed his palm and then winced. "It'll be fine. I'd prefer not to get the hospital bill."

"We have paramedics here. They can get you checked out."

He shrugged. "Nah. I'm okay."

"As long as you're sure. What happened after Hella Billy broke down the door? Who went in there first? Him?"

Raye shook his head. "No, that was me. Hella Billy kind of took a step back. He didn't look like he had any intention of going inside."

"But you did?"

"Yeah. I knew there was a young couple living there, and I thought someone needed help."

"That was really brave of you," she said with admiration in her tone. "Not many people would run into a burning building to rescue people."

"Well, it's not exactly a building, is it? And no one else was going to do it. I'm sorry I didn't get there on time."

"That's not your fault, Raye. I don't think anyone could have got there in time."

"Does this mean my DNA is going to be all over the place now?"

"Don't worry," she told him. "We'll make sure we take prints and samples from you to rule you out of the investigation."

He seemed uncomfortable.

"Is there something else you need to tell me?" she asked.

"It's just that you might find me already on the system."

"You got any outstanding warrants on you?"

"Raye isn't my real name," he admitted. "It's David Reynold, and yeah, you might find something outstanding on me."

She let out a sigh. "Shit, Raye. How bad?"

"I skipped bail. Misdemeanor drug charges."

That was the trouble with trying to work in a place like Sandtown. People didn't want to get involved because they often had their own secrets to hide. She appreciated that Raye at least had the balls to risk his own freedom in order to help a couple he barely knew.

"I'll do my best to keep your name out of it, okay? Let's hope we got lucky and you didn't touch anything."

"Thanks, Law. I'd really appreciate that."

"I am going to need to take a statement from you, though." She raised her voice. "I'm going to need to take statements from everyone who had any contact with the couple or witnessed the fire."

She sensed people slinking away. This wasn't going to be easy. No one in Sandtown liked to talk to the cops. It was an unspoken rule here that the police weren't welcome, and if you were seen to be making them welcome...well...then the locals would make sure you weren't.

She turned back to Raye. "Did you know the couple who lived there?"

"Only to say hi to. She was called Emily. He was Stephan. I don't think they wanted anyone to know their surnames."

"Were they close to anyone else? Anyone who might know a bit about them?"

Raye pinched his lips and shook his head. She understood. It was one thing for him to be talking to her, but it was something else for him to point a cop in the direction of another of Sandtown's residents. It wouldn't go down well. But until they knew otherwise, they needed to treat this as a potential double homicide, and simply being nice wasn't going to cut it.

"I need to know, Raye. If I think you're holding back on me, I can arrest you for obstructing justice, and by the sound of things, you don't want me doing that."

"I can't end up behind bars. It'll be the end of me. Men like me don't do well in prison, Law."

"So point me in the direction of who I need to speak to."

She felt for him. If someone thought he'd opened his mouth when he shouldn't, then he'd probably end up paying for it.

"All I can say is that the girl was more reserved than her boyfriend. I saw him hanging around the club on a number of occasions. She preferred to stick to the art scene, though I saw her down at the chapel as well."

"The chapel. Was she religious?"

"I don't know any more about them, I swear I don't."

"Okay, thanks. You've got my number, right? If you see or hear of anything else that might help, will you give me a call?"

"Sure."

Normally, Lawrey would have been asking around for CCTV footage, trying to track the movement of the victims and anyone else who might have been around the property, but there was no point here. No one in Sandtown used CCTV. If anyone attempted to, they'd be accused of spying. They were mistrustful of anything like that. Only recently had some of them started using the internet, setting up YouTube channels as a way of making money. Before then, even cell phones were frowned against because of the way apps 'listened' or mined people's data. Sandtown, and the people who lived here, were off-grid for a reason. They didn't want the place to become like the rest of America.

There was one person in Sandtown who she really should be able to make talk, though considering what their relationship was like, he'd probably be the most close-lipped out of all of them.

She wasn't the only one asking questions. Uniformed officers were also doing the rounds, and Abel was chatting with some of the residents as well. She didn't know why she always felt responsible for everything, but she did. Just because her son lived in Sandtown didn't mean that she should automatically oversee everything here, but somehow, that's what happened.

Tommy was still hanging around. Was he waiting for her? She hadn't seen him for a few weeks. Normally, he'd come down to visit her in Calrock, and she'd make them both something to eat.

She always felt she had to watch herself with him, certain she'd do or say the wrong thing, and he'd blow up over it. That scenario had happened so many times before that she was constantly on edge, preparing herself for it. Sometimes, she wouldn't even need to say anything. The wrong look would be enough to set him off. She knew he acted that way when he felt guilty about something—he was high and hoping to get money off her, most likely.

She wished things could be easier between them. Sometimes she watched her sister with her two kids and her chest ached. Even when things were tense between them, their arguments never got out of control like they did with her and Tommy. She'd never seen her nephew call her sister a bitch or threaten to hit her—something Tommy had done countless times.

"Hey, Tommy. How are you doing?"

"All right." He jerked his chin at the trailer. "Any idea what happened?"

"Not yet. It's still early. Did you know the victims at all?"

"Not really. They'd only been here a couple of months."

"It's unusual, though, isn't it, for new arrivals to come at this time of year."

He shrugged. "Most people do come in the winter, so they can acclimatize better, but people arrive in the summer, too. They tend not to stay that long. It's not easy living out here in these temperatures, and newbies aren't prepared for it. They might think they are, but the heat can be unbearable. We have the misters set up, and some people have air, but if you don't have that and you've arrived here with only an RV, it's going to be a shock."

"They stayed, though," Lawrey said.

"Yeah, but I heard they had a reason for that. Rumor was they were hiding out here. They were on the run, I think."

This sparked Lawrey's attention. "On the run from what? The law?"

"No, I don't think so. Think it was the girl's ex-boyfriend. Apparently, she'd taken out a restraining order on him, but he kept driving past her house, slow and threatening, like, or parking outside for hours on end. The cops never did anything, despite them having the order. Said there wasn't any proof that he was doing the things they claimed, even though the boyfriend had messages on a phone that the ex had sent. He threatened to kill both of them, and I guess they took it seriously, 'cause they left and ended up out here."

"Who did you hear that from? Them?"

"Not sure. Just people talking. It might have even been the girl who said it."

"Do you know where they originated from?" she asked.

"Nope. I guess they wanted to keep as much information back as possible to reduce the chance of this ex-boyfriend catching up to them."

Lawrey grimaced. "Looks like he might have anyway."

"You think the ex-boyfriend might have kept true on his promise to kill them both?" Tommy asked. "And then set fire to the trailer to cover his tracks?"

"I'm unsure yet, but it's definitely a lead we need to follow. Thanks for that information, Tommy. I appreciate your help. I know it's not easy."

Her son glanced around, as though he was checking out who might have been watching him speak to her. That she was his mother gave him an excuse, but you never knew who might not take kindly to him talking to a cop. She didn't want to get him in trouble either.

Lawrey left Tommy and found her partner. She filled Abel in on what she'd learned.

"I know it isn't much, but we're going to need to run a search on recently issued restraining orders that include the name Emily."

Abel pursed his lips. "We have no idea if that's even her real name. If they were hiding out, there was nothing stopping them telling people fake names."

"That's true, but we've got to work with what we have right now, which isn't much. If this couple were on the run from someone they thought was capable of killing them, we can't rule out the possibility that he caught up to them and did exactly what he'd threatened."

Abel nodded over to one of the trailers nearby. "I might have found something interesting myself. The neighbor over there, Stormi Faith—presumably not her real name—says she saw the couple arguing outside a few hours ago. She was over at the club singing on stage when the fire happened, but she saw them when she was leaving to go to the club. They were really going for it, apparently, yelling at each other like they didn't care if anyone overheard."

"Did she say if she picked up on what they were arguing about?"

He shook his head. "Nope, but Emily shoved Stephan in the chest, and, according to her, he pushed her back. She went inside right after, and everything quietened down, or at least it did until the fire started."

"Did Stephan follow Emily inside?"

"Yes, he did."

"Did the witness see if they shut the door then? Locked it?"

He pursed his lips. "She didn't know. Once they'd gone in, she didn't really pay them any more attention."

How long did the fight go on for?"

Abel checked his notes. "Not long. Minutes. Maybe five."

"After they went inside, did she see anyone else join them? Or did either of them leave again?"

"Not that she saw, but the way they've got their trailer positioned right on the outskirts means you can't see much of anything when it's dark. Someone could easily have come and gone, especially if they arrived around the other side in the dark. No one would have seen them."

That was true. Plenty of the other trailers were closer to each other, so they shared each other's light in the same way a regular urban street would, but this trailer was stuck out in the area many of the snowbirds used when they came during winter, so they were out on their own.

Lawrey let out a sigh. "Plus, it doesn't help if most people were over at the club, hanging out."

The club was situated at the other end of town. No one there would have been able to witness the fire starting or the events that had led up to it.

Areas of Sandtown tended to be divided into the different groups of people. Though it was touted as being an inclusive place, where everyone could be who they wanted to be, just like in any other part of society, people tended to be drawn toward those they could relate to. One area was for those who identified as being LGBTQIA+, another for the bikers, another for the stoners. Some people were looking for community, while others simply wanted to be left alone. For the most part, people recognized and respected those differences in each other. The place wasn't some kind of eutopia though. People still fell out. There was a far higher-than-average incident of mental health issues and drug use.

"Finding a trailer on fire in Sandtown isn't exactly unusual, is it?" Abel said. "It's what people do out here when they want to get rid of someone."

Lawrey narrowed her gaze. "Get rid of someone? Like, kill them?"

"No, I didn't mean like that. I meant let them know they're not welcome here no more. If someone's been caught stealing from another member of the town, or they hear some guy is beating up his old lady. That person is likely to come home and find their trailer on fire."

Chapter Four

U niformed police would guard the scene until the arson squad showed up to investigate. The specialists should be able to tell them if the fire was an accident, or if it had been started on purpose. They'd also be able to say where the fire originated from, and even if there had been an accelerant used. From the pattern of the burns, they were able to paint a whole picture of the scene and the events leading up to the fire.

Lawrey was relieved to be able to get back in her car and get the air blasting. Abel flapped the front of his shirt, creating a breeze.

"I'll be glad to get into the office," he said.

"I don't often hear you say that."

He chuckled. "No, you don't."

They drove the four miles back to Calrock. There was nothing between there and Sandtown but the expanse of desert. The landscape was dominated by sand dunes and rocky outcroppings, and sparse vegetation such as cacti. The air itself seemed to ripple with the heat. People thought the desert to be an ugly place, but to Lawrey it held its own kind of beauty. The vast dunes rose and fell like ocean waves, and the sky above was an endless deep blue she didn't think you'd find anywhere else in the world.

Soon enough, the few more remote homes of Calrock appeared on either side of the road, and within minutes, they were driving back into town. She arrived at the station and pulled into the parking lot outside.

Someone was waiting outside of the station, and her stomach sank.

"What the fuck is he doing here?" she muttered.

"You want me to handle this, Law?" Abel offered.

"No, it's okay. I'll go talk to him."

She hadn't had enough sleep, and she was already tired and hot. Her tolerance level for dealing with idiots had already been breached, and now she knew the dam was about to burst.

She stayed in the car for a few more seconds, appreciating the chill of the air conditioning. With a sigh, she opened the door, and the summer heat hit her in the face like a slap. Already, temperatures must be close to a hundred degrees. The back of her shirt clung to her spine, and sweat pooled in her cleavage.

Mitch Pearce was one of those men who thought he could use his size to bully everyone around him. He acted as though the world owed him a favor, and that he should be respected simply because he was a white, male American. His job as a Border Patrol agent only helped to solidify that opinion. She'd arrested his son for a suspected burglary a few weeks earlier. Clayton was only a couple of months off his eighteenth birthday and was certainly a chip off the old block. Both had entitlement written all over them.

Mitch saw her coming and turned to face her, his arms folded with his hands pushed under his biceps in that way men did to try to make themselves look bigger. He jutted out his jaw and lifted his chin, his nostrils flaring.

"What can I do for you, Mitch," she said as she approached the station. She didn't want to give him the slightest inkling that she was bothered about finding him here.

Behind her, the car door slammed shut, and she sensed Abel was close behind her, ready to act as backup, if needed. She doubted Mitch was going to do anything stupid. He only wanted to make some noise, act like the big man, and feel he was making himself heard.

"You know Clayton didn't do what you're accusing him of."

"That's the problem, though, isn't it? I don't know that. We have two witnesses who say they saw him around the property right before the break-in happened and then we picked up your son's prints on the inside of a window frame. You think he would have been smart enough to put on gloves before touching the fucking window."

"He does odd jobs around town all the time. He cleaned their windows not long before that. He already explained that to you."

Lawrey pursed her lips, not buying it. "He cleaned their windows out of the goodness of his heart and didn't even tell the homeowners about it. Because they say they didn't know anything about him cleaning the windows, they hadn't employed him, and he didn't try to send them an invoice for the job either. Does that sound likely to you?"

Mitch shrugged. "They're old, they forget what they've asked, and Clay said he hadn't gotten around to dropping them off a bill yet."

"A bill for the work they never even asked for. And I've got to say, considering those windows were supposed to have been cleaned, they looked pretty filthy to me. Your son didn't do a very good job, that's if he's telling the truth."

He flushed red. "I don't know about that, but you need to drop the charges against him."

"It's not up to me to drop the charges, Mitch. If the prosecutor believes there is enough evidence to charge him, which there is, then there's nothing I can do or say about it."

"You shouldn't have arrested him in the first place. Your family should never have even stayed in this town after what your father did."

He hawked up phlegm and spat just far enough away that she couldn't claim assault, but close enough that he made his point.

His words still stung. "I'm not my father, Mitch, and you know that."

He looked her up and down. "What do they say about blood being thicker than water? Genes get passed down."

She didn't let him intimidate her. "Maybe you should think about what you're saying, considering your son is currently in juvie for stealing from a defenseless old couple."

"Yeah, whatever, Law. I won't let this go, I promise you that."

He marched back to his car, shaking his head.

"Asshole," Law muttered, probably loud enough for him to hear.

He yanked open the door, climbed behind the wheel, and slammed it shut louder than needed. Then he stamped his foot down and pulled away from the curb with a screech of tires on asphalt.

Lawrey was pleased to see him go, though she doubted it would be the last she'd see of him. Dust billowed out from behind his wheels.

It was going to be a long fucking day.

Abel spoke from behind her. "You okay, Law?"

"Yeah, it's just too early and too fucking hot to have to deal with idiots like that."

"Let's get inside before we both melt."

She had to run her boss through what they'd learned up at Sandtown and then she'd need to do a roll call and fill the rest of the team in as well. It wasn't unusual to have a death in Sandtown, but two young people dying who hadn't been there very long was bound to get some people asking questions. She was surprised the press weren't already buzzing around like flies on horse shit.

"I'm sorry for what he said about your father," Abel said. "You know the rest of us don't think like that, don't you?"

"Thanks, but I'm sure some people do. Small towns have long memories."

"Have you ever thought of moving someplace else? I'm not saying that you should have felt you had to, but why didn't you?"

"Why should I? I never did anything wrong."

"I know that. I just think it would be understandable if you wanted to. Move to some place no one knew your history so you could start fresh."

She shrugged. "I don't know. By the time it had even occurred to me that such a thing was possible, I was already married and had a baby on the way. Besides, this town has always been my home. All my friends are here—the ones who stuck by me anyway—and my family. I couldn't abandon my mom and my sister. They needed me, too."

"I get it."

Lawrey repressed a smirk. "I once punched Mitch Pearce's older sister in the face for saying that it was my fault about those other girls, you know. We were sixteen at the time."

He chuckled. "And then you arrest their son thirty years later. No wonder that family doesn't like you."

"You'd think they'd have gotten over it by now, but clearly not."

"*Your* sister never got the same kind of aggravation you did, though."

"No. I guess it was because she was that much younger. It's easy to blame an older teen than it is a kid."

"No one should have blamed you at all. How could you control what your father was doing?"

She sighed. "No, but it doesn't change the gossip mill, does it? People are still going to talk. My mom had the same, people saying that she must have known what he was up to. Honestly, I thought the same thing myself, at first, blamed her as well. She was the adult, after all. But then I realized that if I thought it was so wrong that people were blaming me, then I could hardly blame her. No one else was to blame except for him."

"You and your mom don't exactly have a close relationship though."

She snorted a laugh. "That's got nothing to do with what my father did. We have a personality clash."

"Because you're too alike?"

"Maybe. She definitely gets on better with my sister. Even when the kids were younger, I noticed how she always babysat for my niece and nephew, but she'd rarely look after Tommy. Maybe it was simply that Tommy was never an easy kid, or that she was still struggling after what happened with Dad, but I always felt some favoritism there."

"I'm sure she loves you all the same."

Lawrey wasn't so sure about that.

Iris Bartlett was watching the station desk as they walked in.

"How was it out there?" Iris asked them. "Did you see Tommy?"

Lawrey offered the older woman a smile. "Yeah, he's fine. Thanks for asking about him."

"No problem. I know how it is to have a son. You don't stop worrying about them, no matter how old they get."

"Ain't that the truth." And Tommy had given her more reasons than normal to worry.

Abel followed her into the office. "Let's get some coffee before we do anything else," he suggested.

"That's an idea I can get with." She needed to eat something too. She hadn't managed any breakfast. But first she'd get caffeinated and then go and speak to her boss about the incident at Sandtown.

Twenty minutes later, Lawrey peered through a window that led off the corridor, peeping through the slats of the blinds on the other side. She caught sight of her boss, Lieutenant Dustin Monroe, sitting at his desk. He didn't look to be with anyone and wasn't on the phone, so she reached the door and knocked.

His voice filtered through the wood. "Come in."

Lawrey entered.

Lieutenant Monroe was younger than her by a number of years—she wasn't going to ask him directly how many—but then he hadn't needed to take time out of his career to raise kids or deal with a problematic son. Not that she wanted the responsibility of being a lieutenant, plus it was too much time spent behind a desk for her liking. Though at this time of year, that didn't seem like such a bad thing.

She took a seat opposite him and filled him in on what they'd learned about the case so far, which wasn't much.

"Currently, the only names we have for the victims are Emily and Stephan, and we don't even know if that's their real names. We've got a partial plate for the trailer, which I'm assuming will be registered to either one or both of them, but the plate was too damaged to show where it originated from."

"Hopefully forensics will be able to clean that up enough to get a better look," he said.

Lawrey continued, "We've also got reports of the couple fighting only a matter of hours before the fire. There's also a possibility that the woman, Emily, had a restraining order out against her ex-boyfriend. We have multiple witnesses to the fire, but since they're all from Sandtown, I'm sure you all understand how forthcoming they've been with their information."

"It's not an easy town to look out for," he said.

"It certainly isn't," she agreed. "Our first priority needs to be finding out the identities of the victims. Once we know that, it'll make our jobs a whole lot easier.

He tapped his pen against the desk. "What was the state of the bodies?"

"Mostly unrecognizable, but not so badly damaged that we can't get DNA samples from them. I'd say prints will be a struggle."

"What about phones or other devices? What kind of condition would they be in after the fire?"

She leaned back. "We're still waiting for the arson squad to arrive, but they should be there by mid-afternoon. They'll recover that evidence."

"Don't envy them working in the afternoon heat," he said.

"Nope, me neither, but then I guess they're used to being in the heat, considering their jobs," she joked.

He returned her grin. "Good point."

"There's a chance this was simply an unfortunate accident that cost two people their lives, but until we know that for sure, we need to be mindful that someone else might be responsible."

Monroe steepled his fingers. "Keep up the good work, Sergeant. If there are any more developments, let me know."

Lawrey excused herself and left his office.

She managed to find five minutes to grab some breakfast, though, checking the time, it was basically lunch now. As she was finishing the last bite of her bacon, egg and cheese bagel, her phone rang.

It was Sergeant Darrell Potts. "Got a call to say the arson squad will be in Sandtown within the hour. Thought you'd want to know."

"Thanks. I'll head back over there and catch up with them."

She ended the call and told Abel.

"You want some company?" he offered.

"Nah, you stay here, in the cool. Focus on finding out the identities of the victims."

Chapter Five

Lawrey stopped her car on the road adjacent to the blackened trailer. Yellow crime scene tape hung slack around the scene, creating the outer cordon. There wasn't even enough breeze in the air today to make the tape flutter. A uniformed officer sat in the small amount of shade created by the half-burned trailer, holding a battery-powered fan against the back of his neck.

The fire inspector hadn't arrived yet, and she debated what to do. She wanted to revisit the trailer, to allow her trained eye to take in any details she might have missed previously, when so many people had been around, but she also didn't want to leave the cool interior of her car for any longer than was strictly necessary. The ground had been scorched beneath the trailer, but with this heat, it almost didn't need a fire for that to have happened.

She was aware that she was attracting attention from the residents. A couple—an older man and a woman of around the same age—scowled in her direction. Across the street, a young male with the kind of scrawny body and bad skin that screamed meth user had stopped to stare in her direction.

Refusing to be intimidated, she lifted her hand in a wave and then climbed out of the car. The young man thinned his lips, his brow furrowing. He reminded her of a stray dog—unsure if he should attack or run away.

She couldn't lean against her car. The metal was hot enough under the sun to leave a serious burn mark.

"Hey, what's your name?" she called over to him. "Did you know the couple who were killed?"

He quickly shook his head and then darted away, leaving the road to weave between the permanent trailers that were people's homes.

The woman spoke up. "They weren't one of us, you know."

Lawrey took a few steps in their direction so she could hear better. "I'm sorry?"

"They might have been here in the summer, but that doesn't make them Sanders. They weren't long-termers like the rest of us here at this time of year."

Lawrey realized she was referencing the victims. "Did you know them at all?"

"No, they were young. They weren't interested in getting to know a pair of old wrinklies like us."

"Damn shame what happened to them, though," the man added. "Far too young to die."

The pair turned to head in the opposite direction.

"What are your names?" Lawrey called after them, but the man only raised his hand in a goodbye, not even pausing to consider giving it to her.

Lawrey turned her attention back to the scene. The victims' trailer was situated on the outskirts of the town. Though no one officially owned any of the land in Sandtown—other than the state—the long-termers had picked out areas which they now called their own, and, for the most part, others respected the boundaries they'd set out.

She remembered a science teacher at school telling her atoms are like people on busses; they'll always select the spots farthest apart from each other. It was about the only piece of information she'd retained from high school. She guessed some of the people in Sandtown were the same. On the outskirts of town, many had selected spots that were the greatest distance from their neighbors, and the same was true for the young couple.

Lawrey walked around the area, but instead of looking toward the burned-out vehicle, she focused her gaze outward. What was around it? Did anything, or anyone, overlook it?

To the rear of the trailer stretched the desert. In front of it was the road. The young woman who lived directly opposite, Stormi, ran the café as well as singing on occasion at the club. She'd reported seeing the couple arguing.

On the corner stood another trailer, but it appeared to be empty, abandoned. Most likely someone who'd arrived in spring, thinking they'd be able to handle the summer temperatures, but who had eventually decided they couldn't hack it. There were plenty of those around.

There was something about the sun that drove people a little crazy.

Sweat gathered in her hairline, prickled her top lip like a mustache, and trickled to the base of her spine.

The sense of someone watching her hit her, the weight of another person's gaze on her back. She turned to find two men standing in a patch of shade on the other side of the road. They both had a similar style—bearded, with shaved heads. Their chests were bare, but leather cuts covered their shoulders and back. At a guess, she'd say these were Hella Billy's crew. Had word gotten around that she was here so they'd come to check her out? Or had they come over to this side of town for a different reason?

Who were those men? Did they know something?

She wondered if Tommy was around. She hadn't told him she was coming. The last thing he'd want was to feel like he was being pulled into an investigation. It was already hard enough for him having a detective as a parent. She didn't take it personally. He'd been young when she'd first joined the force, so he'd grown up with her always having been a cop. Even when he'd been a preteen, it had embarrassed him. If she'd needed to get involved with home disputes or had been forced to arrest someone who also had kids in his school, for some reason it was Tommy who'd been made to look like the bad one, rather than the other kid being embarrassed that their parent had been arrested. Tough kids tended to come from tough homes, and they'd rather blame someone else than take responsibility for their actions.

Their relationship had gotten worse once he'd become a teenager. Things hadn't been good between her and Patrick either. They'd been arguing all the time. Looking back, she wondered if they should have broken up sooner. Maybe it would have saved everyone—including their son—a lot of pain. But she'd been stubborn. She hadn't wanted to give up, no matter how unpleasant home life had become. So Tommy had started staying out more, missing his curfews, saying he hated living there. It was understandable. Had he rebelled against the fact he'd had a cop as a mother? Was that why he'd first tried alcohol and drugs? Was he trying to prove to others and himself that being the son of a detective didn't influence who he was?

Despite her bravado, Lawrey was relieved to hear the hum of a car engine, and then the fire scene investigator pulled up behind her vehicle. She shaded her eyes with her hand, squinting at the person beyond the windshield to make sure she had the right man. The bright sunlight glinting off the glass made it hard to see.

The car door opened, and the tall frame of a fire investigator, Richard Lund, climbed out.

"If it gets any hotter," he said, "there's a danger that I'll be the one who goes up in flames."

"I know the feeling. Roll on fall." When she glanced over again, the two men who'd been watching her had gone. Perhaps it was a coincidence and they weren't there because of her.

"You know you didn't have to come out here again," Richard said. "We could have done this in an air-conditioned office on the computer."

"I know, but I wouldn't get the same feel for it. There's something about being hands-on that gets the brain cells firing." She shrugged. "Call it an instinct. It's harder to pick up on things when you're staring at it on a screen."

"I hear you." He grinned. "With this heat, it does make it feel like we're living through the fire for real."

Richard went to the trunk and opened it to remove the equipment he needed.

"You any closer to finding out who might be responsible?" he asked.

"Nope. We don't even have the IDs of the victims yet. As to what actually happened, we're still working on speculation, rather than proof, so I'm hoping you can help me with that."

"I'll do the best I can."

She liked Richard. He was an easy-going guy who'd been a couple of years ahead of her in high school. He lived in one of the bigger nearby towns now but always came out for incidents such as this.

"Shall we get this done before we both melt?" he suggested.

"Good idea."

It didn't help that they both needed to pull on protective outerwear before entering the scene. The extra layer became a kind of torture device in this heat. Within seconds, her skin had grown clammy. She was literally going to have to peel it off her.

Together, they signed in with the officer guarding the scene.

"Go and sit in my car," she told him, tossing him the keys. "Cool down awhile."

"You sure?" the officer asked.

"Absolutely. You look like you could use a break from the heat."

"Thanks, Sarge."

Lawrey and Richard ducked under the inner cordon and approached the trailer. Richard paused to take photographs of the outside and the surrounding area.

"I assume the victims didn't have this place insured," he asked Lawrey.

"If they did, it wouldn't be for much. I highly doubt someone burned it down, with them inside, just to claim the insurance money."

He lowered the camera. "I agree, but it's always something that should be considered. These things can go wrong. People can still die. I had a case where a desperate mother set fire to her home in the hope of cashing in on the insurance. She thought her teenage daughter was out, staying with friends, but didn't know the daughter had actually had a fight with the friend and had come home early. The mom set the fire and then went on a date, hoping that would give her enough of an alibi to make it seem like she hadn't had anything to do with it. The daughter had gone to bed. She must have been asleep, but by the time she woke up and realized what was happening it was too late. We found the girl's body in a position on the stairs where it appeared as though she'd been crawling, trying to escape."

"Jesus Christ," Lawrey said, shaking her head. "How could the mother live with herself?"

"She couldn't. She killed herself two days later. Left a note confessing everything."

"That's terrible." It was, but it didn't surprise her. Terrible things happened all the time. It was the way of the world.

"I'm only saying we need to consider all possibilities," he added.

"Agreed."

Richard led the way, stepping up into the inside of the home, taking photographs as he went. "First, I need to rule out any common causes of fire—electrical, smoking, cooking, that kind of thing. Then I need to find and locate the origin of the fire. The closer we get to the point of origin, the deeper the alligator charring will be."

Lawrey kept back as he continued to take photographs, starting at the area of least charring and working his way toward the bedroom. He paused to take samples of the carpet and flooring, storing them in new metal canisters and labelling them.

In the bedroom, he stopped to examine the broken windows. "Do you know what happened here?"

"The locals broke them so they could fight the fire with extinguishers. They managed to keep it at bay until the fire department arrived."

He moved around the bed. "From the pour patterns on the floor, I'd say the fire started at this end of the trailer, right beside their bed. See this area of intense burn? I'd say someone's poured an accelerant here."

She walked over to the window. "Could this have been open? Even if it was only a crack?"

He twisted his lips. "If you're thinking that someone poured something through it, the scorch mark is in the wrong place. The angle is all wrong."

"What about if they used something to funnel the fuel to a different spot—a hose, maybe? Then when they decided there was enough, they reeled it back in, tossed in a match, and pulled the window so it was mostly shut, knowing the fire would do enough damage so that it wasn't obvious where the fuel came from. The security chain was on the door when the fire started, so we know whoever did this didn't leave that way."

He tapped his fingers together as he thought. "It's certainly possible. Were there any signs of anyone being outside, footprints, or any sign of the accelerant?"

She shook her head. "There might have been, but the town's residents made a mess of the scene outside the trailer. I don't blame them. They were trying to figure out a way in, in case anyone inside was still alive. It's not like Sandtown has its own fire department, so they had to wait for help to arrive. People here are used to handling things on their own."

"They might have made a mess of the scene outside, but they also managed to save some of it. If it wasn't for what they did, this whole place would have been charred to the bare bones, and that's even harder to work with."

Lawrey agreed. "Plus, the victims were badly burned, but there should be enough left to be able to get blood samples and DNA, which is more than what we'd have been left with if the residents hadn't acted when they did. We're not going to get anything back from the medical examiner until tomorrow, at the earliest, so until we know if the couple were dead before the fire started, it's all speculation."

"What are your theories?" Richard asked.

She ran him through them. "They're all very loose right now. If the couple were both dead *before* the fire started, it's possible the male victim might have been responsible, but he didn't kill his girlfriend and then himself, and somehow then get outside to start a fire from the window."

"Didn't he?" He arched an eyebrow. "Maybe he killed her, set up the fire, and shut the window and door and hooked on the chain, then killed himself?"

"Perhaps, though what reason would he have for doing that? I guess we'll know more once we've got the report back from the medical examiner. I'm keeping an open mind on events. We know the female victim had what can only be thought of as a stalker, so there's a chance he finally caught up with her and murdered the new boyfriend at the same time. Things might have been set up to hide his tracks."

Lawrey gave Richard some space to allow him to get on with his job and went out to the car to grab a couple of bottles of water from a cooler in the trunk. These kinds of investigations could take days, even weeks. Because the trailer was only small, he hopefully wouldn't need that much time.

The uniformed officer was still sitting in the car, so she gave him a bottle as well and then took another back to the trailer.

Richard climbed out and then pulled off the protective outerwear, flapping his hands at his face. Lawrey pressed the chilled bottle of water to her forehead and rolled it over her cheeks.

Richard cracked open the bottle and took a sip. "Did you hear Jess and I separated?"

"Shit, no, I didn't. I'm sorry to hear that, Rich."

"It's fine. Things hadn't been going well for some time. We all think we're going to be the same people we are in our twenties forever, don't we, and then middle age creeps in and we find we want different things."

"What kind of different things?"

"Turns out she wanted someone thirteen years younger."

"Ouch." Lawrey winced. "If it makes you feel any better, Patrick wanted the same."

"I'm sorry to hear that, too. He must have been crazy for leaving you."

She laughed, the sound cold. "I'm sure he doesn't think that."

Lawrey didn't think the years had been kind. What with gravity, and hormones, and the loss of collagen in her skin, it was as though she'd hit forty-five and nature had decided to play a cruel joke on her one night while she'd been sleeping. When she'd woken up and stared at herself in the mirror, a middle-aged woman had been staring back at her. But she told herself she was far more than her appearance. That shouldn't be the first thing that's valued in a woman. Her brain, her job, her role as a mother and aunt and sister and daughter, those were the important things, and that wouldn't change because she had a few lines on her face and her tits hung a little lower each year.

Richard pressed his lips together in a strange smile. "It's the never-ending search for youth, isn't it? People start getting older and then think the person they're with is also older, which makes them feel like they're getting on a bit too much, so they seek out someone who'll make them feel like they're in their twenties or thirties again."

"Honestly, I don't want someone in their twenties or thirties," Lawrey said. "I couldn't keep up. Older people already know where they are in life, and they don't expect another person to make them happy."

"If that were true, our exes wouldn't have run off with younger people."

She pointed at him. "That's very true. I'll rephrase to *some* older people."

He chuckled. "Well, look, if you ever feel like going for a coffee some time, so we can commiserate together about how old and ugly we are now, I'll happily buy."

She eyed him curiously. "Are you asking me out, Richard?"

"Just as friends," he added hurriedly. Then tagged on, "Unless you think differently, of course."

"I'm sure we can go for a coffee, as friends," she said.

She enjoyed his company, so why shouldn't she go? He was an intelligent man, and maybe they could even talk about the case some more. Work was her favorite topic of conversation, and while most dates didn't like talking about autopsy reports over dinner, Richard would be used to that kind of thing.

"Okay, great. I'll give you a call then."

"Sure, and let me know if you think of anything else about the case."

"Will do. I'd better get back to it."

Richard returned to the trailer. Lawrey remained there for a moment. She didn't plan to leave Sandtown yet. She wanted to do another walk around the scene, on her own this time. That was when she did her best thinking. There might be something else she'd missed.

Chapter Six

It had been a long day, and Lawrey was glad to get home and finally be out of the heat. The first thing she did was take a cold shower, rinsing the grime of the desert and her own sweat off her skin. She washed her hair as well, and shampooed it twice, trying to get the stink of smoke out of it.

She towel-dried off and dressed in a pair of baggy sweatpants and a cami without a bra. If she couldn't be comfortable at home, where could she be?

Wandering out into the kitchen, she tossed a TV dinner into the microwave and grabbed herself a beer from the refrigerator while she waited for the ding to sound.

The truth was, she didn't really mind living alone. It wasn't as though she was here much anyway, and her days were filled with noise and people, so she appreciated the quiet when she got home—no one asking her to do anything for them or wanting anything from her. It was when she finally felt at peace.

A *ding* alerted her to her food being ready. She didn't even bother to dump it out onto a plate, but instead ate straight from the tray to save on the washing up. She ate without really tasting it, her thoughts still lost in the case. Though Abel had pushed the idea that the couple's death could have been an accident, her gut told her otherwise. She always believed that good policing was at least fifty percent sharp instincts, and this time her instincts told her that the couple had already been dead, or at the very least unconscious, when the fire had started.

Trying to switch off her brain, she turned on the television to find something to watch and settled back, hoping to relax. Her couch was approaching twenty years old and had torn covers and was sagging at the back, but she imagined it had molded around her shape over the years, and thought if she ever bought a new one, it wouldn't be the same.

Lawrey finished her beer and turned off the television, ready to go to bed.

The ring of her cell phone caught her attention. Her sister's number flashed up on screen.

Her chest tightened. It wasn't like her sister to call so late at night. Lawrey always teased her about how Maddie liked to be in bed before ten p.m., even on a weekend. She wouldn't be calling at this time just to have a chat.

She swiped the screen to answer.

"Everything okay, Maddie?" she asked.

"Not really. It's Cara. She hasn't come home, and she's not answering her phone."

Cara was Lawrey's sixteen-year-old niece.

"Shit. What time was she supposed to be home by?"

"Ten. Eddie is out driving around looking for her, but there's no sign. I'm getting really worried, Law. She should be home by now."

Lawrey checked the time on her phone. It was past eleven at night.

She wanted to reassure her sister. "Cara isn't the sort of kid to get into trouble."

Maddie paused. "She's been acting up recently. The other weekend, we found empty bottles of vodka and some vapes hidden down the side of her bed. I'm worried she's gotten herself involved with a bad crowd."

Vapes and vodka wasn't exactly terrible, but Lawrey knew her perception of 'bad' was skewed. She used to find crack pipes and bags of meth in Tommy's room. She'd have been happy with vodka and vapes.

"What bad crowd?" Lawrey asked.

"I don't know exactly. Some older kids who've been hanging out with the girls after they've finished their basketball practice. I think they might be a year or two above them at school. I don't know why they started taking an interest in them now."

Lawrey was on her feet, hunting for her car keys. She didn't tell her sister what she was thinking—that sixteen-year-old girls were easy prey for older boys. The girls would be flattered that the older boys were paying them attention, and the boys would tell them things they wanted to hear, like about how they were so mature for their ages and different to the other girls. With hormones blazing, most girls of that age didn't think straight, and they didn't yet have the experience to understand when someone was leading them on for their own benefit.

"Don't worry, we'll find her."

"I am worried, Law. You know, after that young couple was killed up at Sandtown. It's not that far from us."

"That's a completely different situation," Lawrey reassured her. "You know what Sandtown is like. Besides, we have no idea what happened there yet. We're still investigating. It could have been an accident—kids who got wasted and didn't put out a cigarette."

Deep down, though, Lawrey didn't believe her own words. Yes, it might have been an accident, but why were they fighting before they were killed? And who was the abusive partner they were running from? She didn't believe much in coincidences. That someone had threatened to kill the couple, and they'd believed the threat enough to take out a restraining order and then run, set alarm bells ringing.

"I hope you're right," Maddie said.

Lawrey left her house and headed to her car. She kept the phone pressed to her cheek, her sister still on the line.

"I'm leaving now. I'll check the park, and the mall, and the canal. Anywhere else you can think of that they might be hanging out?"

"Only at one of their houses, but if she's gone to one of the boys' homes, I won't have any idea where that might be."

The town was small, but not so small that it was possible to know the names and addresses of every person who lived here. Lawrey might know a family name, and that they had a son, but that was about it.

"We'll find her, Maddie. It's normal for girls of her age to act out."

Her sister sniffed down the line. "I wish I could go back to when she was young again. I thought it was hard at the time, but now I'd give anything to have that little girl back. I'm sorry I wasn't more supportive of you when you were going through all that shit with Tommy back then. I thought you handled it, but now I realize how hard it must have been."

Lawrey didn't like to talk or even think about those days. They'd been some of the worst of her life—up there even with when her father had been arrested and the truth of what kind of man he was had come into the open. Nothing was more painful than watching the person you loved most in the world slowly destroy themselves and being completely helpless to do anything about it. She and Patrick had suffered through it for years, Tommy getting himself clean for periods of time, and them thinking this was finally it—he was on the home stretch to a better life—only for him to fall off the wagon again, and they'd be back to square one. Things still weren't great. Lawrey had no doubt that he was using again, but he seemed to have at least found his place in Sandtown. He was surrounded by people who understood him, so he was more likely to fall on them for help than he was her. Did that make her a bad mom? Maybe, but sometimes you have to admit to yourself when you can't help a person anymore.

"It's okay, Mads. Don't worry about it. I'll find Cara, okay? Can you call around her friends' moms, see if any of them made it home, and if so, do they know where she went."

"I'll do that now."

Lawrey ended the call and slid behind the wheel of her vehicle. How much should she be worried? While she felt sure this didn't have anything to do with what had happened in Sandtown, that didn't mean Cara wasn't in trouble. Bad things happened to young women all the time.

Before she set off, she placed a call to the station, making sure the officers working were aware of what was happening. She gave them Cara's description—aged sixteen, shoulder-length brown hair, five feet four, slender build. They all knew Cara was her niece.

Lawrey drove slowly, watching the sidewalk for any sign of Cara or her friends, or even a group of young men who they might have either been with or else who might have seen the girls. She kept an eye on her phone, praying that Maddie would phone her back with the news that Cara had made it home already and was in big trouble, but was safe.

She hated the churning dread in the pit of her stomach, the way her imagination went to the possibility of Cara being dead, of how it would change all their lives. She wanted to believe Cara was fine—which she most likely was—but she'd experienced too much death, too many lives destroyed, to have the safety bubble of believing that bad things didn't happen to good people.

Though it was past eleven p.m., there were still people around, most of them coming back from the bar, or on their way home after late shifts at work.

She spotted a couple she knew walking arm in arm and pulled over and lowered her window.

"Oh, hey, Law. Everything okay?" the female half of the couple asked.

"You seen Cara, my niece, anywhere?"

"No, sorry. How long's she been missing?"

"I don't know she's missing exactly. She hasn't come home by her curfew and isn't answering her phone."

The woman shook her head. "Sorry, I hope she shows up soon."

"Yeah, me, too. Thanks anyway."

She slid the window back up and kept going. Where the hell had the girl gotten to?

Her phone rang, but instead of it being her sister, it was one of the uniformed officers from her station, Steve Litching. Her stomach flipped. She was poised between being desperate to answer so she could find out what was going on, and not wanting to know in case it was something bad.

She had no choice, however, so she pulled over and answered the phone.

"Did you find her?" she asked in a rush before Steve had even gotten the chance to speak.

"We've got her, Sarge."

She blew out a long breath and sank back in her seat. "Where is she?"

"Down by the canal. We're with her now."

"I'll be right there."

She ended the call and then quickly made another one to her sister. "I've found her, Maddie. She's safe."

She could hear the relief in her sister's tone. "Oh, thank God. And she's not hurt or anything?"

"No, she's fine."

"Should I tell Eddie to come find you?"

"No need. I'll bring her home. I'm going to have a word with her first, if that's okay with you?"

"Of course it is, Law. She'll probably listen to you more than she would either of us."

Lawrey wasn't so sure about that, but she appreciated the vote of confidence anyway.

She tossed the phone to one side and drove the short distance down to the canal. She spotted the cruiser first, the wash of blue and red lights against the dark sky, and then saw two uniformed officers standing with a group of youngsters. The teenagers stood with hands in pockets, heads down, scowling at the world. Lawrey picked out her niece among them, flanked by some girls she recognized as being Cara's friends. What were those girls' parents thinking? Did they not realize their teenagers were still out at almost midnight on a school night? Or did they simply not care?

Cara caught sight of Lawrey. The girl pursed her lips and folded her arms across her chest in defiance. There was no sign of any remorse in her body language.

"Thanks, Steve," she told the other officer. "I appreciate you tracking her down. I'll take it from here."

He drew his dark, bushy eyebrows together. "You sure? They've been drinking, by the looks of things."

"It's fine. Can you make sure the other girls get home safely?"

"Sure thing, Sarge."

Lawrey tried not to judge her teenage niece. The girl was wearing a top that was smaller than some of Lawrey's bras. While she understood it had been particularly hot out when Cara had left the house, she didn't think for a minute that the heat was the reason that particular item had been chosen. It bared the girl's tan midriff, and Lawrey tried not to experience a flash of jealousy at her slim, flat stomach. It had been a long time since Lawrey's belly had looked anything like that.

"Get in the car, Cara." Her tone didn't leave any room for argument.

Her niece said something to one of her friends, then stormed over, her head down, her hands shoved in the pockets of her shorts. She yanked open the passenger door, threw herself into the seat, and slammed the door shut behind her again.

Steve had already ushered Cara's friends into the cruiser, while the others they'd been with stood by, watching.

Lawrey looked over at the other teenagers. "The rest of you get home as well. Your parents will be wondering where you are, I'm sure, and you won't want me to send my colleagues to your front doors to let them know exactly where you are and what you've been doing."

They all muttered to one another, but they dispersed, the remaining girls heading away from the canal and to the sidewalk, while the guys walked along the canal. Lawrey waited long enough to make sure they were definitely leaving, and then she got back behind the wheel of the car and braced herself for the wrath of her niece.

Cara was sitting in the passenger seat, her entire body knotted in a ball of tension. Her arms folded tight, her jaw clenched, her lips thinned.

Lawrey let out a sigh, and apparently that was enough to set Cara off.

"I can't believe you had the goddamn *police* pick me up. Do you have any idea how embarrassing that was? I bet someone recorded it on their phone, too. It'll be all over school in the morning."

Lawrey twisted in her seat toward the girl. "You know a good way to ensure that doesn't happen? Make sure you're home when you say you're going to be home. And, if for whatever reason you can't make it, call your mom and let her know. Your parents thought you'd been murdered and left in a ditch somewhere. Frankly, so did I."

Cara rolled her eyes. "My phone died, that's all. It's no big deal."

"Look at all the police who came out to help find you. Clearly, it is a big deal."

"If my parents gave me a normal curfew instead of expecting me home ridiculously early, I wouldn't have been late. I don't know anyone else who has to be home at ten o'clock. Some of my friends don't have to be home until midnight. We're sixteen now, we're not babies."

"While you're living under someone else's roof, you need to follow their rules."

"Mom's rules are bullshit," Cara muttered.

"Who were the young men you were with? They were older than you."

"No one. They're seniors from school."

"What are they doing hanging out with a bunch of sophomores?"

"Nothing. We're just friends."

"They can't get friends their own age?"

Cara covered her face with both hands, let out a growl of annoyance, and sank down in the seat. "Oh my God. This is so stupid."

"It's not stupid, Cara. You have people who love you and who worry about you. Trust me, life would be a lot worse if you didn't have that." She shoved her phone at her niece. "Now, call your mom and tell her you're on your way home."

Lawrey was used to playing the bad guy, at least when it came to her family. She wished she could be the fun aunt, but she felt as though her ability to have fun had been drained out of her most of her adult life. Maybe she did take herself, and life, too seriously, but when you'd gone through the sort of shit she had, it was hard not to.

Chapter Seven

Lawrey yawned and scrubbed her hands over her eyes. She hadn't gotten to bed until way past midnight, and then hadn't been able to sleep. She'd turned over the confrontation with Cara in her mind, wondering if she could have handled things differently. She wanted her niece and nephew to feel like they could come to her if they were ever in any kind of trouble, but she didn't think that was going to happen. Maybe she just wasn't that kind of person. It wasn't as though Tommy had ever come to her either.

She headed into the office, making sure she picked up coffee on the way. She was in before eight, aware that they hadn't made enough progress on finding out about the two victims and what had happened to them. Today should bring some new developments. She hoped to hear from the medical examiner about the autopsies of both victims. The ME would be able to tell if they'd still been alive when the fire had started. If they weren't, and something else had killed them, Lawrey would find herself with a homicide investigation on her hands.

Abel was already at his desk when she got in.

"You're in early," she commented.

"Yeah, Marlene was awake at five, and I couldn't see much point in trying to get back to sleep. She dozed off, though, so I thought I might as well make myself useful."

"I'm sure you're useful at home as well, Abel. If you need to be there instead, we can manage."

He flapped a hand in her direction and changed the topic. "How's your niece? I heard there was a search party out for her last night."

Lawrey thought to how Cara probably hated her now. "She's grounded but otherwise fine."

"She's at that age. Bound to start pushing boundaries."

"True. Glad she's my niece so I can at least hand her back to her mother."

They both laughed.

"Oh, hey, I almost forgot something." She went to her desk and opened her drawer and took out a box of Girl Scout Cookies. "They're for Marlene. They came knocking a few evenings ago, and I knew she liked them."

Abel glanced down at the box. "Thin Mints. Thanks, Law. They're her favorite."

"Yeah, I remembered. I know she's not eating much right now, but I thought they might tempt her."

"Thanks. I'll let her know they're from you. Or why don't you come visit, give them to her yourself?"

"Things are crazy right now. I'm not sure when I'm going to have the time."

"Oh, sure. I understand. I think she'd love to see you, though."

A pang of guilt went through her. He was completely right. She did need to visit. When Lawrey had still been married to Patrick, the four of them had hung out all the time. They went to each other's houses for cookouts, invited each other to their kids' birthday parties, even spent the occasional holiday together—if Lawrey and Abel were ever to get the same time off. It was so hard seeing Marlene like that, and Lawrey always felt like she didn't know what to say, or that she was going to say the wrong thing.

Distracting herself, she ran her gaze over her desk. A small pile of mail waited for her, so she picked it up and rifled through for anything interesting. One letter caught her attention, and she paused. A cold rush of goose bumps ran across her skin. The name and address were handwritten, unusual in this day and age, but she recognized it. She tore open the envelope and took out the letter.

Printed across the plain white sheet of copy paper in black typeface, all in capitals was:

YOU KNEW WHAT HE WAS DOING. YOU LIKED IT. PERVERTED BITCH!!

She dropped the letter, instantly wishing she hadn't handled it.

"You okay, Law?" Abel asked.

"Yeah, fine."

This wasn't the first nasty letter she'd received, and she doubted it would be the last.

It had been almost thirty years now since her father had been caught in the sport's equipment closet with one of the girls he'd had on his soccer team. She'd been the same age as Lawrey's younger sister at the time. In the same school as well.

Abel frowned, concern etched across his face. "It's another one, isn't it? You'd think after thirty years, they'd give it up already."

"Thirty years probably feels like nothing to one of his victims. I imagine every time they close their eyes, they're taken right back there again."

"They still don't have any right to send you threatening letters. You were a child yourself when it all happened. How anyone can blame you, I don't know."

She understood. How often had she blamed herself?

He put out his hand. "We should get the letter to forensics."

She sighed and dropped it into the wastepaper trashcan beside her desk. "There's no point. They're too careful. Forensics won't get anything off it."

"You don't know when they might slip up."

"And if they do, what then? I go to them and challenge them on sending me a few letters after what my father did to them?"

"You don't know that whoever is sending these is one of his victims."

She did though. In her gut, she did.

Several people had come forward, but she was sure more existed who hadn't been able to bring themselves to talk about what had happened. It haunted her that she might come across them in everyday life, and yet she'd never know. Her father had taught at that school for fifteen years, pretty much since she'd been born, before he'd been caught and arrested. The shame it had brought on their family was unbearable, but even then, she knew it was nowhere near as bad as what the victims had gone through.

She had always been a daddy's girl. Where her sister had been closer to their mom, Lawrey had always had her dad around her little finger. Or so she'd thought.

Now, looking back, she wondered if anything about the close relationship she'd had with her father had been inappropriate. Had things happened that she'd unconsciously blocked out? It made her question everything. Those games they'd played doing tickling matches—was that really all they'd been?

People had said she must have known because the two of them were so close. Thick as thieves. Two peas in a pod.

It made her question her own reality.

What had been the truth?

Maybe she'd have felt better if she could have confronted her father about their past, ask him directly, but he'd taken his own life in a prison cell shortly after he'd been arrested. Everyone said that clearly made him guilty of the atrocities he'd been accused of, though he never got to have a trial. Lawrey hadn't been so sure. Her father had never seemed suicidal. He'd been confident, a charmer, someone who'd always been quick to make her smile. It didn't make sense to her either, but then little had back then. But everyone knew that no one liked a kiddy-fiddler in prison—not the other prisoners, nor the staff.

Was that why she'd become a cop? To prove to everyone—and maybe even herself—that she was nothing like her father? Most likely. It didn't take someone with a psychiatric degree to figure that out.

She forced a smile. "Let's forget about it, okay? We've got more important things to focus on, like the Sandtown case."

"You sure?" He didn't seem convinced.

"Positive."

She called that morning's briefing. It wasn't a big team, so roll call didn't take long.

"Finding out the identities of the two victims needs to be our priority," she said. "They'll most likely have people out there who love and miss them, and who need to be informed of their deaths. It'll open up a number of much-needed lines of inquiry, too, if we know who they are. How are we doing with running the partial plate?"

"We're narrowing it down," one of her detectives said, a young woman by the name of Annie Fletcher. "Hopefully forensics will be able to clear up the plate so we can at least get what state the vehicle originates from."

"What about interviewing any more of the residents of Sandtown? Have we got anyone who's seen anything more?"

"No, sorry, Sarge," Abel said. "No one's talking."

She thought for a moment. "It's a shame we can't find someone who has taken a photograph or video of the trailer before the fire damage. We might get the full plate then. Maybe we need to work harder to find some video footage of the area, even if it's from days or even weeks before the fire."

Heads were nodded around the room.

The trouble with crimes happening in Sandtown was that people simply weren't forthcoming. In other towns, if a crime had occurred right on their doorsteps, Lawrey could almost guarantee that people would come forward with information. It went the other way here. The residents clammed up, and it was highly unlikely anyone would voluntarily come forward with information, but especially not video footage. Who knew what else they might have caught on camera.

"We should hear from the medical examiner at some point today," she continued, "and we might even get a report back from the arson squad. That'll give us something else to go on."

She looked across her team. "Anyone have anything they need to add?" She waited a moment. "No? In which case, you all know what you need to be doing. Let's find out what happened to that couple."

Chapter Eight

The fire and the two deaths had affected Raye more than he'd thought possible. He couldn't get the scent of skin burning out of his nostrils. He was glad he was already a vegetarian as he doubted he'd have ever been able to eat meat again anyway. It wasn't as though this had been the first fire in Sandtown, and it hadn't been the first deaths either, but they'd been the first ones he'd needed to face head-on like that.

He stood in front of a large canvas, the paints he needed for the work already decanted from their bigger pots into smaller ones to avoid waste. It was so hot, the paint dried within minutes, and he'd learned from experience that it was better to keep the lid on the bigger tub and only use what was needed. He'd laid out his favorite brushes and already had the image he wanted to create on canvas in his mind.

He hadn't slept well. That wasn't unusual—especially in this heat—but it was more than that.

Addiction gnawed at him like invisible termites burrowing into his self-resolve. He'd been clean for twenty-six days now, which was the longest he'd managed in years, and he was proud of every one of those days. It wasn't easy getting clean anyway, and the prevalence and access to drugs in Sandtown made things even harder. Maybe he'd have been away from temptation if he lived somewhere else, but it wasn't as though that was ever going to happen.

Sandtown was his home now, and ever since he'd come to this place, he'd never considered living anywhere else.

Even if he wanted to, it wasn't as though he stood any chance of getting a mortgage to buy—not that he could afford to—or renting a place. He had no references, no deposit, and couldn't promise a steady income. At least here, he had a roof over his head and no one to answer to. Besides, it was his home. These were his people, and he didn't want to start over someplace else.

The best alternative he could have hoped for was family taking him in, but his brother wouldn't have him. Brad was married with two young kids, and though Raye knew Brad loved him, he couldn't have Raye living with him. Raye was too much of a liability. They'd tried it several times before, when Raye had been living on the streets, and Raye had promised to stay clean. But he'd inevitably fallen off the wagon, and his behavior had spiraled out of control.

He was deeply ashamed of how he'd treated his brother and family. It was no wonder Brad's wife despised him. He'd stolen from them multiple times, had lied, and manipulated—anything to get the money for that next hit. One time, he'd even faked that there had been a break-in, to make it appear as though someone other than him had stolen from them. He'd smashed a window, and trashed the house, and then had called the cops saying he'd got home and found the place like this. Of course, they'd busted him right away. Not only did one of the neighbors opposite have a Ring doorbell camera, so caught him going around the side of the house at the exact same time that he said the break-in must have happened, but they also found the items that had apparently been stolen—jewelry, cash, iPads, a credit card—hidden in a vent down in the basement where he was staying.

Addicts might be conniving and manipulative, but with the amount of brain cells killed off by the drugs, they weren't always the smartest of people.

Raye picked up his paintbrush, the wood digging into the fleshy part of his palm where the door handle had burned him. He sucked air in over his teeth and was instantly transported right back to that moment he'd realized the door was locked and he couldn't get to whoever was trapped inside.

Sweat broke out across his forehead at the memory. If he'd only been a little quicker, could he have saved their lives?

Raye hadn't had much interaction with the couple, but he'd seen them around. The girl had been young and pretty, with long wavy blonde hair and perfect teeth. She'd seemed altogether too wholesome to be living in Sandtown. The boyfriend had been a little older, but there had been something harder about him, a watchful glint to his eye. Raye had noticed the way he always seemed to have the last word, the way she'd fallen silent when he spoke over her, and how he often hooked his arm around her neck in a way that seemed less overprotective and more possessive.

There had been something else, too, something he wondered if he should have told the police sergeant about.

There was a rule in Sandtown that was similar to prison—snitches got stitches.

Even when something as serious as the deaths of two young people had occurred, it was still frowned upon to talk to the police. The residents of Sandtown were mistrustful of the cops, and many for good reason. They'd been homeless, and, despite not bothering anyone, had been forced to move on and move on—as though the cops actually thought they had anywhere to go, like they were living in underpasses and sewers and abandoned train stations for no reason. The police didn't want them to move on. What they actually wanted was for them to simply not exist. Plenty of them had experienced violence at the hands of cops, too, and of course, no one ever believed them or cared.

Sandtown was a refuge from all of that. A place they were accepted and felt safe. To go against that moral code of keeping the cops out was an action that meant maybe next time *you'd* be the one who found your RV burned to the ground.

The only reason people spoke to Lawrey Winters was because she was Tommy's mom. Tommy was liked in Sandtown. Yeah, he could get into trouble, just like they all could, but he was attractive and easy-going, always happy to drink beer and chat the night away.

Raye had seen Tommy and the girl who died in the fire a couple of nights before the fire, sitting around at The Crowbar, looking closer than two people who weren't supposed to be into each other should. Raye didn't know what had happened to the boyfriend—maybe he hadn't been feeling well and had stayed in the trailer—but the girl seemed to be enjoying her newfound freedom. Enjoying, in particular, her time with Tommy. Their heads had been close together, and Tommy had even been messing with the girl's hair, twisting it around his fingers, making her laugh.

Had the boyfriend been jealous? Was that what they'd been arguing about? Could he have decided to kill the girl and then himself rather than risk losing her to Tommy?

Raye didn't know much about police work, but even he knew that was a motive.

But if it was a motive for the boyfriend, then didn't it also mean it could be a motive for Tommy wanting them dead?

It made him antsy, having this information, and not knowing what to do with it. It played constantly on his mind, and he swayed between keeping it to himself and making contact with Lawrey.

Doing so was going to attract attention to himself, and it would be the wrong kind of attention, too. He already had people in town who didn't like him, and giving the cops information wouldn't look good for him.

Raye turned his attention back to his art, but still, a combination of guilt and need gnawed at him.

What if his information could catch a killer?

Chapter Nine

L awrey was knee-deep in paperwork when one of her detectives got her attention.

"Sarge, we've had a hit on the partial plate."

Lawrey spun around in her chair. "That's good news, Annie. What have you got?"

"We found one that's registered to twenty-three-year-old Stephan Porter from Portland, Oregon. With a bit of digging, I was able to pull up his driving insurance documents and discovered that he's got an Emily Clark as a named driver."

"Emily and Stephan," Lawrey repeated. "Those are the same names the witnesses from Sandtown gave us."

"That's right."

"They must be our victims. Did you run a NCIC check on their names?"

"Yes, and I found out that Emily Clark has a restraining order against a man called Zack Jones."

"Good work," Lawrey said. "That definitely fits with what we've learned so far. What about their families?"

"I've asked local officers to visit Emily's father to inform him that a young woman's body who we suspect to be that of his daughter has been found. We still need a formal identification to be done, though the body isn't in much of a state to be identified. We'll probably have to go down the DNA route, just to be sure. According to our records, Emily's father reported her missing two months ago."

"What about her mother?" Lawrey asked.

"No mother. Looks like she's not in Emily's life."

"What about Stephan Porter's family?"

Annie shook her head. "Haven't tracked anyone down yet. Mother died several years ago in a car accident. From the obituary, there's a half-brother, but we don't know where he is."

She let that sink in. Some people's lives seemed plagued with tragedy.

"Any priors, for either of them?"

"Yeah, for Stephan, but all misdemeanors." Annie checked her notes. "Drug possession, disorderly conduct, nothing too alarming. He's also got some parking tickets outstanding."

"No violence against women?"

"Not on record anyway." Annie moved on. "I expect Emily's father will want to come here, speak to us directly."

"Okay. Maybe he can consider identifying the body when he's here." Lawrey wasn't sure how she felt about that. While it was often useful to speak with the family, sometimes they got in the way. A grieving father in Sandtown, swinging his weight around, might be more of a hindrance than a help.

"What else do we know about the man Emily has the restraining order against? I assume that's her ex-boyfriend."

"He's twenty-six and has priors for petty theft and assault. He spent a short time behind bars when he was twenty-two."

"Sounds like a real catch."

"I've got local police heading around to his last known address, seeing if they can speak with him."

Abel was on the next desk over and overheard. "If he's responsible for killing the couple, will he even be there?"

"He could have driven here and back in that time, I guess," Lawrey said. "We'll run his plates, too, see if ANPR picked him up on the roads between those times."

"He might have driven a different vehicle, covered his tracks," Annie suggested.

Lawrey turned back to the young detective. "Good point, but we won't know until we've started with the basics. I should hear from the medical examiner later today so we'll hopefully know the causes of death, but personally, I think we've got too many things in play for this to have been an accident. If someone killed that young couple, I want to know who."

Abel cleared his throat "I heard that forensics also located two cell phones. They're badly damaged as well, but they've been sent off to digital forensics to see what we can get off them, if anything. With any luck, we might find some threatening messages or something from a number we can trace, but I suspect the phones will be disposable cell phones if they're on the run."

Lawrey twiddled a pen between her fingers. "Let's check for social media accounts. See if either of the victims posted anything recently. Same for Zack Jones. Might give us an idea as to their recent state of minds, too."

"Will do," Annie said. "Though I don't know if they'd have posted anything recently if they were in hiding."

Lawrey considered this for a moment. "If no one in Sandtown knew their surnames, if they were using disposable cells, if they didn't touch their social media accounts, how, exactly would this ex-boyfriend have tracked her down? The United States is a big place. She could have been anywhere."

Abel stepped in. "We don't know that he did. Right now, we're assuming he's our main suspect. They could have just as easily pissed off someone in Sandtown, and they decided to run them out of town. It's happened before."

"Yes," Lawrey nodded slowly, "but they don't normally burn down the trailers with the residents still inside them."

Abel cocked his head. "True. Maybe they didn't know. They might have thought they were out."

"It wouldn't exactly have been difficult to check that they weren't." Lawrey licked her lips. They were dry and cracked. Going from the desert heat into air-conditioned rooms was wrecking her skin. "I think we need to talk to some of the Sandtown residents in more detail. Find out what they know of the couple. One of them might have seen someone hanging around."

Abel checked his notes. "We've already had our officers take formal statements from the witnesses."

"Yeah, I've read them. No one saw anything, apparently."

She couldn't help the sarcasm in her tone. She only managed to get a toe in the door because Tommy was so well liked, and she didn't want to put Tommy in a difficult situation by pushing her luck. But, if it turned out two people had been murdered, she wouldn't have much choice.

"Did Emily's father know she was in Sandtown?" she wondered.

"He'd filed a missing person's report, remember?" Abel said. "That indicates he didn't know where she was."

"Yeah, but that doesn't mean he didn't know. Think about it. If he knew someone was causing trouble for his daughter, then he might have wanted that person to think Emily was missing. Maybe he thought it would stop whoever she had the restraining order against from hassling her?"

"That seems like a stretch. Making up that kind of lie and bothering the police, starting an investigation even."

"If you were worried someone wanted to kill your daughter, would you be worried about wasting a little police time?"

A muscle ticked in Abel's jaw. "If someone wanted to kill my daughter, they'd better hope I didn't get to them first."

"I thought we're supposed to believe in the law," she said. "No vigilante justice here."

"Hmm." He didn't seem convinced.

"Anyway," she moved back to the case, "my point is that we don't know the full story yet. It just seems like it's not a coincidence that a girl who needed to take out a restraining order on an ex-boyfriend ends up dead, together with her new boyfriend."

"You're right," he agreed.

Lawrey filled the rest of the team in with what they'd learned. Discovering the names of the victims was a big step. It meant they could request phone and bank details, try and track their movements. Of course, everything was harder when two people were living off-grid, but they might get lucky.

Lawrey's phone rang, distracting her once more. She answered it. "Detective Winters."

"Hi, it's Doctor James Anderson. I'm working on the two victims from the fire over at Sandtown. I've got some answers for you and thought you'd want to know ASAP."

"Doctor Anderson, hi. I absolutely want to know, thank you. Do you want to do this over the phone, or shall I come down there?"

"Might be better if you come down."

"No problem at all," she said. "Give me thirty minutes, and I'll be with you."

She ended the call and got to her feet.

"Going somewhere?" Abel asked.

"Medical examiner just called. He's got some info for us about the case."

Chapter Ten

Calrock was too small to have its own hospital and morgue, so she had to do the eight-mile drive to the next town, which was substantially larger, to speak with the medical examiner.

Lawrey didn't mind the drive. The interior of the car was cool, and she was able to sit and think while the tires ate the miles. Lots of people thought the desert was a barren, empty place, but she didn't see it that way at all. It was teeming with plants and wildlife, if you took a moment to take in the details. And the desert skies were like no other place on earth, how they stretched endlessly, uninterrupted.

It didn't take her long to arrive at the morgue. She got out and hurried between the car and the building, eager to escape the midday sun beating down upon her head and shoulders.

She signed in and then made her way down to the basement where the autopsy rooms were located. The corridors were cool, her shoes squeaking against the linoleum flooring. Pictures of the local area had been framed and hung on the walls, as though they would help make this place more cheerful somehow. The smell of cleaning fluid, together with something more organic, permeated the air.

Lawrey reached the doors for the examination room and pulled on some protective outerwear from a rack positioned against the wall. She knocked and then entered.

Music played from somewhere in the corner.

James Anderson, the medical examiner, looked more like someone's kindly uncle than a person who spent all day chopping up bodies. He was British and spoke with what sounded like a very proper English accent to Lawrey, which always made her smile.

"Sorry to interrupt," she called.

He was deep in his work, quite literally, his gloves covered in bodily fluids as he leaned over a cadaver.

"Oh, Detective, my apologies. I didn't hear you come in."

He gave a voice command to the speaker, and the room fell quiet.

"Thanks for coming down," he said.

"Happy to. I'm hoping you're going to be able to tell me if we're looking at an accident or if this case is a homicide."

"All I can give you are the facts," he said. "You're the one who'll have to decide how to interpret them."

In the windowless room, several metal operating tables were positioned at regular intervals. Today, only two of those tables were being used. The burned bodies of the two victims from the trailer in Sandtown were laid out on their backs, as best they could be, considering the fire had caused some of their limbs to curl in on themselves like a boxer holding his hands up in front of him, something called the pugilistic attitude. Exposed muscles contracted and shrank because of the heat, leading to a deformity of the limbs.

"There are a number of questions I ask myself when working on burn victims," he said, walking steadily around the tables. "First of all, what can we use to identify the victims? Are there any possible sites for fluid analysis or to take DNA samples? Luckily, these victims aren't so badly charred that those things are impossible. I also check for any foreign bodies that can help to identify the victims, tattoos that are still visible via macroscopic examination, for example. They might have been wearing a watch at their time of death or perhaps a wedding ring. Even dental fillings or medical devices can be matched with a victim's medical history. So you see, we have a lot to work with."

"Yes, you do," she agreed. "We might have found the identities of the victims via the plate that was on their trailer. Names are Stephan Porter and Emily Clark. We have the girl's father coming, so if you're able to get a DNA sample—which, considering the condition of the body, I guess you can—we can compare it to his DNA. The young man might be a little harder, as we're still working on tracking down next of kin."

James nodded. "That's good news, but yes, we'll need to confirm their identities to know for sure."

"What about how they died?" Lawrey was keen to get onto the good stuff.

"Yes, of course. That was my second point. I always ask myself, are there any obvious causes of death, other than the fire? Now, I saw photographs from the scene when the bodies were in situ. The positions of both the bodies still lying in bed is suspicious. It suggests neither of the victims made any attempt to escape the fire, and we have to ask ourselves why. Were they so intoxicated that they didn't wake up?"

"I thought the same."

"So let's look at the bodies. Are there any wounds that suggest they were dead before the fire started, therefore indicating that arson was a way of covering up two underlying homicides? I also carried out specific toxicology screening to test for blood levels of substances such as alcohol, cyanide, and also carbon monoxide, to try to understand whether or not the victims were alive before the fire started." He walked around to the other side of the table and motioned to the lower half of Emily's body, where the charring wasn't so bad because she'd been pressed against the mattress. "We got lucky that the other residents were able to douse some of the flames. I've seen some burn victims' bodies that have been completely carbonized in a fire, and believe me, that makes my job a hell of a lot more difficult."

"I can imagine."

"Yes, it complicates dissection and means things like bullets and traumatic fractures, or even prosthetic limbs, can be missed."

Lawrey was itching for him to get on with it. "Were they dead before the fire started?"

"Yes, I believe they were."

"How can you be sure?

"The percentage of serum carboxyhemoglobin in both their blood samples was low, plus, there was no presence of smoke in either of their lungs. Neither of them were breathing at the time of the fire."

Lawrey's pulse picked up its pace. That changed things. They knew for certain now that their deaths weren't an accident, and so, most likely, neither was the fire.

"If they didn't die from the fire," she said, "how did they die?"

He pursed his lips, his nostrils flaring. "I'm sure you understand that these things are far harder to see when a body has been badly burned, but I've used cross-sectional imaging and autopsy computer tomography to give me a better overall view of the body. From what I can tell, the female victim has multiple injuries that weren't caused by the fire. She has a fracture of her hyoid bone. She also has fractures of her third proximal phalange on her right hand, and of the third and second metacarpal of her left hand. She also had a complete break of her left clavicle."

"Are these older or newer fractures?"

"Newer. They hadn't had the chance to heal before she was killed."

"So they most likely happened during the attack that killed her?"

He pursed his lips. "That's the most likely interpretation of events. Again, because of the burning, it wasn't so easy to tell, but the imaging also revealed multiple areas of bruising, particularly around her throat and wrists, but also vaginally and anally."

"What are you saying? That she was sexually assaulted?"

"From what I've been able to tell from what remains of the tears and bruising, especially that they're still detectable even after the fire, it was definitely assault rather than consensual sex."

A terrible image of Emily Clark's final hours was starting to form in Lawrey's mind. "She was raped and then murdered?"

"And then her body burned."

"Any traces of DNA?" Lawrey asked. "Semen inside any of the cavities?"

"Unfortunately, the heat from the fire denatured any possible samples we might have taken. I did find something in the back of the throat, but there's a good chance it'll be the same."

"So we won't know if it matches the DNA of the male victim?"

"I've sent it off to the lab, but it's going to take a couple of days to get the results."

"Can we put a rush on it?"

"We can try. Not sure we'll get anywhere yet. I've also taken samples from beneath her nails, so we might get something from that, but again, the fire has made that difficult. One hand is basically charred, but the other came off better."

Lawrey glanced at the poor woman's hands. One was completely blackened, the fingers curled in toward the palm. The other hadn't been so badly burned, and Lawrey was even able to make out a couple of perfectly shaped nails, from which he would have taken the samples.

"What about the male victim, Stephan Porter?"

The medical examiner crossed to the next table and stood by the victim's head. "He has several stab wounds. Two are more superficial, but I believe he died from a deeper one, which was made by a puncture of a flat blade between the ribs which perforated the victim's left lung. It then filled with blood, effectively causing him to drown to death in his own blood."

"Jesus," Lawrey said. "Is there any possibility he did this to himself? The couple were arguing before they went into their trailer. Maybe he killed the girl and was so overwhelmed with grief that he killed himself, too."

"It's difficult to tell, because of the fire damage, but I'd say that was unlikely, but not impossible."

She couldn't remember seeing a knife anywhere near the bodies, or one being found, but with the fire damage, it could have been missed—possibly fallen between the burned floorboards. She made a mental note to check if the arson squad had found anything. If there was no knife, then whoever did this must have taken it with them. They must have killed Stephan before raping and murdering Emily. But why did no one hear or see anything? Surely, if someone attacked Stephan, Emily would have screamed and perhaps tried to get help. The person would have needed to act with extreme speed to stop her from getting away.

"I have one final question," Lawrey said.

"Shoot."

"How long before the fire started had the two victims been killed?"

"It's not an exact science, I'm afraid, and with this amount of damage to the bodies, it makes it even harder to tell."

"Ballpark figure?" she suggested. "Minutes or hours?"

She knew it couldn't be any longer than that, as both victims had been seen arguing outside of the trailer several hours before the fire. It might help her build up a picture of how events had taken place. If Stephan had killed Emily shortly after they'd gone inside, but he'd been alive hours later, it might mean that he'd tried to cover up her death, but things had gone wrong.

On the other hand, if Stephan had died first, and Emily had suffered the sexual assault after he'd been killed, they'd know they were looking for a third party.

"Going purely on facts, it's impossible to know for sure. The way the heat from the fire affects the blood in the body means our usual methods go out of the window. But if we're speaking purely on experience and gut instinct, I'd say the girl was dead first. Just don't ask me to prove it in court."

"I understand, and thank you."

"I'll upload the final report when it's ready."

She left the morgue and drove back to Calrock, her thoughts whirring. Right now, the most obvious suspect for the murders was the same man Emily had a restraining order against. If he'd found her, her rape and murder would be punishment for her trying to escape him.

They needed to track him down.

She got back to the station. Her partner was there to greet her.

"How did it go?" Abel asked.

"We're looking at this being homicide." She filled him in on everything she'd learned, including how they were missing the murder weapon that had been used to kill Stephan Porter. "At least we know now that we're dealing with a murder investigation. Someone killed that young couple and then tried to burn down the trailer to cover up the deaths."

Abel pursed his lips. "You don't think Stephan was responsible then?"

"I think it's highly unlikely. He'd have had to sexually assault and murder Emily, then stab himself, set the fire, and then lie down on the bed beside Emily and wait to die."

Abel shrugged. "Crazier things have happened."

"I'm not ruling it out, I just don't want to get blindsided by the theory. It's more likely that Emily's ex-boyfriend showed up. The only thing that doesn't fit is the possibility Emily died before Stephan. If Zack Jones is responsible, surely he'd kill Stephan first, since Stephan would be more of a threat to him."

"Unless he knocked Stephan unconscious, or had him locked in the bathroom or something, while he assaulted Emily. We don't know much about this Zack Jones yet. He might be one of those sick fucks who wanted to torture Stephan by making him hear what he was doing to Emily before he killed them both."

"That's a good theory," Lawrey said, "but why didn't anyone hear anything? If Stephan was alive, wouldn't he have banged and shouted?"

"Maybe someone did hear something," Abel said. "But you know what Sandtown is like. They decided to mind their own business."

"And let a young woman die." She clucked her tongue against the roof of her mouth. "How are we getting on with tracking down Zack Jones?"

"Uniform went to his last known address, in Portland, Oregon, but there was no sign of him. The place didn't appear to have been lived in for a while. They peered inside the mailbox, and there were a ton of letters for him. They went around to the neighbors and asked if anyone had seen anything of him, but no one had seen him for the last week or so, at least."

"So he could have been on the trail of Emily Clark and Stephan Porter."

"It's something we need to consider."

She nodded. "He has a motive, and so far we haven't been able to track him down in order to get an alibi from him. You have to admit it's suspicious. Maybe Emily cracked and called him or something, slipped up and let him know where she was. Violent men tend to have a hold over the women they abuse, even long after they've gotten out of the relationship. We know Emily and Stephan were fighting. That might have been going on for sometime, and Emily felt she wasn't in a good relationship with him either and turned back to the ex. Stephan could have found out, and that's why they were arguing."

"It's certainly a possibility. Until we can track down her ex, it's one we're going to need to keep open." Abel seemed to be thinking. "Here's something I don't get. If Zack killed them and set the fire, why was the security chain on the door?"

"He must have got out through a window," Lawrey said, "and pulled it shut behind him. The guy from the arson squad suggested that an accelerant had been used, and the pour pattern was close to the window, too."

"But no one saw him?" Abel didn't sound convinced.

"Or they did, but they're keeping their mouths shut."

"Would they lie to protect a stranger, though? An outsider who's come into Sandtown, murdered two of their own, and then run again?"

Lawrey remembered what the older couple had told her—that Emily and Stephan hadn't been one of them. That they weren't 'Sanders' even though they were there during the summer.

"Maybe they never thought of Emily and Stephan as their own?"

"Even so, I still think someone must have seen something. Or heard something, even. How does someone murder two people, set fire to a trailer, and walk away as though nothing has happened?"

"I do agree. Strangers get noticed in Sandtown, especially at this time of year. Maybe if it had been winter, with all the snowbirds and tourists, I could buy that happening, but in the height of summer?" She sucked air in over her teeth and shook her head. "It doesn't make sense to me."

"You think someone from Sandtown might have done this?"

"I'm not pointing any fingers," she said.

"No, but I know that face." He angled his head. "You're considering it."

"I wish we had some idea of what they were arguing about. Had Emily been in touch with Zack again? Or had she heard from him? Maybe one of them felt they needed to move on, while the other thought they should stay? Or it might have had nothing to do with that. Maybe we're being blindsided by the fact Emily had a restraining order out against her ex-boyfriend. One of them might have met someone new and decided to break things off."

"Met someone new at Sandtown?" Abel checked. "I guess it's possible."

"I think we need to get back up to Sandtown and ask some more questions. Someone up there knows more than they're letting on, and it's our job to find out what."

Chapter Eleven

They'd already decided between them that Lawrey would take the lead on the questioning. The residents of Sandtown knew her better and were more likely to open up. She'd told Abel to hang back, close enough to be nearby if she needed him, but not so close that people refused to speak to her.

They grabbed something to eat on the way. Lawrey never liked dealing with potential conflict on an empty stomach, and it felt like forever since she'd eaten breakfast.

The first place they went to in Sandtown was Raye's trailer home. Abel parked a short distance from the structure Raye had built up around it to create his studio, sheltered from the sun.

Lawrey climbed from the car and paused at the entrance. She spotted Raye standing at a canvas. He had on a wig of long dreadlocks today, a leather miniskirt, and a T-shirt tied at the sides.

"Hey, Raye. You mind if I have a word about yesterday?"

Raye Diante jumped at her voice and spun around. He had a paintbrush held cautiously in one hand, but, from the look of the canvas in front of him, he wasn't actually doing much painting.

"I spoke to you already," he said. "And I gave the other cops a formal statement and told them everything I knew."

"I know, and thank you for that, but things have changed. Yesterday, we believed this still might be an accident, but today we're investigating a double homicide."

His blue eyes went wide. "A double homicide? Someone killed them?"

"It certainly looks that way, and it's our job to find out who. I'd really appreciate your help with it."

"But I don't have anything else to tell you." He glanced down, his foot—which today was pushed into a pair of wedged mules—scraping on the dirt ground.

"You might think you don't, but any information could be of help to us right now."

"I-I really don't think it's a good idea."

She cocked her head. "Raye, you seem to be forgetting that outstanding warrant and that I know your real name. You wouldn't want me to follow those up, would you?"

He paled. She felt bad using it against him, but this was far more important than a couple of driving tickets and misdemeanor drug possession charge.

"I don't know what to tell you."

"Tell me about the couple, Emily and Stephan. When did they arrive?"

"I don't know exactly. A couple of months ago. Right before summer."

Lawrey frowned. "It's unusual for people to arrive at that time, right? Normally people are leaving."

"True, but they were hiding out from someone."

"Emily's ex-boyfriend?"

"Yeah." He scowled. "If you know all this already, why do you need me to go back over it?"

"In case we've missed something important." She checked her notebook. "How did they seem to you?"

"How do you mean?"

"Were they friendly? Happy? Worried?" She widened her eyes at him. "I can go on feeding you adjectives, but I'm sure you get the point."

"At first they kind of kept to themselves. They didn't really speak to anyone more than they needed. But after a month or so, they started to warm up. They got to know people and socialized some more. He always seemed really protective of the girl, especially at first, but I guess they relaxed a bit, decided they were safe here."

A big mistake on their part, she thought but didn't say.

"There have been reports of the two of them fighting. Do you know anything about that?"

He shrugged. "No, but people fight, and out here, it ends up being everyone's business. The walls of a trailer ain't so good at keeping the sound in, if you know what I mean."

"But you don't know what they were fighting about?"

"Sorry, no idea."

Lawrey moved on. "You said they were socializing a bit more. Can you tell me who with?"

His lips tightened, his nostrils flaring. "If I do that, you're going to go and speak to them and then they're going to come looking for me."

She lowered her notebook and pen. "I swear I won't tell them who else I've been speaking to."

"You won't need to. They'll know. People see everything in this place. I guarantee there will already be word spreading that the cops are back and asking questions."

"See, here's the thing that bothers me, Raye. You say people see everything in this place, yet a couple wa murdered and their trailer set on fire, but it seems no one saw a single thing. Curious, isn't it?"

"I told you everything I know. I'm not protecting anyone."

"Who were Emily and Stephan friendly with?"

He let out a sigh. "Stephan hung out over at The Crowbar." He pursed his lips again, hesitating.

She could tell he was holding something back. "Tell me, Raye."

"And word is that Emily was getting a little too friendly with Tommy."

She blinked up at him. "Tommy? My Tommy?"

"Yeah. That might have even been the reason Emily and Stephan were fighting. But I don't know that for sure. I wasn't lying when I said I didn't know."

"Shit."

Her stomach knotted. She hated confrontation with Tommy. She always worried she was going to say something that tipped him over the edge. She dealt with confrontation every single day in her job, and normally she'd face it head-on, but it was different with her son.

Could he have had something to do with the young couple's deaths? No, she couldn't believe it of him. He'd done some fucked-up shit in his time, but murder? Besides, if he was friendly with Emily, why would he kill her? He had no motive.

People would say she was blinded where Tommy was concerned. Maybe they were right, but she thought that would be true of most people and their kids. No one wanted to think badly of them. Even though she knew Tommy was capable of theft and violence and drug and alcohol abuse, she'd never be able to convince herself that he was a killer.

Speaking to Hella Billy wasn't going to be fun either. The big ex-biker was notoriously anti-police. She didn't know the full story, but rumor was that his daughter was killed and for some reason he blamed the police for it.

"Thanks, Raye. I appreciate you telling me. I know that won't have been easy."

"Can I get back to my work now?"

"Sure."

She left him to his painting.

Tommy's trailer was on the other side of town. Abel was waiting down the road for her, and she envied him the air-conditioned cool of the car.

"How'd it go?" he asked as she opened the passenger door and climbed in.

"Can you drive me over to Tommy's. Seems he knew Emily better than he'd mentioned to me."

"Sure thing. What did Raye say?"

"That the two of them had gotten close, maybe too close. It might have been the reason Emily and Stephan were fighting."

"Well, damn."

"Yeah." She let out a sigh. "I can't believe he'd have anything to do with their deaths, though."

Abel shot her a look. "I should probably be the one to talk to him. Conflict of interest and all that."

"Yeah, I know. Can you let me speak to him first, though. You know I won't cover up for him. If I think for one second he's done something so terrible, I'll throw him behind bars myself."

It hurt her to say such a thing, but it was the truth. It was her job to protect people from crimes, and if someone she'd created was involved, she'd feel even more responsible than normal. She wouldn't let him walk, no way.

"Whatever you want, Sarge."

He drove her to the other side of town, to where Tommy's trailer was located. A heavy stone had lodged in her chest. What was he going to say?

They found Tommy sitting in a camping chair out the front of his trailer. He'd built a shade over the door and fitted a misting system to keep cool. He looked well, and her heart broke a little. He was a functioning addict, but she loved him with every piece of her.

"Hey, Mom," Tommy greeted her. "I heard you were in town again."

"I've gotta ask you some questions, Tommy. It's about the couple from the trailer fire."

"Thought you might need to do that." He spotted Abel sitting in the car and lifted his hand in a wave. "Hey, Abel. How's Marlene?"

Abel climbed out and slammed the door shut. "Not good, to be honest, Tommy. Think we're almost at the end now."

Tommy drew on his cigarette. "Fuck, I'm sorry, Abel."

"Thanks," Abel said, his voice tight.

Tommy flicked the cigarette, and the embers bounced across the road. "So, what do you want to ask me, Mom?"

"How close were you with the female victim, Emily?"

He shrugged. "Not close at all. We chatted a couple of times, but I barely knew her."

"That's not what I've heard." She didn't say that it was Raye who'd told her. It wouldn't be fair to put that on him.

"I don't know what you've heard or why I'm being singled out. Maybe because people know you're a cop, so they're fucking with both of us?"

Lawrey thought that Raye was telling the truth. Did that mean Tommy was the one lying to her now? If he *was* lying to her, it meant he had something to cover up.

"Who were you with before the fire started, Tommy?"

He barked a cold laugh. "You asking me for an alibi, Mom? You really think I'm capable of burning down someone's trailer with them inside it?"

"I'm not only investigating a burned-down trailer. We have reason to believe the couple were already dead when the fire started."

His eyebrows shot up. "They were murdered?" Realization dawned. "You think I might be capable of murdering two people? Jesus, Mom. I know I've done some bad shit in my time, but not that. Never that."

"Then tell me what you were doing in the time before they were killed and the trailer was set on fire."

He dragged his hand through his hair. "Jesus, I don't know. Just hanging out."

"Where?"

He gestured at the trailer. "Here, I guess."

"You guess?"

"Yes, I was here."

She wasn't just going to let it go. "But you can't prove that."

He waved a hand. "I don't know. Go ask around. Someone might have seen me leaving my trailer when people started shouting about the fire."

"See, it's not easy to get that kind of information from people, because no one around here ever seems to say anything."

"That doesn't mean I'm responsible. I haven't done anything! I can't believe you'd even think I'd murder someone because I'd talked to them a few times. I mean...what the fuck, Mom?"

"Don't make out like you're some kind of angel, Tommy. I know you. Don't forget that."

He rolled his eyes, and she was taken back to him being a teenager. Sometimes it felt like nothing ever changed.

"Yeah, and you'll never let it go, will you? You can't think because someone says I spoke to the girl a couple of times that I'm responsible for killing her? Why the fuck would you jump to that conclusion?"

"I haven't jumped to that conclusion. I'm asking questions. That's what my job is all about. I'm asking you exactly the same questions as I'd ask anyone else."

"Now, I'm no cop, but I always thought you needed things like actual evidence, or maybe even a motive before you started accusing people of things."

Abel stepped in. "No one is accusing anyone of anything. Like your mom said, she's simply asking some questions. If you knew this girl, you might be able to help us find out who killed her and her boyfriend. Maybe she said something to you about what they were doing in Sandtown."

His shoulders relaxed. "There was some ex-boyfriend she was trying to hide out from, though, if you ask me, the one she was with here wasn't exactly a catch."

"What do you mean by that?" Lawrey asked.

"He was overbearing. Always wanted to know where she was. Possessive, and jealous."

She raised an eyebrow. "Jealous of you?"

"Nothing happened," he insisted. "We spoke a few times, shared a beer and a cigarette. Normal stuff."

"But she mentioned she was frightened of her ex?"

"Not frightened, exactly. More relieved. I think she was happy to be here. It was the new boyfriend, Stephan, who she seemed more worried about. She was always checking over her shoulder, or saying he'd be asking where she was, and that she needed to get back. I guess she had a type, and that type was asshole men."

"Did you ever see any sign that Stephan was hitting her? Bruises or anything like that?"

He shook his head. "Nah, nothing like that. She was jumpy around him. Different to how she was when it was only the two of us."

Only the two of them? That sounded cozy. Was it possible Tommy was the reason Emily and Stephan had been fighting?

"What about Stephan? Who did he know in town?"

Tommy jerked his chin. "He hung out at the club mostly. Saw him talking with Hella Billy more often than not."

"Okay, thanks, Tommy."

She exchanged a glance with Abel. "Guess we're paying Billy a visit, too."

"For fuck's sake, don't tell him I sent you." Tommy lit another cigarette.

"We won't. Don't worry."

They probably didn't need to. Enough people had seen them talking that it would be all over town within an hour or two.

They left Tommy and drove to the part of town where The Crowbar was located. Like the rest of Sandtown, The Crowbar was an open-air, semi-permanent structure made out of whatever could be sourced for free or cheap. It had the vibe of a tiki hut rather than a biker bar, with a bamboo roof and a wooden structure. To one side, a stage had been created that hosted the bands that liked to play here, and at the far end, inside what had once been a metal storage container, was the bar. The furniture was an assortment of random items, chairs and tables that had been scavenged.

They climbed out of the car and approached the bar.

A man in his late twenties with a shaved head stood behind the bar, wiping down the surface. Lawrey wasn't sure why he was even bothering since a place exposed like this meant it would only end up covered in a fine dust within thirty seconds anyway.

She didn't know this guy's name, but she knew he wasn't Hella Billy.

The man scowled as he caught sight of them. "What do you want? We don't much like cops around here."

"Tell me something I don't know," she said. "I'm Detective Winters, this is Detective Kavanagh. We need to talk to Hella Billy. Is he around?"

The scowl didn't leave his face. "He's not in town right now. He's gone on a job somewhere."

"What kind of job? Isn't his job right here, in the club?"

He shrugged. "It's something to do with the club. Meeting with a new beer supplier or something."

Lawrey arched her eyebrows. "A supplier of *something* sounds about right to me."

The man took a packet of gum out of the top pocket of his shirt, unwrapped a stick, and folded it into his mouth. "Now, now, Detective, you can't go accusing people of things without there being any truth to it."

"I didn't accuse anyone of anything. I only want to talk. What do you know about the young couple who was killed the other night?"

"Not much. The guy came to the club on the regular. The girl, too, sometimes. She was pretty, though, got too much attention from the men, and I don't think he liked that."

"You don't think who liked that? Stephan?"

"If that was his name, yeah. He seemed the possessive type. That doesn't go down so well around here. We prefer to think that people can't belong to people."

That was something she could agree with.

"When's Hella Billy coming back?" she asked.

"Dunno. Tomorrow maybe."

She gave a brief nod. "Okay. I'll be back." Then she paused. "Oh, and what's your name again?"

"Robin," he told her. "Robin, Prince of Thieves."

She rolled her eyes. "Sure it is."

She spotted a wallet sitting on the counter and quickly grabbed it.

"Hey, that's mine!"

The driver's license was in a plastic sleeve inside. She read the name. "Landon Hawkins. Good to meet you, Landon."

His scowl deepened. "The feeling isn't mutual."

Lawrey put down the wallet and turned to leave.

"People round here don't like the cops poking around," he called out to her.

She shouted back, "I don't give a fuck what people around here do or don't like. Tell Hella Billy I want to talk to him."

She sensed his glare penetrating her spine as she walked away and headed to the car. She climbed into the vehicle, slammed the door shut behind her, and sat back.

"What do we know about Hella Billy?" she asked Abel.

"Not much. Ex-biker. History with the cops. Much the same as a lot of people around here."

"He was the one who broke down the door of the trailer. Do you think that was because he was friendly with Stephan?"

"It's a possibility."

"But then why didn't he go inside? He left it up to Raye?"

"Maybe he didn't want to put himself at risk. It's understandable. I'm not sure I'd run into a burning trailer either."

"Raye did, though," she said thoughtfully. "He didn't give a thought to his own safety. He ran straight in there."

"Raye seems like a good guy," Abel said.

Lawrey's phone buzzed, and she checked the screen. It was a message from her sister.

Don't forget, dinner at seven at Tipsy's.

"Shit," Lawrey cursed.

Abel looked at her expectantly. "Everything all right?

"Yeah, I promised my sister I'd have dinner with her and Eddie tonight. You want to come? Might do you good to get out?"

"Nah, thanks, though, Law. I appreciate the invite. I'd better get back to Marlene."

She patted his hand. "No worries, Abel. I understand. Don't forget to give her those cookies from me and send her my love."

Chapter Twelve

H eat.

Cloying heat.

Her tongue stuck to the roof of her mouth. Her eyelids were so dry they seemed to be glued to her eyeballs. Was that why she couldn't open them?

She couldn't seem to get her body to respond at all. Her limbs were lead weights, far too heavy to move.

Her head pounded.

A humming came from somewhere nearby, though she couldn't quite place it, and she couldn't open her eyes to see where it was coming from. Where was she? What had happened? Her brain didn't seem to want to work either. No coherent thought formed in her mind. She struggled to remember much of anything at all—even her name was vague and distant, a dream she couldn't quite hold on to after waking.

The creak of a door opening, followed by a male voice, filtered through to her.

"Fuck, look at the state of this one."

A different voice. "Is she even still alive?"

"She'd fucking better be. Won't be much good to us if she's dead already."

Footsteps grew closer, near her head. The shove of a foot against her ribs. She wanted to respond, wanted to cry for help, but she didn't think it would do any good, even if she was able to. These men must have something to do with the state she was in.

Did she recognize their voices? She couldn't be sure. Something about one of them pinged a memory inside her, but since she couldn't even remember her own name, how was she going to remember his?

She needed water. That was the only thing she could be sure of. That, and it was hot, and everything hurt.

Was she in Hell? Could this be what Hell was like? The voices around her were those of demons? No, she didn't think she was dead, though she couldn't be sure. The voices were too human.

"No, she's still with us. I saw her fingers move."

Strangely, she took hope from his words. Her fingers moved? Had they really? She couldn't even figure out where her fingers were...well, at the ends of her hands, and her hands were at the ends of her arms...or at least she hoped.

"She gonna be awake by the time we need her?" one of the men asked.

"Yeah, it'll wear off by then. Leave her the food and water. She'll want it when she wakes."

Water.

It was as though a part of her brain came alive at the word. She suddenly found she wasn't as deep as before, not floundering quite so much. Her focus was to drive herself upward, and then she'd be able to get what she needed most. But though she tried, she couldn't break free from the weights holding her down. She kicked and struggled, but it was like being stuck in weeds beneath the surface of a deep dark lake.

Footsteps faded, followed by a clang of a door shutting once more.

She had used all her energy trying to fight her way to...to what? She wasn't even sure she remembered anymore.

Like what had happened to her, her name, where she was, it all faded into nothingness.

Chapter Thirteen

Abel got home shortly after six.

"Hey, sweetie." He kissed the top of his daughter's head. Sometimes, he still had to shake himself at the idea that he had an adult daughter now. He didn't feel anywhere near old enough, though, when he looked in the mirror, he was reminded by the face staring back at him that he was. "How did today go?"

"Oh, you know. Ups and downs. She's sleeping now."

"I'm sorry I wasn't able to pop back today. Had my hands full with a case."

She looked up from her book. "That young couple killed out in Sandtown?"

"That's right. How did you hear about it?"

"I popped out to the Mini-Mart to grab some groceries, and someone was talking about it there."

"Should have known word would get around fast in this place."

"Yep. No keeping secrets here."

"If only the same could be said for Sandtown. Those people's mouths are clamped tight as a clam. No one's talking, but someone must know something about what happened."

"Do you know who the victims are yet?"

"We've got some names, but no confirmation of the bodies actual identities as of yet. I'm sure we'll find out, though. Most people out in that place tend to be on the system, so we'll hopefully be able to match prints or DNA."

"Good. I'm sure they'll still have loved ones out there who'll want to know what happened."

He thought of the case. "They're not the only ones who want to know what happened."

She changed the subject. "You want some dinner? I kept some lasagna back for you. I can reheat it, if you like?"

"You're a good girl, Suze, thanks."

"Tell you what, I'll even crack you open a beer."

"What more could an old man ask for?"

A healthy wife, he thought. What was he going to do when Marlene passed? Suze wouldn't stay forever. He wouldn't want her to. A young woman her age should be out living her life, meeting a possible future husband, or getting ahead in her career. He felt overwhelmed with guilt that she was here instead, but he knew she wouldn't have it any other way. Suze wanted to be here for her mother, and she wouldn't miss these final few months.

When Marlene did eventually go, be it weeks or even months from now, he was going to need to figure out who he was without her. They'd been together since they were in their early twenties, and he didn't know how to live without her in his life.

He left the living room to go to the back of the house where the bedrooms and bathrooms were located.

He was glad their house was all on one level. They'd have struggled if they'd had to contend with stairs when Marlene was so weak. While she wasn't able to get out of bed much anymore, at least she'd had her independence for as long as possible.

He knocked lightly on the bedroom door—even though it used to be his bedroom, too—and then entered.

Marlene was sitting up in bed, propped by numerous pillows. Her appearance would never not shock him. The amount of weight she'd lost recently had turned her skeletal. She'd never been a big woman, but now she looked as though she could blow away in a breeze. His heart broke anew every time he saw her.

"Hey, sweetheart," he said softly, "you're awake."

He went over to her and kissed her forehead. She smiled at him, but the expression was forced. He recognized the tension around her eyes, the pinched lines of her mouth.

"The pain bad again?" he asked.

"Yeah, but I didn't want to worry Suze."

"Suze is an adult," he said. "She can handle it."

"She might be an adult by age, but she's still my little girl, and if I can save her from suffering while I can, then I will. God knows she's going to have enough of that ahead of her."

Marlene was a stubborn woman when she wanted to be, and Abel knew there was no point in fighting with her. She'd rather be in physical pain herself than cause any more emotional distress for their daughter.

"Okay, well, let me get those pills for you."

She was on patches to ease some of the background pain, but when she had breakthrough pain like this, the only thing that touched it was morphine.

"Thanks, love," she said with another weak smile.

He found the medication and a glass of water and waited while she swallowed the pills. He took the glass back off her again, and she sank back into the pillows, waiting for the drugs to kick in.

"Are you hungry?" he asked. "I could make you something light?"

Stupidly, he wanted her to eat, wanted her to keep her strength up, even though he knew there was no point. She was never going to get any better, no matter what kind of nutrition she consumed. He wanted to cry just thinking about it, and he did, in private, when no one else was around to see.

He'd moved into the guest room some months ago when it had become clear she needed the bed. Her sleep patterns were all over the place, so it was better that she could sit up and turn the light on to read, or watch Netflix on her laptop at any time, rather than worrying she was going to disturb him. Because of his job, he also got calls all times of the day and night, so he didn't want to wake her either.

It broke his heart that this cruel disease had stolen such a simple comfort like sleeping beside the person you loved.

"No, I'm fine. Suze made me something earlier. Thank you, though, sweetheart. I think I'm going to sleep some more."

"Okay, I'll leave you in peace then."

He backed out of the room and closed the door, but not fully. He wanted to be able to hear if she called out for him.

Abel went back into the living room. The meaty scent of lasagna filled the air, and his stomach gurgled. It had been a long day, and other than grabbing a sandwich at lunch, he hadn't eaten.

"How does she seem?" Suze asked him, setting his mea[l] on a tray on the coffee table.

He was pleased to see an icy beer sitting on the tray. H[e] needed it.

"Much the same," he said.

Worry passed like a cloud across his daughter's feature[s.] "You don't think she seems more tired than normal?"

"It's normal for her to be tired with what she's goin[g] through."

"I know. I feel like she'd been sleeping more these las[t] couple of days."

Abel wanted to reassure her. "It's good for her to sleep."

She dipped her chin. "I guess so. I wondered if we['ll] know when the right time is to tell Grace to come."

Though he was aware this would be a necessity at som[e] point, the suggestion still hit him in the chest. A[t] twenty-four years old, Grace was their youngest daughter[.] Suze was suggesting that it might be time for them to sa[y] goodbye, but he didn't think that at all. He couldn't reall[y] imagine it ever happening. Marlene had been sick for s[o] long, it seemed like a battle that would never end.

"It's not that time yet. She's nowhere near that point."

Suze flinched, and he realized he'd spoken too sharply.

"I'm sorry, love. I can't stand the thought—" He ha[d] to cut himself off, his nostrils flaring, his eyes burning wit[h] unshed tears, a lump blocking his throat.

"It's okay, Dad. I understand. As long as we don't leave i[t] too late. She would be heartbroken if she didn't make it o[n] time."

She was going to be heartbroken anyway. They all were.

Chapter Fourteen

L awrey checked the time. Shortly before seven. She wasn't late for once.

She pushed open the door of the bar on Main Street and stepped inside. She glanced around, looking for her sister and brother-in-law. She caught the eye of a few of the locals, nodding and smiling her hellos.

"Hope you're not here on business, Detective," one of the men said.

"Night off, Alfred," she called back. "I'm allowed to have them."

He tipped his fingers to his forehead in a salute. "Yes, ma'am."

Lawrey caught sight of her sister sitting at one of the booths. Eddie wasn't there, though he might have ducked into the restroom.

"Hey," she said, sliding into the seat beside Maddie. "One of those for me?"

She nodded at the silver bucket on the table that was filled with ice and bottles of beer.

"Sure. Help yourself."

Lawrey did exactly that, the bottle icy, and took a deep swig of the beer. "Where's Eddie? I thought you'd both be here."

"He got caught up at work, but he's on his way."

Was it her imagination, or did her sister appear awkward when she said that? She shifted in her seat, not meeting Lawrey's eye.

"He's coming, though, right?" Lawrey checked.

"Sure. He won't be long." Maddie quickly changed the subject. "Thanks for helping out with Cara last night. We appreciate it."

"Hey, that's what family's for, right? How was she after she got home?"

"Angry, dramatic—usual teenage girl. Anyway, how have *you* been?"

Lawrey shrugged one shoulder. "Busy investigating that young couple killed up at Sandtown."

"Did Tommy know them?"

"According to him, he spoke to the girl a few times. Seems like no one knew them much. They'd only been there a couple of months and kept themselves to themselves."

She didn't want to give Maddie any more details.

"And how did Tommy seem?" Maddie asked.

"Oh, you know, as well as can be expected. He hasn't made any promises about being clean, and I'm not going to ask for them either. I think we've gone beyond that point."

"I'm sorry, Law. You never know, he still might decide he wants to get clean one day."

Lawrey shook her head and took a swig of her beer. "I can't see it happening, and I'm not going to hinge my happiness upon it either. That way only leads to heartbreak. I've experienced that for myself more times than I'd like to count."

Maddie offered her a smile of sympathy, and then her gaze drifted over Lawrey's shoulder.

"Oh, look, there's Eddie now." Maddie lifted her hand in a wave and beckoned her husband over.

Lawrey followed her line of sight. Eddie wasn't alone. A man around her age, with wavy dark hair that curled around his neck like it needed a good cut, was with him. The man seemed out of place, smiling nervously, his gaze darting around as though he was looking for someone but wasn't quite sure who.

Lawrey's stomach sank. "Oh, Maddie. Please tell me you didn't."

Maddie's voice rose a pitch. "What? He's a good guy. Eddie couldn't speak any higher about him."

"He could be the best fucking man in the entire world, and I still wouldn't want to sit here making awkward conversation with him."

"Just be nice."

Lawrey scowled. "I'm always nice."

"At least be polite. That's all I ask. It's not his fault he's been set up with you."

"Thanks for the vote of confidence, Mads."

"You know what I mean."

The two men approached the table, and Maddie delivered a swift warning elbow into Lawrey's side.

"Oww," Lawrey hissed.

Both women sat up straight, smiling a little too brightly.

Eddie leaned down and kissed his wife's cheek and then turned his attention to Lawrey.

"Hey, Law. Hope you don't mind, I invited one of my buddies along. This is Joe. We play squash together at the sports club."

"I don't know how anyone can want to play sports in this heat."

"It's air-conditioned and inside, so that's not a problem. You might know that if you went to a gym every now and then."

Lawrey deliberately picked up a chip, dunked it in salsa, and shoved it in her mouth. "I get enough exercise running around after criminals, remember?"

"Yeah, so you say." He glanced at his friend. "Joe, you remember me mentioning my sister-in-law, Lawrey."

Joe put his hand out to her. "Of course. It's good to meet you."

Lawrey forced herself to half stand and place her hand in his. They shook briefly, and then everyone took their seats. Lawrey took a swig of her beer, while the men helped themselves to bottles from the ice bucket.

"Well, this is nice, isn't it?" Eddie said.

An awkward tension settled around the table.

Joe was the one to break it. "Eddie says you're a detective."

"That's right."

"Must be an interesting job."

"It is."

She wasn't giving anything away.

"What do you do, Joe?" Maddie asked, clearly filling in the part of the conversation Lawrey wasn't going to bother with.

"I'm a content creator."

Lawrey almost spat out her beer. "A content creator? Isn't that something kids do these days?"

"Lawrey!" Maddie protested, clearly thinking she'd been rude.

But Joe had the good sense to laugh. "I'm not doing silly TikTok dances or anything like that, if that's what you're thinking. It's essentially advertising for brands."

"Doesn't sound like a real job to me." Lawrey took another pointed swig of her beer. She didn't really understand it. Social media was something she avoided at all costs.

"I promise it pays."

"A job like that must mean you can work anywhere, right? So what are you doing here?"

"A side project on Sandtown."

Immediately, Lawrey's instincts woke up. "What kind of side project?"

"Call it a documentary, if you want. People are interested in Sandtown and the people who live there."

Strangely, she felt protective of the place. Was that because Tommy lived there and she didn't want him to be exploited? Did this Joe know a young couple had died there only a day ago? She couldn't see how it was possible for him not to know, especially if he was researching Sandtown.

Was that the reason he was here now? Had he somehow known that Eddie was her brother-in-law and had wrangled a double date?

The server arrived to take their food orders. Lawrey went for a portion of chili cheese fries, ignoring Maddie's order of a salad. She needed something more substantial to soak up the beer.

The four of them made small talk until the food arrived. They ate, and then the two men got up to go and play some pool, leaving the women alone once more.

"What are you doing?" Maddie hissed at her.

"Nothing."

"You're treating him like he'd got two heads o
something."

"You don't think it's suspicious that he's doing research
on Sandtown right when there's been two murders?"

Maddie stared at her. "Are you serious?"

"Of course."

"What? Like you think he's the killer or something."

"No, that's not what I'm saying. More that he migh
think he's going to get some additional information out o
me or something."

"He's barely mentioned it all evening. Or the deaths."

"He could be playing the long game."

Maddie rolled her eyes. "Jesus, Law. Not everyone is ou
to get something."

"Aren't they?"

It was her job to be suspicious. An important part o
policing was done on a cop's instinct. She trusted hers.

"You trust Eddie, don't you?" Maddie asked.

"I trust you, and *you* trust Eddie."

The truth was that there weren't many people she
trusted, and even them being a relative didn't automaticall
put someone in the trustworthy category. Her own son had
stolen from her more times than she could count, and look
at what happened with her father.

Her sister arched an eyebrow. "That's not the same and
you know it."

"Okay, yes, I trust Eddie."

"Then believe that he wouldn't set you up with someone if he thought for one second that the person was trying to mine you for information."

"Fine." She sighed and sat back. "It's just I'm not in the right place to date yet."

"What are you talking about? It's been almost ten years now since you and Richard separated. You've been divorced for most of that."

"Ten years? Has it really?"

Where had the years gone? Sometimes she wished she could go back, start over, and make different choices this time around. Then she'd be spiked with guilt at the thought. She didn't want to make out like she regretted her life, or her son, or even the years she'd spent with Patrick.

They'd made her who she was.

Considering everything, it was hardly surprising she'd wanted a family of her own. It hadn't even really been about family—she still had her mom and her sister. It had been more about change, about escapism from her own thoughts. She'd been desperate to think about someone other than herself, to get out of the cycle of negative thinking, escape all the shit that was going through her head. She wanted something else—someone else—to worry about.

Talk about 'be careful what you wish for', because all she'd done was worry about Tommy since the first moment he'd been born. She'd sit by his cot, night after night, certain he'd stop breathing. And that hadn't even been the worst of it. He'd been a serious little boy, prone to accidents, who'd grown into an awkward, anxious teen whose desperation to escape his own thoughts hadn't led to a baby but to drugs.

She'd never considered what the repercussion might be for her son. That at school, people would talk about who his grandfather was and what he'd done and tease the boy about it.

In a town as small as this one, there was no escaping your past, no matter how hard you tried.

"Yes," Maddie said, "and it's about time you moved on."

"I *have* moved on," Lawrey insisted.

"Not with a man."

"I don't need a man to complicate my life, and anyway, there have been men. It's not like I'm a born-again virgin."

Maddie laughed. "I don't want you to waste what's left of your youth."

Lawrey snorted. "My youth? I'm forty-five years old, Maddie. In fact, I'm turning forty-six at the end of the week. I'm hardly youthful."

"You won't be saying that when you're seventy-five. You'll look back on you at this age and wonder why you were feeling so old."

"Hmm...my perceptive little sister." She lifted her beer bottle, and they clinked the necks together. "Point taken."

Lawrey finished her beer and then tossed down some money to pay for her meal.

"Anyway, I'm going to call it a night. I've got a busy day tomorrow."

Joe must have spotted she was leaving, and he hurried back to the table, practically at a jog. "You going already, Lawrey?"

"Yeah, early start."

"Mind if I walk you back?"

"I only live a few blocks from here."

"I can manage a few blocks."

Behind him, Maddie was nodding at her like a demented wobbly head dog on a dashboard. Lawrey thought her sister might spontaneously combust if she dared say no.

"Sure," she relented. "Why not."

"Great."

They said their goodbyes and then left the bar, Joe holding the door open for her as she stepped out onto the street. It was night, but the air was still warm.

"This way," she said.

They walked side by side, not speaking.

He shot her a look from the corner of his eye. "You didn't really want to be there tonight, did you?"

"That obvious?"

He grimaced. "Yeah, a bit."

"Sorry, it's not you. It's me. And that's a total cliché, so I'm sorry about that as well. I've got a lot going on at the moment, and I'm not in the right headspace to even think about having a relationship."

He lifted both eyebrows. "A relationship? Wow. That jumped ahead fast. I thought we were only having dinner."

Heat rose to her cheeks. "That was presumptuous of me, wasn't it? You probably didn't even want to see me again, never mind jump into anything more."

He held up one finger. "Now, hang on a minute. I never said anything about not wanting to see you again."

"I wanted to make sure we both know where we stand. I didn't want you to think I was leading you on or giving you the wrong idea."

"Thanks. I appreciate that."

They continued to walk, their pace slow.

"So...what made you want to become a cop?" he asked.

"I guess all the usual reasons. I wanted to help people. I wanted to make my life mean something, to make a difference."

He seemed troubled. "Oh, right."

"You're not buying that?"

He shrugged. "I assumed it was more to do with who your father was."

Instantly, she froze, all her insides seizing up. "You've been looking into my background?"

Her fight or flight instincts had been activated. She couldn't decide if she wanted to punch him or run away.

"No, not at all," he added hurriedly. "Eddie mentioned it, that was all. I didn't mean to upset you."

It was too late for that.

"Anyway, thanks for walking me. I can get the rest of the way home myself."

He reached out and took her arm. She glanced down at where his fingers wrapped around her elbow.

"Lawrey, wait. Don't go running off. I was having a really nice time tonight."

A part of her wanted to soften, to give in and accept this man's company, but eventually she would end up having to have those conversations with him, and she didn't want to let anyone in. Life was easier when it was only her she had to take into consideration. People wanted things from you—your time, your patience, your understanding—and she simply didn't have anything more she could give.

"I'm sorry, I do have to go. Thank you for an enjoyable evening. It was better than I'd anticipated."

He gave a rueful smile. "You're welcome."

Lawrey returned the smile, stuffed her hands in her pockets, and walked away. She sensed him still standing there, watching her go, and fought against every instinct to glance back again.

Maybe she should have invited him home. It had been a while, after all. Then she could have let him down afterward. But he seemed like too much of a decent guy to be messed around like that.

No, she'd done the right thing, even if she felt as though she'd disappointed herself.

Chapter Fifteen

Raye clutched the selection of cozy crime novels to his chest as he headed back to his trailer. He'd been at the community library—one of his favorite places in Sandtown—until well after sundown, picking out the books and gossiping with some of the other residents who'd been there.

He arrived at the entrance to his studio. Solar lights meant the place was lit, despite it being nighttime. He covered his mouth with the hand not holding the books, and his eyes pricked with tears.

"Oh, my lord, Jesus Christ."

Someone had destroyed his studio. Paint was splattered everywhere, up walls, across the floor, over every available surface. The paint tins were all open and now lay discarded and half dried out on the floor. Hundreds of dollars' worth of paint, materials that he couldn't afford to simply replace. Brand-new, as yet unused, canvases had been stripped from their protective plastic coverings, and someone had run a knife through them, cutting them into shreds so they fluttered like bunting in the hot desert wind.

He took a step farther into his studio and caught sight of his most recent work. He hadn't quite finished it, and now he never would.

Someone had thrown paint across it, ruining the imagery of the desert that he'd worked so hard to create. Not only that, but they'd also taken a blade to the canvas, shredding it down the middle.

Tears welled and slipped down his cheeks. He stood in the middle of the destruction, staring around, unable to believe that someone hated him enough to do this. It could have been any number of people. His studio was open air, the sides created out of whatever he'd been able to scavenge—metal and tarpaulin mostly.

Despair filled him, and with it came a fresh wave of longing for the nothingness a hit of heroin would bring him. What was he supposed to do now? He didn't have the cash to replace all this stuff, but in order for him to raise money, he needed to replace his paint and canvases.

The fuckers who'd done this deserved to pay, but Raye was more of a lover than a fighter. Actually, since he'd turned forty, he didn't feel like much of either.

This wasn't the first time someone had messed with him. He was fully aware that not everyone liked him. Though he'd never done anyone in Sandtown any harm, simply existing as who he was seemed to scare some people.

He'd always felt at home in Sandtown, as though he'd found his people, and for the first time, he felt unwanted.

Movement came from behind him, and he spun around, his heart lurching. He half expected to find whoever had done this standing behind him, ready to finish the job. Instead, he discovered the small frame of his neighbor, DeeDee. Her mouth hung open, her eyes rounded, as she stared around at the destruction.

"Oh my God, Raye. What happened?"

"Someone doesn't appreciate good art," he tried to joke, but his voice came out strangled.

She must have seen he was on the verge of tears. "Oh, sweetheart. Are you okay? You're not okay, are you? Come here."

She held her arms out to him and beckoned him with her fingers, and he found himself folded against her small frame. He was always more likely to cry when someone was being kind to him rather than being mean, and he found himself sniffling on her shoulder.

When he pulled himself together again, he straightened. "Is there any chance you heard or saw anything?"

He wasn't sure what he'd even do if he found out who was responsible. It wasn't as though he could go and beat them up. Any fights he'd gotten into, he'd always been the one who'd come out worse.

"No, sorry. I've been on the other side of town all day, helping Tye with something. Do you have any idea who might have done this?"

"Someone who wants to send a message," he said.

"What kind of message?"

"I'm guessing they didn't like that I spoke to that detective."

Who would even know about that? Tommy, probably, since Lawrey would have needed to speak to him about his relationship with the girl. But would Tommy really do this to his place? He didn't think so. Tommy always seemed like a nice guy, but some people were really good at putting on a front. Maybe the nice guy thing was an act. After all, he was a drug addict, and there was no one more sneaky or manipulative or conniving than an addict. Raye was sure Tommy's mother could attest to that, and she was a detective. Or maybe Tommy had told someone else that Raye had spoken to the cops, and they were the ones responsible.

"Are you going to tell that detective about this?" DeeDee asked.

"Are you kidding? Talking to her has done me enough harm, wouldn't you say?"

She gave a sympathetic twist of her lips. "You definitely think that's the reason someone smashed up your stuff then?"

"I can't think of any other, can you?"

Unless they'd done it because he'd tried to save that young couple...

Or maybe someone out there simply didn't like a man in a wig and hot pants? As much as Sandtown boasted about its inclusivity, a home for all outcasts, there were still the same issues here that one could find in the rest of society. Racism, homophobia, and violence against women was as alive and kicking here, as it was in the rest of the country. Maybe this had nothing to do with the dead couple, or him speaking to the police.

It was a coincidence, though. He'd lived here for six years without anything this drastic happening before. Sure, he'd been the victim of the occasional burglary or gotten into the odd fight, but that was all.

DeeDee squeezed his forearm. "Let me round up the troops. We'll help you get all this cleaned up in no time."

"Thanks, DeeDee. You're the best."

She smiled. "And don't you forget it."

Chapter Sixteen

It was still dark outside when her phone rang the following morning.

Lawrey groaned. What now? It wasn't as though she ever expected to sleep in, but it would be nice if the sun could at least break the horizon before someone called her.

She reached for her phone and shoved it against her ear. "Yes?"

An older woman's voice came down the line, crackly with age.

"Lawrey, it's Carol Hayes. I'm so sorry to bother you, but can you come over?"

"What is it, Mrs. Hayes?"

"I heard someone downstairs. I think someone's broken in to steal from me."

Lawrey checked the time. It wasn't even six a.m. yet.

She sighed. "You could call the station, you know?"

"You're on my side of town, and I know you. I'd feel safer if you came."

She'd probably know most of the uniformed officers, too, but Lawrey realized there wasn't much point in arguing with her. It was better that she get over there and get this done with. She didn't think for a minute that Mrs. Hayes actually had an intruder. She was an older woman who lived alone and got spooked by the raccoons knocking over the trash cans.

Would that be her one day?

Lawrey used the bathroom and threw on some clothes. Within ten minutes, she was in her car, driving toward Carol Hayes' home. It wasn't far. She pulled up outside the house and climbed out. At least it was still cooler, the sun barely above the horizon.

Carol Hayes lived alone right on the outskirts of town. Her property backed onto the desert, and her nearest neighbor was almost half a mile away. It was no wonder she felt the need to reach out to the local law enforcement every now and then. Trouble was, it was getting to be more than every now and then with Carol. This was the third call this month.

Carol was waiting for her on the porch, her housecoat wrapped around her body.

"Thanks for coming, Law. I'm sorry to have gotten you out of bed."

"It's fine, Carol. How can I help?"

Her lips were pinched, causing the lines around them to deepen into valleys. "It's those goddamned people from that town again, I'll bet. Bunch of drug addicts and criminals. I wish they'd never settled in that place."

"I understand your frustrations. Are you sure it was them on your property?"

"Damned, Law, I'm sorry. I wasn't including your boy in with them."

The truth was that their town would have probably dried up and blown away if it was not for the proximity of Sandtown. As much as the locals had issues with the place and its inhabitants, Sandtown brought in a steady influx of tourists and snowbirds. Since Sandtown didn't have any infrastructure of its own, it meant those people were using Calrock to pick up supplies, to stop and eat at the restaurants, to fill up their tanks with gas. Towns, similar to theirs, but that were farther from Sandtown had shut down in the end, as more and more of their young folk decided they couldn't handle living with the heat and wanted more opportunities closer to the city. She understood the old-timers didn't see things that way, however. They only saw the drugs and the crime and couldn't help but think back to when things had been simpler.

"Don't worry about it, Carol. Now, why don't you show me what's missing."

The older woman's brow furrowed. "Oh, I don't know that anything is missing."

"I thought you'd said you'd had a burglary."

"No, I said I heard someone downstairs, and when I came down, the window in the laundry room was open."

Lawrey pinched her lips and frowned. Had she really come out at this time just to take a look at an open window?

"Show me," she said.

Mrs. Hayes led her inside and through the house. "In there."

She flicked on the light. Sure enough, the window was standing open a few inches.

"Could you have forgotten to shut it properly?" Lawrey asked.

"Listen, I might be getting on a bit, but my brain is sharp as a tack. I'd have remembered if I hadn't closed it properly."

"But you don't think anything was taken?"

"I must have scared them off."

Lawrey wasn't sure how scary Carol would be to some thieves if they wanted to steal from her. She'd seen plenty of cases where they'd been interrupted in the middle of a job, and instead of running, they'd attacked the residents of the house.

"If that was the case, you were lucky not to have been harmed."

"*If* that was the case? Of course it was the case. Now," she waved a hand in the direction of the window, "are you going to do some investigating? Dust for prints or something like that?"

There wasn't even proof that a crime had happened. At worst, it was trespassing, but Lawrey didn't even have proof of that having happened. It could simply have been an old lady's forgetfulness and imagination working together to create a crime.

"Leave it with me, Carol."

"Okay. I'll go and make us both some coffee."

Lawrey waited until Carol had shuffled off and then she crouched and frowned at the floor underneath the window. Was that a dusty partial shoe print? She used her phone to take a couple of quick snaps of it. The shoe print didn't mean anything, though it did seem larger than any size Mrs. Hayes would wear.

"Have you had anyone in here recently?" she called out.

Carol's voice drifted out from the kitchen.

"I had Phil Tayer in to look at the spin-dryer," she said. "It was making a strange sound the other week, like there was metal inside it, and he said something about the drum coming off its bearings. Something like that anyway. He was able to fix it, and that's all I really care about. I could hang the clothes outside, but, when the wind comes up, they get covered in dust and I end up having to wash them again."

The print most likely belonged to Phil Tayer then, but Lawrey didn't say so. "I'm going to head outside, make sure no one is hanging around."

"Thanks, Lawrey. I appreciate it."

Lawrey left the house and stepped outside. Dawn crickets chirped, filling the air with their song. The sun was up now, and already it was warmer. She found herself flapping her shirt away from her skin to create a breeze. She crossed the porch and took the couple of steps down to the yard. She paused and checked the surroundings. Carol wasn't overlooked by any neighbors out here. On the outskirts of the town, there was only the road and desert scrubland either side of the property. It was no wonder Carol got herself spooked, living out here on her own. Lawrey would probably feel the same way. She knew if she dared suggest to the older lady that she might be more comfortable moving into town, it wouldn't go down well. The property had been in Carol's family her whole life—she'd most likely even been born there, and she'd probably die there, too.

It was a lot for anyone to handle on their own. She had several acres, including some outbuildings that were falling into disrepair. It wasn't Lawrey's place to comment on them.

Somewhere in the distance, a dog barked, angry and loud. Another dog heard it and decided to join in, until there was a chorus of the animals barking. That wasn't unusual for out here. People kept dogs around to chase off any unwanted visitors. Maybe she should suggest that Carol got herself a pet as a way of giving herself a little security.

Lawrey moved around the side of the house. She wasn't expecting to see anyone, and she was right. She reached the part where the window opened out onto and drew to a halt. The ground was parched, no chance of there being any footprints. If one had been left in the dust, it would have long blown away by now. Still, she studied the area more carefully, wanting, if nothing else, to be able to report to Carol that she'd taken this seriously. She continued, walking the perimeter, ensuring no one was hanging around who shouldn't be.

Other than the crickets and the dogs, no one else was around.

She let out a sigh and went back inside the house, to where Carol was waiting in the kitchen, the air redolent with freshly brewed coffee.

"All clear," she said brightly. "If anyone was hanging around, they're long gone. You must have scared them off."

"It was those damned Sandtowners, I'll bet my life on it."

"Unless I have some kind of proof, I'm afraid I can't go accusing people, Mrs. Hayes." Lawrey took a sip of her coffee, willing the caffeine to hit her veins already. "You don't have any security cameras around here?"

"Cameras? No," she scoffed. "What would I need with cameras? Everyone's watching our every move these days. I refuse to be a part of it."

"Might bring you some peace of mind, though. You could check them if you felt someone was outside."

Carol sniffed. "No, thanks."

"Or you could get a dog?"

Carol stared at her like she'd lost her mind. "Noisy, smelly things. I'm more of a cat person, but I don't like keeping them cooped up inside, and out here the coyotes will get them. Anyway, it's not as though I'm completely on my own. I have my family to watch out for me. My granddaughter, Francis, is always popping around, and my son, Gordon, is around a lot more now he's back in town. They check out any sounds that worry me."

Lawrey knew nothing she could say was going to change the older woman's mind. Some people lived exactly how they wanted to live, and nothing anyone else ever said was going to change that. She finished her coffee and set the mug down in the sink.

"Right then, if there's nothing else, I'll be off. Thanks for the coffee."

"Okay, Law. I appreciate you coming out."

"Oh, one last thing." Lawrey went back to the laundry room, pulled down the window, and locked it. "Better safe than sorry."

Chapter Seventeen

Lawrey stopped by the local diner to grab some breakfast before heading into the office. She could never think straight on an empty stomach.

The moment she stepped through the station's front door, she knew something was wrong.

She flapped her hand through the muggy air. "Fucking hell, it's hot in here. Why isn't the AC on?"

"Oh, we thought we'd try a day with it off, see what it's like to work in one-hundred-degree heat," Iris said from the reception desk, wafting at her puce face with a folded piece of paper.

"Seriously?"

"No, not seriously. The damned thing's broken, isn't it? I've called out an electrician, but he says he might not be able to get here until tomorrow."

Already, the underarms of Lawrey's shirt were damp, sweat running between her cleavage and trickling down her spine. The heat made everyone exasperated and irritable. She was not going to survive this temperature all day. At forty-five, she was already having hot flashes, and it wasn't as though it always happened at night either. Sometimes, she could be standing in one spot, and, all of a sudden, she'd come over all hot and dizzy and nauseous. Stupidly, she'd been hoping all those symptoms of her age would somehow miraculously bypass her, that she'd be one of the lucky ones, but as the months passed, her hope for that was fading.

Before she'd even made it to her desk, Lieutenant Monroe called her into his office. The AC wasn't working in there either, and he was red-faced and sweating.

"How are we doing with tracking down the man our female victim had the restraining order against?" he asked.

"Still working on it, boss," she said. "It's like he's vanished into thin air."

"You considering him your main suspect then?"

"Right now, yes, but I don't think we've uncovered all the facts about what happened up in Sandtown. We're doing everything we can."

"I know that, Law. I just don't want the state to decide we don't have enough resources and send someone in."

"Understood." She turned to leave, but he cleared his throat.

"Actually, there is one more thing. I've had a complaint about you from Mitch Pearce."

It was all she could do not to roll her eyes. "Seriously? What's that asshole got to say?"

"That you called him an asshole," Monroe said.

"That's it?"

"You can't go calling people names in public, Law."

"He implied a lot worse about me," she said. "Brought up my dad…"

Even all these years later, she still felt herself shrink inward with shame at the mention of him.

People still claimed she shouldn't be a detective because of who her father had been—that it was some kind of conflict of interest. That was bullshit, but it gave people who didn't like her a reason to talk behind her back. And there were plenty of people who didn't like her. She didn't normally give a shit about that, but when it affected her work, it pissed her off.

"You knew when you became a cop that your past would be held against you. You need to find a way of dealing with it that doesn't involve you lashing out."

"Yeah, I know. Sorry, boss."

"I'll let Mitch know it's been dealt with, but I am on your side, Lawrey."

She nodded and left the office, happy to be out of there.

"Everything okay, Law?" Abel asked as she came out of the office and approached her desk.

"Fine. How are we getting on with tracking down Zack Jones?"

"We've got a BOLO out on him, but it looks like he's gone into hiding."

"Wonder if that's because he murdered his ex-girlfriend and her boyfriend?"

Abel was red in the face, sweat prickling on his hairline. "Or he's got another reason for staying low. Or maybe he's on vacation and has no idea Emily Clark is dead."

"Who have we tried to contact who might know where he is?"

"Everyone. Friends, family—what few he has of them. He's between jobs right now, but we still made contact with his old boss and some of his coworkers in case he mentioned having any plans to take a trip. We've requested a warrant to get his phone and credit card records, see if we can track him down that way."

"Good. That's bound to turn up something."

Lawrey sat at her desk and turned on her computer. The report from Richard Lund at the Office of Fire Investigations had been uploaded. She took a moment to read it through and examine photographs of the scene with fresh eyes. One particular detail caught her attention.

She leaned out to get her partner's attention. "Hey, Abel, it looks like the accelerant used to start the fire was denatured alcohol."

"Denatured alcohol? Like the kind artists use to clean their brushes?"

"Exactly."

There was only one person who came to mind when she thought of an artist. Raye Diante.

"When I spoke to Raye," she said, "I noticed that was what he was using."

Abel's eyebrows drew together. "He wouldn't be so stupid to set a fire using his own equipment, would he?" He thought for a moment. "Unless he was high. Not thinking."

It didn't ring true for Lawrey. "Raye said he was clean and he was trying really hard to stay that way. I believe him, too. Besides, why would he set the fire and then alert everyone to it? If it wasn't for him, the whole trailer would have gone up in flames."

"He was first on the scene. Isn't it true that arsonists often like to watch the result of their work?"

She huffed air out of her nose, mulling it over. "But what about the bodies? If he was also responsible for killing the couple, in what way could it possibly benefit him to keep the fire contained, so leaving evidence for us to uncover if he was the one who set it? Plus, Raye has no motive. What reason would he have for wanting that couple dead? Also, we know that Emily was sexually assaulted before she died, and I'm fairly sure Raye doesn't swing that way."

"Doesn't mean he's not capable of rape, though," Abel pointed out. "Rape is more about control than sex. Maybe he simply hates women."

"That doesn't sound like Raye at all."

She did remember Raye warning her that his DNA and prints might be inside the trailer. Had he been trying to cover his own back? Was that the reason he'd gone inside, so he had a reason why they might find evidence of his presence?

Abel shrugged. "Like I said, maybe he wasn't thinking straight. Don't tell me you've never come across a criminal do something stupid before?"

She laughed at that. So often, criminals thought they were being smart, when they'd done some dumb shit that led the cops straight to them.

"True, but I don't think Raye is one of those people. It's not as though his home or studio has any locks on it. The studio part is practically open to the public. Anyone could have walked in and grabbed some denatured alcohol. Hell, we don't even know for sure that it came from Raye's. Whoever did this could easily have got it from elsewhere."

"I know you want to think well of Raye, but don't let that cloud your judgement."

"I won't, but I will need to talk to him again. I want to talk to Hella Billy, too. Find out what he knew about Stephan Porter and ask him why he didn't go inside the trailer after he busted down the door the night of the fire.

Can you focus on finding Zack Jones? I've got the boss on my back about it. He's still our primary suspect right now, and that we can't find him makes him appear even guiltier."

• • • •

LAWREY WAS HAPPY TO get out of the office. There was still no sign of an electrician coming to fix the air, so at least she got some reprieve from the heat while she was driving.

That reprieve was short-lived, however. She reached Sandtown before she knew it and drove to the road Raye's trailer was located on. Not wanting to make it obvious who she was visiting, she stopped on the corner and climbed out. The heat hit her, and she found herself needing to take an extra breath, as though the desert air didn't contain enough oxygen.

She found Raye lying on a daybed beneath the mister. His eyes were closed, and she felt bad for waking him, but she had no choice.

"Raye?"

He jolted upright, his eyes wide with alarm. Had he been expecting someone else?

He saw her standing there and exhaled a shaky breath and slouched back against the daybed again. "Jeez, Detective. You gave me a fright."

"Sorry to disturb you, Raye, but we need to talk."

He swung his legs off the side and twisted to sitting. "That sounds ominous."

She fully entered the makeshift studio. The place seemed emptier than normal, though she couldn't quite put her finger on why. "We got the report back on the fire. The accelerant used was denatured alcohol. What do you know about that?"

"Nothing. Should I?"

"I know you keep some here for your work. Can you check for me and make sure everything is accounted for?"

Raye didn't move but wrung his hands between his knees. "I don't need to."

"Why's that?"

"Because I already know someone stole some from me last week."

"When you say 'last week,'" Lawrey said, "can you narrow that down for me?"

He thought for a minute. "Think it was Thursday morning I noticed it gone, so could have been stolen any time between Wednesday afternoon and then."

"But you didn't report it?"

He shot her a look that said, 'Yeah, as if.'

"You don't have any security cameras around here? Maybe secret ones?" She knew it was a long shot.

"Nope." He tucked a strand of his blond wig behind his ear. "I don't trust those things. You think you're on the watching end of the lens, but there's someone else who's taken control of it and is staring right back at you." His leg juddered up and down. The idea seemed to make him nervous.

She tried a different angle. "Do you have any idea who might have taken the denatured alcohol?"

He glanced nervously left and right, in case anyone had spotted them talking. She felt bad that she was potentially getting him in trouble just by being here, but a young couple were dead.

"No, I don't. Sorry, Law."

She tried again. "What about someone hanging around? Looking or acting suspicious?"

He gave a small laugh. "Isn't that everyone in Sandtown?"

She smiled back. "Okay, anyone acting more suspicious than normal?"

He let out a sigh. "Honestly, Law, I don't know what to tell you. I don't know who took the denatured alcohol. I feel bad that it was used to set fire to the trailer, but I haven't got any more information for you than I've already told you."

"Okay. You realize I'm going to have to speak to your neighbors, too, see if anyone else saw anything?" She doubted any of them would tell her anything, though, even if they had, but she hoped the threat would get Raye talking.

He glanced down at the ground. "Do whatever you have to."

"Suit yourself."

She left Raye and went to the next trailer along. It was owned by a skinny woman called DeeDee Sign who ran a clothing store out of a separate trailer on the same plot. She had a hammock strung up in front of it and a fire pit a short distance away.

"Had a feeling you'd come knocking sometime soon," DeeDee said from the steps of her trailer.

Lawrey guessed DeeDee was around her age, though probably had half her body weight. The combination of the summer sun and the lack of weight gave DeeDee's skin a crinkled appearance that aged her.

"Technically, I haven't actually knocked," Lawrey pointed out.

DeeDee shrugged and folded her arms across her narrow chest. "You know what I mean."

"I need to ask you questions about a bottle of denatured alcohol that was stolen from Raye's place last Wednesday or possibly early Thursday morning. You know anything about that?"

"Nope."

Lawrey knew this was going to be hard work. "Did you see anyone hanging around Raye's who shouldn't have been?"

DeeDee pursed her lips and shook her head. "I don't know why you're focusing on Raye. Shouldn't you be talking to your son?"

Lawrey immediately found herself getting defensive, her shoulders straightening, her chest lifting. "I already have."

"Yeah? And asked the right questions? Word is that he was sleeping with Emily."

A jolt of adrenaline went through her. "What?"

"Yep. The two of them were screwing behind Stephan's back. That's why they were fighting that night."

"You know this for a fact?" Lawrey asked.

"Well, it's not like I was there at the time. I suggest you ask your son. Wouldn't surprise me if he was involved in what went down that night."

"Shit," Lawrey muttered.

She should be focusing on tracking down the bottle of denatured alcohol, but now all she wanted was to find Tommy, grab him by the collar, and demand to know the truth. It occurred to her that this was exactly what DeeDee wanted to achieve, to stop her asking questions, but she'd worry about that later.

She took one of her cards and tossed it onto the hammock. "Call me if you think of anything else."

Preparing herself for a fight with her son, she went back to her car and drove across Sandtown to Tommy's trailer. Like most of the residents, he was inside, hiding from the midday sun.

She took the steps up to his front door, rapped her knuckles on it, and entered before he'd gotten the chance to call her in. She found him in bed, lying beneath the fan.

He sat up, blinking in the light, frowning in her direction. "What are you doing here, Mom? Ever heard of a thing called privacy?"

"Yeah, well, you gave up your right to privacy when you lied to me."

"I didn't lie to you."

"No? Then why has someone told me that you were sleeping with Emily? You told me you barely knew her."

"I did barely know her. Sleeping with someone once doesn't make us besties."

"Christ." She shook her head, so disappointed in him. She was always disappointed in him, and she hated that. "I need to know these things. It might be important in the case, Tommy. You must realize that."

"It's hard enough for me living here when everyone knows my mom is a cop. How do you think it helps me by talking to you?"

Her frustration mounted. "This isn't about you. Two young people are dead. Don't you care about that?

"Sure, but it really doesn't have anything to do with me."

"You don't know what it has to do with. Finding that out is my job, and you make my job a thousand times harder if you hide things from me. The same goes for everyone else in Sandtown. I understand you all want to protect your own, but if someone knows something, they need to tell me about it."

He let out a long sigh, like she was boring him.

Lawrey changed tactics. "Emily was sexually assaulted before she was killed. You ever get rough with her, Tommy? The medical examiner was able to get a sample of semen from the back of her throat. You know how bad it will be for you if it's a match."

A muscle in his jaw ticked. "For fuck's sake. No, I was never rough with her. Who do you think I am?"

"You were sleeping with another man's girlfriend behind his back."

Tommy snorted. "It wasn't as though he was a good boyfriend."

"What do you mean by that?"

"I dunno. She seemed scared."

"Scared of what? The ex-boyfriend?"

He twisted his lips. "I dunno. Might have been the current boyfriend."

"Didn't she say?"

"Not really. We didn't talk about them."

"Seriously? What did you talk about then?"

He glanced up. "Fun shit. Like the stars, and how there must be another planet out there with lifeforms like us."

Lawrey released a breath. "This story isn't the same as what you told me before?"

"Yeah, well, I didn't want you to know the whole truth then, did I?"

"And you do now?"

He shrugged.

She tried again. "So what made you think she was scared?"

"Her body language." He pursed his lips and twisted his hands together. "I lied before when I said she was more relaxed."

"Explain what you mean."

"You know how someone jumps at the slightest movement? How she seemed overly aware of her surroundings all the time. She didn't seem to relax, like she was constantly watching out for someone." He thought for a minute. "She had this nervous tic, where her knee was always bouncing up and down, and she kept chewing on her nails. They were chewed right down, and I kept thinking she needed to stop because she was making them sore."

Something pinged inside Lawrey. "Hang on, wait a minute. You sure she was chewing her nails?"

"Yeah, absolutely. It was making me uncomfortable."

"Fuck." Lawrey got to her feet. "I have to go."

"What? Why?"

"I can't explain it right now. If you think of anything else, call me, okay?"

"Okay?"

She drilled him with her gaze. "Promise?"

"Yeah, Mom. I promise."

Lawrey resisted the urge to throw her arms around his neck, but she knew he wouldn't appreciate it. Besides, she needed to make a call—an urgent call. The first one was to the medical examiner.

In a hurry, she raced back to her car, pulling her cell phone out of her pocket. She turned the engine on to get the air going and then made a call to Doctor James Anderson.

His voice came down the line. "Detective, how are things?"

"I need to ask you a question."

"Go for it."

"You said you'd sent scrapings from beneath the victim's fingernails off to the lab. Can you remember how long they were?"

She wanted confirmation that her memory wasn't playing tricks on her.

"How long her nails were? I'm not sure. Average length, I guess. Nothing that stood out to me. And, of course, parts of her hands had been burned in the fire."

"Nothing that stood out to you," Lawrey repeated, "like if she chewed her nails so badly, there wasn't much left for you to scrape out from under them."

"No, nothing like that. Why do you ask?"

"Just something I'm considering." He'd confirmed her recollection of the female victim's hands. "I'll have to call you back."

She ended the call and then dialed a different number.

Abel answered it. "Sarge?"

"It's a different girl," she said in a rush. "I don't know who the girl is who burned in the RV, but it's not Emily."

Chapter Eighteen

Silence came down the line at her announcement, then Abel spoke.

"What? How do you know that?"

"I spoke to Tommy, and he said Emily chewed her nails, that they were so far chewed down it made him uncomfortable. I remember what the nails were like of the girl on the ME's table and they weren't chewed."

"Holy shit."

"Exactly. We haven't done a DNA match on her yet because she wasn't in the system, and we need a sample from her father. I bet when we get one, we'll have proof that she's not Emily."

"Hang on a minute. How do we know that the person Tommy described is the real Emily? Maybe that girl is the fake Emily and the one found dead in the RV is the real one."

She hadn't even considered that possibility. Her head was spinning. She had that rush of adrenaline she always experienced when something of significance happened in a case.

"Okay, but either way, someone had switched them out. The girl who's been living in Sandtown these past couple of months isn't the same one whose body was found in the trailer."

"Why would someone switch them out?" Abel asked.

"That's what I'm wondering." She thought of something else. "Shit. Emily's father is on his way here. He believes his daughter is dead."

"No, he believes a person matching his daughter's description is dead. Without a definite ID, we wouldn't have told him it was her for sure."

Lawrey exhaled slowly. "True. Right now, we have no way of knowing."

"Can the father ID the body?"

"I don't think so. It's not in a good shape. I wouldn't like for that to be the final image he has of his daughter—assuming there's the slightest possibility it's her. Unless he insists on seeing her, it's better if we go down the DNA route."

Abel fell silent down the line for a moment, and then he spoke. "If it turns out the girl in the trailer isn't Emily, we have two big questions that need answering: whose body do we have in the morgue, and where the hell is Emily?"

Lawrey sat back in the car seat. "Someone clearly wanted us to believe Emily is dead, but why?"

"So she could vanish," he stated. "So no one would come looking for her."

"But why kill the boyfriend as well?"

"Maybe because he'd have been able to tell right away that the girl who died in the trailer wasn't Emily. Or because he was involved somehow and someone wanted to keep him quiet."

Lawrey considered this. "That definitely sounds like a possibility. Finding out the real identity of the dead girl will help us figure all this out."

"Someone out there might be missing her."

"Good point. Let's get onto missing persons, see if they've got anyone matching our Jane Doe's description."

"Someone other than Emily Clark, you mean?"

Lawrey let out a sigh, her brain whirring. She always appreciated having Abel to bounce ideas off. She didn't think she'd work anywhere near as well without him.

"If you were going to find a young woman to put in the place of another one, where would you start looking?"

"Prostitutes, drug addicts, homeless girls," he replied. "Someone who's less likely to be missed."

"Who does that sound like you're describing?"

"A resident of Sandtown, but it's different there. I think someone in Sandtown would miss one of their own."

She shook her head, even though he couldn't see her. "Not necessarily. The population of the town swells by a thousand during the winter. You can't tell me that one of those girls going missing would be noticed."

"If that was the case, and she went missing in the winter when it was busier, then she's been missing months. Someone took her, held her, and then killed her, all so they could use her in the place of someone else? It doesn't make sense. The person responsible wouldn't have even known Emily was going to come to Sandtown then."

"Maybe they didn't plan it. Maybe they saw Emily and decided they wanted a change."

She turned over this possibility in her head. "I'm coming back into the office. Can you let everyone know about this latest development? Make sure they all know that Emily Clark might still be alive."

Chapter Nineteen

L awrey had barely been back for an hour when a call came in from Iris on the reception desk.

"Sarge, there's a man at the front desk, says he's Emily Clark's father. He's not very happy."

"Okay, thanks, Iris. I'll be right there."

She rose from her desk and left the office to go to the front of the station. In the waiting area, in front of the reception desk, a man sat on one of the cheap plastic chairs. His legs were spread wide, his elbows planted on a pair of meaty thighs. He clutched at his shaved head, his fingers digging into his bare scalp.

Iris jerked her chin toward him and widened her eyes, though Lawrey didn't need any help figuring out that this was Emily Clark's father.

"Mr. Clark," she greeted him. "I'm Detective Winters. I'm heading up the case here." She didn't say 'your daughter's case' for good reason. There was a good chance the burned victim wasn't his daughter and that Emily was missing instead.

He shook her hand begrudging. His palm was hot and clammy, and she resisted the urge to wipe her own on her pants.

"I want to see her," he said. "I want to see her right this instant."

Clark had a thick neck and a gut to match. Cheap tattoos ran over the backs of his knuckles and up the side of his neck. His expression was one of a permanent scowl, and she wondered if what had happened to his daughter had put the expression there, or if this was simply what he looked like.

She held up her hand. "First of all, Mr. Clark, remember that we don't know for sure that the victim we found in the trailer is even Emily. There's the possibility that it isn't—"

"In which case, I need to know. I'm not waiting for days for some goddamned DNA test. Do you have children, Detective?"

She nodded. "Yes, I do."

"Then wouldn't you want to know for sure, as soon as you could? Do you know the kind of torture I'm in right now, not knowing whether my baby-girl is alive or dead? These past few months have been hell. That son of a bitch stole her from me, and now she's dead."

Lawrey hesitated. "Who are you talking about when you say someone stole her from you?"

"Stephan. Emily always did have bad taste when it came to men. The last one was violent toward her, so instead of finding a good man, she runs straight into the arms of one exactly like him."

Lawrey had to wonder how much Emily's taste in men came from her father. Then she shook that thought out of her head. If that was true, what would it say about her own taste in men? She certainly wouldn't want anyone who was anything like her daddy. Was that what Mr. Clark was like, however? Had Emily grown up in a violent household, so that was all she'd ever known?

She wanted to ask him if he'd ever hit his daughter, ever shoved her, or intimidated her with his size, but she knew that would only put him on the defensive, and if she wanted information from this man, she had to be more subtle about it.

"Where's Emily's mother?" she asked instead.

"No idea. Ran off when Emily was only tiny. Waste of space. What kind of woman abandons her only child?"

Maybe a woman who feared for her life?

"And Emily hasn't had any contact with her?" Lawrey asked.

"Nope. Not even a birthday or Christmas card."

Had they done a background check on Mr. Clark? Did he have any history?

He put back his shoulders. "Now, are we going to see if this is my daughter or not?"

"The morgue isn't in this town," she told him. "It's an eight-mile drive away."

"Then what are we waiting for?"

"I have to warn you that there was significant damage to the victim's body. It's not a pretty sight."

"I don't care about that. Do I look like I let a little blood bother me?"

Lawrey had seen some of the strongest men felled by a crime scene in the past. People might think they were tough, but when it came to being faced with what might possibly be their loved one, lying on a cold metal slab, it could bring the toughest of men to their knees. She'd seen police officers turn white and have to stumble away at the sight of victims of a road accident, and others attend incidents that involved small children and discovered it played on their minds so badly that they were forced to leave the department and seek out an alternative career.

"It's up to you, Mr. Clark."

"Then let's go."

Lawrey made a call to the morgue to let them know they were on their way and then informed her team about where she was going. She led Emily Clark's father out to her car. They drove the desert road, with windows up and the air blasting.

"What do you do for a living, Mr. Clark?" she asked.

"Why do you ask?"

"Just passing the time." She didn't look at him.

"I'm a mechanic. I own my own shop back in Portland."

"How long have you been doing that?"

"My whole adult life. I mean, I didn't own the shop right out of school, of course, but I worked at someone else's, and they trained me up. Eventually, I was able to buy my own place."

"And still managed to raise your daughter on your own. That's impressive."

"Not really. My parents both helped out a lot. I couldn't have done it without them."

"They must be really worried about Emily, too?"

"They died years ago, when Emily was a young teenager."

"Oh, I'm sorry. That must have hit her hard."

"Yeah, it did." He hesitated as though he was unsure if he was oversharing, but then continued. "That's when she started going off the rails, you know. Never coming home for her curfew, hanging out with the wrong kinds of people, dating older guys. She didn't want to listen to me. She just wanted to do what she wanted to do."

"I understand. I've got a sixteen-year-old niece who is getting to be a bit like that. It's a difficult age. They see themselves as young adults, which they are, but they also don't have the experience or brain development to make adult decisions."

"Emily was a bit younger when it all started, about fourteen, I think. In a way, I feel like I kind of lost her then."

Despite herself, Lawrey found her heart going out to him. He might look like he could bang a few heads together, but from the tone in his voice, he really loved and missed his daughter.

His description of her was helpful, as was his opinion of Stephan. If Stephan wasn't already dead, she'd be asking some serious questions of him. There was still a possibility he was involved. Maybe he did stab himself, or perhaps he'd gotten on the wrong side of whoever had switched out Emily's body. Was it possible Emily herself was involved in the changeover? Had she wanted to disappear?

They arrived at the morgue. She pulled into the small parking lot outside the building. She opened the car door, only to be smacked in the face with a blast of heat.

"Jesus fucking Christ," Clark muttered. "How do you stand living out here?"

"You get used to it."

"You say that Emily has been living in this?"

"That's right."

He shook his head. "She always loathed the heat. Used to love fall—Halloween and all that. She couldn't wait to pumpkin spice everything. Gross stuff. I don't know why she'd choose to come and live out here. She must have hated it."

"The people in Sandtown get used to it, and they also tend to have solar panels and generators so they can have the air running twenty-four-seven. Some of them even have misters for outside so they can feel cool."

"I can't imagine Emily had something like that set up."

"No, she didn't, but there are communal areas there where people hang out that have them. It can be more comfortable than you think."

"But still fucking hot," he said.

"True. Let's go inside. It'll be cooler in there."

He gave a curt nod and followed her inside the building. They had to sign in, and then Lawrey led the way down to the morgue which was situated in the basement. It was windowless—a way of keeping out the heat—and also had the air humming all day and night. Dead bodies and warm temperatures were not a good combination. They were refrigerated most of the time, but obviously that couldn't happen when the medical examiner was working on them.

She took him into one of the adjoining rooms. "Wait here. I need to make sure they're ready for us."

"Okay."

The man had paled. Now the reality that he might be about to identify his daughter's body had sunk in, all his bravado had faded.

Lawrey spoke to the people in charge and returned and handed him a set of protective outerwear and some gloves. "Normally, we'd be able to do this through a window, but we're going to need to go in so you can get a closer look due to the charring of the victim's body."

His lips thinned, but he nodded and took the protective items. Lawrey put on her set. The body—whoever it belonged to—was still a matter of a criminal investigation, and they needed to protect any evidence that potentially hadn't been found yet.

"Are you ready?" she asked.

"I think so."

"I'm sure I don't need to warn you that it won't smell pleasant either. If you feel nauseated, please leave the room. We can't afford to have the body contaminated with someone else's vomit."

"I understand."

Together, they went into the examination room.

The body lay on a table, a white sheet covering her. Lawrey tugged it back enough for Mr. Clark to be able to see. Normally, only the face would be needed, but because of the charring, it was best if he could see the whole body.

Clark approached the table slowly. His shoulders were rigid, his back straight. Tension radiated from him. Lawrey remained silent, giving him both the physical and mental space to do what he needed. Seeing another person's remains in such a bad state would be hard on any normal person, but also knowing that the body could be that of someone you loved the most in the world made it even harder.

Could he really tell if that was his daughter or not? The body was badly burned, the hair all but gone, one side of her face blackened, the other mottled with burn marks.

Would she be able to recognize Tommy in that kind of condition? Yes, she would. Even the tiniest detail would make her know it was him. The way his smallest toe curled in under the one next to it. The scar he had on his hairline from falling off his bike. The large mole he had on the back of his leg. When he was a young child, she'd have thought she knew his body as well as she knew her own—as though he was an extension of her. Now he was a grown man, so of course she didn't feel that way anymore, but that didn't mean she didn't know him. She wouldn't be able to see all of those details on a body so badly damaged as this one, but there would be something she would recognize.

Clark stopped and stared down at the body. His head moved slightly as he took in the sight, his gaze traveling from head to toe.

Then his shoulders dropped, his entire body seeming to fold in on itself.

"I don't know who that is, but it's not Emily."

Lawrey stepped forward. "You're sure?"

"One hundred percent. I'd recognize my own daughter, and that's not her. Her hands are all wrong, as is the shape of her nose and mouth. She's not so badly burned that I can't see that. I feel terrible for whoever this girl is, but I promise it's not Emily."

"Thank you, Mr. Clark. Let's get out of here."

She led him out of the room and closed the door behind them. They both stripped off the protective gear and dumped it in the trash.

"We will still need to confirm it's not Emily through a DNA sample," she told him.

"I understand." He covered his face with his hands. "I can't believe she's still alive. I was so convinced that was going to be her." He lowered his hands and fixed her with his gaze. "But if she's alive, where the hell is she? Does she know what's happened? That another girl was in the trailer when it burned down? Why hasn't Emily come forward? How could she put me through thinking she was dead like that?"

"Please, Mr. Clark, take a seat. This has all been a big shock, I know. We don't know where Emily is, or what her thoughts or motivations might be, so there's no point in beating yourself up about it."

"Wouldn't you think the same? If your child allowed you to think they were dead?"

She'd thought Tommy might be dead more times than she could count. They'd fight—normally because he'd be wasted or had stolen from her again, or both—and then he would vanish for days or even weeks at a time. She'd use all her contacts in the police to try and trace him, terrified he was going to show up dead with a needle in his arm, but each time he came crawling back, saying he was sorry and begging for forgiveness. She'd tried to get him in rehab on multiple occasions, but he'd always refused. It wasn't as though she could force him. By the time he'd turned eighteen, it was his life and he could do what he wanted. She promised herself that she'd harden up, that she wouldn't allow him back in her life when he was going to steal from her and swear at her and break her heart all over again. But he was her son, and while she didn't have many soft spots, she had one for him.

"Can I ask you some questions about Emily's ex-boyfriend, Zack Jones? We're still trying to track him down, and you may be able to help."

"Sure. What do you need to know?"

"It's our understanding that Emily and Stephan came to Sandtown because they were trying to get away from him. We know she had a restraining order against Zack, but it doesn't sound as though he'd paid much attention to it."

He nodded. "That's what she told me. She said Zack kept threatening Stephan, too, sending him text messages saying what he was going to do to him if he ever got his hands on him."

"Did Zack ever come to the house?"

"Not that I saw. I never saw him at all, actually, once they'd broken up and she took the restraining order out on him."

Lawrey frowned. "She was living with you, though, wasn't she? Before she ran away, I mean."

He nodded. "Yes, she was."

"But you never saw Zack threatening her? Or lurking outside the house?"

"Not as far as I can remember. I witnessed the fallout, though, how distressed she was, but she seemed more worried about Stephan than herself. It wouldn't surprise me if he was the reason she ran."

"To protect Stephan?" she checked.

"That's right."

Emily's father's words jarred against what Lawrey had already learned. People had reported Emily as having been frightened of her ex-boyfriend, but it seemed she wasn't so much frightened of him for herself but for Stephan.

"Do you have any idea where Zack might be?" she asked.

"Sorry, I've no idea. Do you think he might have taken her?"

"We really don't know at this point, but he's definitely a person of interest."

"Her church has been praying for her safe return," Clark said.

Lawrey shot him a look. "She was religious?"

"She'd fallen out of practice as she got older, but yes, she grew up in a Christian household. Why, does that surprise you, Detective? You judging a book and all that?"

"Apologies. I didn't mean anything by it." She remembered Raye saying something about Emily being at the chapel, but she hadn't given it any more thought. "Would Emily have likely sought out a church, especially when she was feeling troubled?"

"Absolutely. I believe that would have been one of the first places she'd turn to."

There was a small chapel in Sandtown. She'd go and speak to whoever was running it these days. Maybe Emily would have confided in them, told them her worries when she wouldn't speak to anyone else.

Chapter Twenty

When Lawrey left work that evening, she didn't go straight home.

She lifted her hand and knocked on the door. She didn't want to be here, but she needed to speak to her ex-husband about their son.

Patrick's new wife, Alyssa, answered the door. Lawrey remembered how old she'd felt when she'd been thirty. She'd already been a mom of an eleven-year-old boy by then and had been married for the same number of years. She'd felt middle-aged, but looking back now, she realized how young she'd been. She wished she'd appreciated it. The woman in front of her now seemed so youthful by comparison.

Alyssa's expression fell when she saw who was at the door. "Oh, hey, Lawrey. Can I help you with something?"

"Is Patrick in?"

"No, sorry. He's out right now. Can I help?"

"Not really. I need to talk to him about our son."

Alyssa raised a pair of perfectly shaped eyebrows. "Your son? Your adult son?"

"Yes, you remember. The one who's closer to your age than Patrick is."

She couldn't help herself. Something about this woman always got her back up. Was it that she was younger and prettier and had been the one who'd ended up making Patrick happy? Probably.

Alyssa folded her arms across her annoyingly perky chest. "Lawrey, Tommy is a grown-up now. I'm sure whatever this is can wait. It's not like he's a small child and the two of you are co-parenting."

"No, but he's still our son, and we'll always be his parents, whether you like it or not."

"Fine." Alyssa's shoulders slumped. "You want to come in and wait?"

She didn't, not really, but she really did need to talk to Patrick.

"Fine."

Alyssa stepped back, allowing her through the front door. It felt strange being inside a house that now belonged to Patrick but that also didn't belong to her. She couldn't see any signs of Patrick in the décor at all, not that Patrick was ever into all of that.

"You want to sit down?" Alyssa said, motioning at the couch.

Lawrey perched awkwardly on the edge of it and sought her mind to think of something to say by way of conversation.

"So, how are things with you and Patrick?" Lawrey asked eventually.

Alyssa curled her lip. "Do you really want to know?"

Lawrey glanced away, catching sight of a framed photograph of their wedding day on the wall. "Not really. Just making conversation."

The rattle of keys in a lock caught her attention, and they both glanced toward the door as it opened. Lawrey was relieved Patrick was home.

He stopped short when he saw her. "What are you doing here, Law?"

"Can we talk in private?"

"We're in private. Anything you want to say can be said in front of Alyssa."

"Oh, for fuck's sake." Lawrey barely managed to stop herself rolling her eyes. "Fine. Tommy's got himself caught up in something. I assume you heard about that young couple who were killed earlier this week up at Sandtown?"

"Of course."

"Turns out Tommy was sleeping with the girl, Emily. Only now we've learned that the girl killed inside the trailer wasn't Emily at all."

"Who was it then?" Alyssa asked.

"We don't know yet, and we don't know where Emily is either. Whether she's alive or dead." She let out a sigh. "To be honest, we don't know what the fuck is going on, but Tommy lied to me about how well he knew Emily, and now the girl is missing."

"Tommy lies about everything. I don't think you should look into it too deeply."

She stared at him like he was an idiot. "It's literally my job to look into things deeply, especially when it concerns two people being dead and another one missing. What reason would he have to lie unless he was trying to hide something he'd done or protect someone else?"

"Maybe he just didn't want to tell you the truth because he knew how you'd react?"

She raised her eyebrows. "How I'd react?"

"Yeah, like you always think the worst of him, just like you're doing now."

Lawrey leaned forward, her hands clasped between her knees. "He's been sleeping with a girl who is now missing, and two other people were murdered. Don't you think that's a big deal?"

He threw up his hands. "He's young. Young people sleep around these days."

"Yeah, but those same people don't always turn up dead or missing. This is serious, Patrick."

"I've barely even heard from him, and I can't remember the last time I saw him in person."

She blew out a breath and shook her head. "Jesus, Patrick, he doesn't live that far away. You could visit."

She didn't understand how Patrick could turn his feelings for his son off so easily. It was as though he was able to wash his hands of Tommy and move on. Maybe a part of her was jealous. No matter how much Tommy had hurt her in the past, there was no way she could ever give up on him. He was her son. Even if she discovered he was responsible for the deaths of the couple in the trailer, she would still love him. She'd also make sure he spent the rest of his life behind bars.

"Yeah, and he could suggest meeting up with me, too. It goes two ways." He glanced over at Alyssa. "Besides, we don't want him being in the house. You know what he's like. Turn your back for a second and something is missing."

"Is that your opinion or hers?" Lawrey glared at Alyssa.

He let out a sigh. "It's not an opinion, it's a fact. Where there's Tommy, there's normally trouble."

She wasn't going to have this fight with him again. It was one of the main reasons they'd broken up.

When she'd become pregnant at only nineteen, people had rolled their eyes and talked behind their backs.

She'd told herself—and Patrick—that the pregnancy had been an accident, but had it really? When people, namely Patrick's parents, had accused her of trapping him, she hadn't been able to deny it. Yes, she'd been on the pill, but perhaps she could have been a little more careful about how regularly she took it. But it wasn't as though Patrick hadn't been happy about the pregnancy. They'd both been happy, once the shock had worn off. They were in love, truly, in that deep, passionate, self-absorbed way only teenagers can be, so they'd promised they'd make things work.

After they'd first gotten married, it had worked, for several years. Except then Tommy had started having issues, and, as much as she'd never blame him, it had come between them. Patrick accused her of fussing over him, stifling the boy, while Lawrey felt Patrick was too hard. It was all the usual toxic masculinity bullshit, telling Tommy big boys didn't cry, and to pull himself together, and to fight back if someone was picking on him. That wasn't who Tommy was at all.

But Lawrey had remembered that promise about making things work, and even when they were at the point where they didn't even want to sit in the same room as one another, she'd still clung to the marriage. It wasn't until Patrick met his thirty-year-old colleague and decided life would be better off with her—which it probably was—that she'd released her hold on him. Tommy had almost been an adult by this point, and she'd already lost count of the number of times he'd stolen from them and run away. It wasn't surprising Patrick wanted to leave. Tommy barely even registered that his parents weren't together anymore. When she'd eventually told him, all he'd said was 'finally.' His comment had surprised her, and when she'd asked what he meant, he'd said the two of them should have broken up years ago, that their relationship made the house a horrible place to be, and it was part of the reason he'd run away as often as he had.

The news had been a shock. She'd thought she'd done the right thing by clinging to the marriage, believing, at least in part, that she'd been doing so to give her son a stable home—something he needed more than anything—but her actions had actually done the opposite

Lawrey grabbed her purse and got to her feet. "I can see I'm wasting my time here. If you do hear from him, please let me know."

Patrick didn't make any attempt to stop her from leaving.

Chapter Twenty-One

The air seemed too thick to breathe.

She needed to wake up. If she didn't, she would die in here, she was sure of it.

More than anything, she needed water, and she thought the men who'd been here before had brought her some. If she didn't manage to get her eyes open and her limbs to move, she wasn't going to be able to reach it.

Come on, Emily. You can do this.

With a jolt, she realized she knew her name. Emily. Emily Clark. What else could she remember? Did she know what had happened to her? How she'd ended up here—wherever *here* was?

There was one thing she knew with certainty. She didn't want to die here.

Had Zack caught up with them? Was this him punishing her for evading him? How could he have found her? Even her own father didn't know where she was, though not telling him or even getting in touch had broken her heart. She'd wanted so badly to call him from a different phone, or even write an old-fashioned letter to let him know she was still alive, but Stephan had insisted it was too dangerous. These days, everything and anything could be traced. She'd tried to argue that her father would never tell Zack where she was, but Stephan said that her dad might try to come here to find her, and Zack might follow him.

It hurt, but she'd eventually accepted what he'd said. She didn't want to constantly be on the run. Sandtown wasn't without its problems, but over the past couple of months, she'd finally started to feel like she was part of a community again. Some of the women had taken her under their wing, teaching her how to customize her clothes, or getting her involved with their art projects. No one there poked into another person's past if they weren't open to sharing it. Everyone respected everyone else's privacy. Of course, Stephan didn't like her getting too close to people. He insisted that she needed to be careful about what she said, that she would let something slip that would mean they were found, but it didn't escape her notice that Stephan was more than happy to drink beer up at the club every day. She liked Hella Billy, but some of the others who hung out there sent her mental warning bells jangling.

A stab of guilt went through her. Maybe she *had* gotten too close to one of the residents. She hadn't meant for it to happen. She'd had a few drinks, and Stephan had been ignoring her. She'd felt hurt and rejected, and then *he'd* come along and made her feel beautiful again. So many people in Sandtown believed that one person couldn't own another, that there shouldn't be jealousy or secrets in a relationship. She'd wished Stephan had seen it that way.

Emily drew her thoughts back to her current situation. Zack being responsible for this was the only thing that made sense to her, though she couldn't understand why he'd go as far as locking her up somewhere. But wasn't that what she'd expected from him? That one day he'd go too far and really hurt her?

He'd put his hands on her plenty of times during their relationship. He'd even left bruises on her and had threatened that if she ever left him for someone else, he'd kill the both of them.

She hadn't been the only one who'd experienced his threats. After the restraining order had been issued, Zack had refocused his attentions on Stephan. She hadn't seen it for herself, but Stephan often came home saying that Zack had followed him today or that Zack had been sending him threatening messages from a burner phone. She'd seen those messages, and they were horrifying. They'd even shown them to the police, but they hadn't been interested. She'd felt so guilty that she'd brought Zack into Stephan's life, she didn't feel she had any choice but to go along with things when Stephan said they needed to leave and come to Sandtown.

Her eyelids fluttered. Were they opening? Was she actually awake?

Her throat was so dry, she could barely swallow.

Emily managed to roll onto her side. Everything hurt. She'd never known pain like it. She still couldn't remember what had happened for her to have ended up here. Where was Stephan? What had happened to him?

If he wasn't here with her, did that mean he was still at the trailer? Had he raised the alarm to look for her? What if he decided it was too dangerous to do that, that if he did, Zack would know where to find them?

No, that didn't make sense. If Zack had taken her, there wouldn't be any point in trying to hide her from him anymore, unless Stephan had managed to escape and was more worried about his own safety than hers?

The thought terrified her. Would he really do that? No one knew where she was. If Stephan didn't report her missing, then no one would ever know to come looking for her.

Before they'd come to Sandtown, she'd have said that Stephan would never do such a thing, but now she wasn't so sure. Hadn't he been acting differently recently? He'd gotten overly protective, which she'd put down to him worrying about their safety, but he also got angry when she tried to ask him where he'd been. It was as though he was allowed to control everything she did, but she wasn't allowed to know a single thing about him.

She needed to get out of here. There was no point in lying around, feeling sorry for herself, waiting for someone to save her. She needed to save herself.

With that determination solidifying inside her, she managed to climb onto all fours. Her head hung down, and she wasn't sure she had the strength to lift it. She needed to see where she was, however.

It was dark, but she could make out corrugated iron walls surrounding her. A window, narrow and with bars covering it, was set high in the wall, moonlight filtering through. What was this place?

"Help," she managed, but her voice was a rasp. "Someone help me."

She doubted anyone was close by enough to help her. If someone had locked her in here, they wouldn't have put her anywhere someone might walk by. If they had, they'd have tied her up to prevent her from banging and gagged her to stop her shouting. Unless they thought she wouldn't regain consciousness and so hadn't bothered to tie her up.

The possibility sparked hope inside her. If she did try to bang on the sides of the building and whoever took her overheard her, would they tie her up then? She paused, not wanting to rush into anything. Right now, they probably thought she was still unconscious. If she started to make a noise, they'd know she wasn't.

She took in her surroundings. In the corner were a couple of buckets. Did one of them contain water? Did they have cameras in here? Was someone watching her?

A fan on the ceiling swirled the tepid air around, and she realized the hum she'd been hearing was that of a generator.

She didn't know if the pounding inside her skull was because of whatever they'd drugged her with, or because she was dehydrated from the heat, or because of some injury she'd sustained, but she did know that she wanted the pain to stop.

What did the men want with her? Were they going to kill her? They'd said they didn't want her dead *yet*, so they did plan on killing her?

She wished more than anything that she'd told her father where she was. How had she allowed Stephan to convince her not to do so? Her dad loved her. He'd never made her doubt that. It was the one thing she was sure of, and right now she wasn't sure about much at all. He might never find out what happened to her, and it would torture him for the rest of his life.

She managed to drag herself over to the bucket of water.

The water was stale and warm, but she didn't care. She dunked her filthy hand into the bucket and scooped water toward her lips. Realizing she couldn't drink quickly enough, she gave up using her hand and stuck her whole face right in. She sucked water between her lips, as though they formed a straw, and gulped it down.

She sat back, breathing hard. Her stomach churned and gurgled. Oh, no. That didn't feel good. She'd drunk too much, too quickly. The thudding pain in her head intensified, and she suddenly grew hot with nausea. She dropped to her hands and knees and gagged. The water rushed from her mouth in a gush, splattering across the floor. Her whole body heaved with the violence of the expulsion. Tears filled her eyes, and she sobbed.

Was she going to die in here? What did they want with her?

The room spun around her, dizziness overwhelming her. She needed to lie down again, to close her eyes, if only for a few minutes. She'd feel better when she woke up again, she was sure.

She needed to...sleep.

Chapter Twenty-Two

L awrey had spent a sleepless night tossing and turning. She was sure she was missing something and that it had to do with Sandtown. The possibility that Tommy had been involved continued to niggle at her. She didn't think him capable of murder, but if he'd lied to her about that, what else had he lied about?

Instead of going straight to the station that morning, she decided to do a detour via the town. She remembered how Mr. Clark had told her that Emily had her church praying for her safe return. Emily had been a young woman, in a strange place, frightened of what the future held for her. Could she have sought out the comfort of God here in Sandtown?

Lawrey planned to find out.

The small wooden chapel had been constructed on the edge of Sandtown. Like so many of the structures here, the sides had been spray-painted with bright colors, transforming it into a work of art.

Pastor Saul Payne, who worked out of the chapel, was far younger than she'd anticipated. He was six feet tall, but skinny, had a long Roman nose, and thin lips. Despite his youth, he'd already lost the majority of his hair but had grown what remained longer in order to comb over the balding spot.

"Pastor Payne?" she enquired.

"Yes, but call me Saul."

She didn't bother to smile. "I'm Detective Winters. I'm investigating the deaths of the young couple in the trailer that burned up a couple of nights ago."

He leaned forward, glanced left and then right, as though he was making sure no one was watching them. "You'd better come inside. It's far too hot to be outdoors at this time of day."

He wasn't wrong about that, though Lawrey felt as though he was using it as an excuse to get out of the view of the rest of Sandtown.

Even so, she was happy to step inside the relative cool of the chapel. A tired unit fixed in one of the windows worked hard to churn the lukewarm air.

He gestured for her to take a seat on one of the pews at the front, and then when she did, he sank down beside her. Lawrey felt awkward sitting in church. She couldn't remember the last time she'd been inside one—most likely for a funeral. When she'd been younger, she'd attended church because everyone was getting married or christening their babies. Now her friends were more likely to be getting divorced than married, and their children were all grown.

She looked around. "If you don't mind me saying, this is a strange place to want to work from."

"Is it? Why?"

She raised her eyebrows. "Why? You can fit maybe twenty people in here, at the most. Why not work somewhere you can find a bigger congregation?"

"Maybe I wanted to work where I saw value in helping people rather than bringing the numbers in. Yes, the number in the congregation might be smaller, but their troubles are far greater."

"Where were you working before you came to Sandtown?" she asked.

He shrugged. "Nowhere for any length of time. I've moved around a lot."

"You know, most people who end up here do so because they've been homeless or had mental health issues, or drug problems. You weren't one of them?"

"No, I wasn't, and not all of them have mental health or drug issues. Some people come here because they're searching for somewhere they belong."

"Is that the case with you?"

"Maybe. I wanted to be somewhere I felt I was needed."

Lawrey glanced around again, taking in the sparse furnishing and cheap religious artifacts. Maybe they thought if they put anything of any value in here, someone would steal it.

"Do you live in the chapel, Pastor?"

He gave a small laugh. "No, I have an RV nearby, just like everyone else. But I'm sure you're not here to talk about my living situation."

She appreciated his directness. "No, you're right. I wanted to ask you about Emily Clark. I spoke to her father recently, and he says she was religious and most likely would have sought comfort from the church. I wondered how well you knew her and if she ever told you anything that might help us find her."

His face pinched with confusion. "Find her? I thought she'd died in the fire."

"It would seem not. The body found in the trailer, along with Stephan's, belonged to someone else."

He paled and crossed himself. "That's terrible. I mean, not for Emily, but for whoever else was killed."

"Yes, it is, and I'm sure you understand that it's created more questions than it has answers."

"You have no idea who the person was, or where Emily has gone?"

"Not yet, which is why we need your help."

He let out a breath. "Well, I'll tell you everything I can, but I'm not sure how much help I'll be."

Lawrey shifted in the uncomfortable pew. "I'll be the judge of that. Did Emily come to the chapel?"

"Yes, she did. On a number of occasions. She felt she needed guidance, and I was here to help her."

"Guidance for what?"

"She felt very lost, as so many of the residents here do. She wasn't sure what direction her life was going to head in. She'd never pictured this being where she'd end up. She was carrying a lot of guilt with her."

Lawrey pursed her lips. "Guilt about what?"

"She felt guilty for leaving her family and friends behind, for not telling anyone where she was going. She knew how worried they must have been, but she was worried that if she told anyone, then her ex-boyfriend would get the information out of them somehow."

"Did she seem scared?"

He thought for a minute. "Not scared, no. More anxious. I don't think she wanted Stephan to see us talking."

"Why not?"

"She said he didn't like her faith, that he called it a way of brainwashing and controlling people."

"But she didn't see it that way?" Lawrey asked.

"No, not at all. She only wanted comfort and guidance. I think she wanted me to tell her that she was doing the right thing by hiding out up here and not telling anyone where she was. She missed home. She talked about wanting to go back, but Stephan wouldn't allow it."

Lawrey frowned. "Wouldn't allow it?"

"I thought it sounded controlling, too, but when I suggested that, she said he was trying to protect her. I got the impression he didn't like her talking to anyone but him, though."

"Did she ever mention him getting violent with her?"

He angled his head. "You think she ran from one violent man into the arms of another?"

"I think something bad has happened to her, and the perpetrator is most likely someone she knows, and the probability is that the person is a man. Those are simple statistics."

"I see, but no, she didn't mention him being violent toward her."

"Did she talk about anyone else in Sandtown? Anyone else they were involved with?" Lawrey wondered if Emily had mentioned Tommy's name at all.

Lines appeared between his brows. "They had friends here. Stephan often drank with people down at the bar."

"The bar?" she checked. "The one Hella Billy owns?"

"There aren't that many to choose from here. I don't think she thought Hella Billy was a good influence on

Stephan. There were rumors awhile back that Hella Billy helped run someone out of town. The guy kept beating on his wife, night after night, and they'd all hear her screams and see the bruises the next day. In the end, the residents got so sick of his behavior that they decided it was time for him to leave. They asked nicely—at least as nicely as they could—for him to go and leave the wife in Sandtown, but he refused. In the end, one of the other women took her in, and when the husband was out one evening, they burned the trailer down, just like someone did with Emily and Stephan."

"Except that couple weren't inside it when that happened."

"No, they weren't. The husband asked around about where his wife was, but they kept her hidden. No one would tell him. What was he going to do—search everyone's trailers? They'd never let that happen. You try living out here without some kind of shelter. You can't. It'll quite literally kill you. So the guy moved on, and he never came back."

"And Hella Billy was behind that?" she asked.

"According to rumors, yeah, but then so was the rest of the town. In the summer months, when the place is down to a hundred and fifty residents, people get to know each other damned well. Sure, they tend to stick to their own, so their neighbors are people like them, but that doesn't mean they don't overlap."

She'd been meaning to catch up with Hella Billy for a couple of days now, but he'd eluded her. Was there a reason for that?

Lawrey got to her feet and then handed him one of her cards. "If you think of anything else that might help, I'd appreciate a call."

He took it. "Of course."

She turned to leave, and he walked her out. She stepped outside, the sun bright after the dimness of the chapel's interior.

"Thank you for your time, Pastor. I appreciate it."

"I sure hope you find her and you catch whoever is responsible."

"I do, too." She paused and turned back. "Oh, one more thing. Where were you before the fire broke out?"

"At Bible study. There were at least five people who can vouch for me being there."

"Bible study?" she checked. "At that time of night?"

"It's the only time the temperature is bearable."

Lawrey offered him a nod and an understanding smile. "Thanks again, Pastor."

She got back in her car and drove over to The Crowbar. The place was deserted at this time of the day. The remnants from the night before could be seen everywhere. It didn't look as though there being two murders in town had put much of a damper on the town's party spirits.

Movement came from out back, and then a huge man in his early fifties walked out, a glass in one hand, a cloth in the other. He was at least six feet four and almost as wide as he was tall. Tattoos covered every inch of his skin; he even had tattoos by his left eye, up his neck, and behind his ear. His long hair was gray and wavy and hung between his shoulder blades. He still wore the leather cut that was from the motorcycle club he used to ride with, though he no longer had an affiliation with the club.

He caught sight of Lawrey and scowled. "What do you want?"

"To talk to you about Emily Clark and Stephan Porter."

"I don't know nothing about that."

She cocked her head. "Really? See, I have several people reporting that Stephan in particular spent plenty of nights drinking here, and that you were seen talking with him many times."

He shrugged one meaty shoulder. "So? This is my bar. I'm allowed to talk to the patrons."

"I never said you weren't." She wondered why he was so defensive. What did he know? Was it that speaking to the cops was generally frowned upon in Sandtown? Or was there more to it? "What sort of things did you talk about?"

"Nothing of any relevance."

"There must have been some topic, even if it was just about the weather."

He kept his expression passive. "We talked about the weather."

"Right." The only thing to say about the weather was that it was fucking hot, and that wasn't going to be changing anytime soon. "How did Stephan seem to you?"

"What do you mean?"

"I mean, what kind of man was he?"

He arched his brow. "You expect me to know that through a handful of conversations over a beer?"

"I think someone like you is observant, that you'll watch out for any sign of trouble, and that makes you a good judge of character. I think you'll know within minutes of meeting someone if they're going to cause you trouble or not."

"I mind my own business. It's not like he was in town for long."

"Did he ever mention perhaps moving on? Or had they planned on staying? It's unusual to get someone new coming to town at this time of year."

"Yeah, the heat is normally enough to run most people out of town if they're not prepared for it. People might kid themselves that they can handle it, but once the reality of what it's like to live in hundred-degree temperatures for months on end hits, they soon hightail it out of here."

"Stephan and Emily didn't, though. Maybe they were better prepared."

He snorted. "Or they thought whatever might be waiting for them outside of Sandtown was worse than the heat."

"You know something about who might have been looking for them, then?"

"Only that Stephan said Emily had an ex who was as crazy as a loon."

"Did he tell you anything else?"

"Nah. I don't think he wanted anyone to get an idea of where or who they were hiding out from, in case word got back."

She pointed at one of the chilled bottles of water in the refrigerator behind the counter. "Think I can grab one of those?"

"Sure, as long as you don't think it's on the house."

"Don't worry, I'm paying."

It was like she was constantly dry out here. The air seemed to suck the moisture from the inside of her mouth and nose. She handed the money over, lifted the chilled plastic to her forehead, rolled the condensation around, and then cracked open the lid.

"Though I guess someone found them anyway," Billy commented.

"Unless that was exactly what someone wanted it to look like." She paused and then said, "I've heard rumors that you've been behind the burning of people's trailers before, when they've not been wanted in town."

He snorted. "You've heard rumors, huh? Or are you accusing me of something?"

"Not accusing you. Just asking you if something is true or not."

"I don't know what you're talking about."

She took a sip of the chilled water. "Why did you break down the door to the trailer but left it to Raye Diante to go inside?"

He shrugged. "No idea. He seemed to want to go in there more than I did."

"You weren't worried about Stephan and Emily inside?"

"Didn't think there was anyone inside at that point."

Lawrey felt like she was wasting her time. She wasn't going to get anywhere with Hella Billy. He was definitely someone who knew how to keep his mouth shut. She tossed some money, together with her card, down onto the bar top.

"Oh, one more thing, Billy."

"What's that?"

"You ever use denatured alcohol here?"

He held her gaze. "No, never."

"What about a bottle of denatured alcohol that was stolen from Raye Diante's place the other week. You seen it lying around?"

His eyes narrowed. "No idea what you're talking about."

She exhaled a long, frustrated breath, shook her head, and went back to her car.

Chapter Twenty-Three

Lawrey took the long, straight desert road out of Sandtown toward her home town of Calrock. In the winter months, the road was busy with tourist traffic, but at this time of year, she'd be lucky to pass a single other vehicle. It ran on for miles, with nothing but clumps of prickly pears and Joshua trees breaking up the view.

Though the road was paved, the desert seemed to be trying to claim it back, the sand and dust creeping across the edges, blending the line between road and dirt.

As she drove, she turned over what she'd learned. The more questions she asked, the more she believed that Stephan Porter wasn't all he'd made himself out to be. Emily had trusted him to protect her from her ex, but had Stephan played her? Had he had something else in mind the whole time? Could he have brought her to Sandtown for an entirely different reason, under the guise of keeping her safe.

Lawrey glanced in the rearview mirror. Behind her, a familiar cloud of dust and sand swirled into the hot air, signaling a vehicle behind her. Heat shimmered off the road, and she squinted, the sun in her eyes.

The vehicle behind her was coming from the direction of Sandtown and was gaining fast.

Her instincts sat up.

"Shit."

Within seconds, the vehicle was right on her tail. A black truck, an older model, the license plate deliberately smeared with dirt. A combination of the dust and bright sunlight meant she couldn't get a good view of the driver. Someone was in the passenger seat, too—a man, from the shape and size.

Her heart picked up pace, and her palms grew sweaty on the hot leather of the steering wheel. She forced herself to take a slow breath, to calm both her racing pulse and thoughts.

Acting impulsively could get a person killed.

She didn't think whoever was in the truck wanted her dead. Someone was trying to intimidate her, make her think twice next time she wanted to come into town to ask some questions. She doubted any of them wanted to go down for killing a cop.

Lawrey went over her options. She could get on the radio and request backup, and report what was happening, but she had the feeling this whole thing would be over by the time her colleagues reached her. She could pull over and draw her gun to ensure whoever was driving understood she wasn't someone to be messed around with. Problem with that was the two assholes in the truck were also most likely armed, and once shots started firing, things would get a whole lot more serious. The third option was that she ride this one out, keep going, let them have their fun, and hope she didn't end up dead by the end of it.

Though she hated feeling like someone got one over on her—she always wanted to be a force to be reckoned with—she decided the third option would be the most sensible.

She kept going, keeping a steady speed, not wanting them to think she found them intimidating or that they frightened her in any way. She resisted the urge to put her foot down, knowing they'd enjoy the chase.

The front grille of the Ford truck got closer, until it filled the entire width of her rearview mirror. There must only be a matter of inches between the front of their vehicle and the back of hers now.

Lawrey braced herself for impact, certain they were going to ram her.

Sure enough, a crunch and screech of metal filled her ears, and she was thrown forward, the seat belt snapping tight across her chest.

"Motherfuckers." She ground her molars and tightened her grip on the steering wheel, keeping the car on the road.

They'd pulled back a little now, but she wasn't sure that meant they were done with her. They were probably having too much fun. She fixed her gaze on the rearview mirror once more, trying to memorize any details about the truck or the driver and passenger that she could use later to figure out who was doing this. Why did someone want her to stay out of Sandtown so badly? This was more than simply the residents' general disliking of the cops. They were warning her to stay away. Did it have to do with the deaths of the young couple, or was there another reason someone didn't like her asking questions?

It wasn't as though it was a secret that plenty of dodgy dealings went down in Sandtown. While many of the older, longtime residents made their livings in perfectly respectable ways, offering up services to the town's other inhabitants or selling to tourists, there were plenty of generally younger ones who didn't. Being this close to the Mexican border meant the opportunities for both drug and people smuggling were rife. She'd had to work with border patrol on a number of occasions due to illegal immigrants making it across the border.

Still, she resisted the urge to put her foot down. Starting a road chase might look like fun and games in the movies, but the reality was that it was more likely to get someone injured or worse. And since she was the one being chased, rather than the chaser, she preferred not to ramp things up.

The road was still empty, other than them. She hadn't seen any vehicles coming in the other direction, and no one in their right mind would be on foot out here in the middle of the day. That was suicide.

That was another reason she didn't want to be run off the road. She kept water in the back—no one drove out here without bringing a decent supply with them. A car breakdown could mean dying if no one came along to pick you up again. People had died out here, normally tourists who didn't understand how dangerous the heat could be. Their cars broke down, and, instead of staying with the vehicles, they'd decide to try to walk for help. There were plenty of spots out here where it was impossible to pick up service so they could phone for help. If they didn't have enough water or even something as simple as a hat, it could kill them.

Behind her, the black truck approached again.

"Fuck," she muttered.

They were nothing more than bullies.

How far away from town was she now? A couple of miles, at least. She didn't think they'd follow her right into

Calrock. There would be too many witnesses. Which meant she only had to wait this out another five minutes or so, and then she'd be free of these assholes.

They slammed into the back of her again. This time, her tires hit a pothole, and instead of her car shunting forward, the steering wheel yanked to one side, and she found herself veering off the road and toward the desert beyond. The car bumped and shuddered as the asphalt became dirt.

Her chest hurt where the seat belt had snapped tight each time, preventing her from smacking her face into the steering wheel, or, even worse, flying out of her seat and going straight through the windshield.

She managed to pull the car to a halt, turning into the skid, the car veering on an angle so the driver's side was now facing the desert. Dust and dirt billowed up all around her, making it hard to see.

Her heart raced, her mouth running dry. Left with no choice, she unholstered her gun and prepared herself for the possibility of gunfire. She wished she could see the truck. Had it stopped as well? Were the people who'd been chasing her now approaching her car to finish the job?

Sitting there, she felt like a goldfish in a bowl. She unclipped the seat belt and shoved open the driver's door. Using the side of the car as cover, she slid out and dropped down beside it. She strained her ears for approaching footsteps, but instead she caught whoops of laughter over the top of the roar of the engine. The crunch of tires on the road, and the screech of brakes. It sounded as though they'd turned around. The engine grew quieter, more distant.

Still holding the gun in both hands, Lawrey let out a long breath and sank against the side of the car. She wouldn't have admitted to anyone that the incident had shaken her up, but it had. Who the fuck were those assholes?

The sun beat down on her, and she knew she couldn't sit this way for much longer. Besides, she didn't want to still be here if they decided to come back.

Lawrey got to her feet, hating how shaky her legs felt. She went to the trunk and grabbed a bottle of water and chugged almost the whole thing. That spike of adrenaline combined with the heat had left her parched. She looked back up the road again and then took out her phone.

In the dirt, where the truck had turned around, tread marks had been imprinted. There didn't seem to be anything special about them, but she still used her phone to take some photographs. If only the license plate hadn't been obscured, but she assumed that had been done on purpose. Even if she had been able to make it out, it would probably have been a stolen one or fake.

With that done, she went back to her car and got behind the wheel. She started it up again and continued to town. The whole time, she kept a watch in her mirror, making sure they hadn't returned, but the road remained quiet.

Not long after, Lawrey arrived at the station.

Iris, behind the reception desk, took one look at her. "You okay, Law?"

"Yeah, just had a little run-in with a couple of Sandtowners. They tried to run me off the road coming out of town."

Iris frowned, her lips pursing, deep lines from her twenty-a-day cigarette habit. "Those sons of bitches. Think they're above the law."

"Not all of them are like that."

"Shit, Law. I didn't mean Tommy, of course."

"I know you didn't." She flapped a hand. "Don't worry yourself."

"What would Tommy think of people he associated with running his own mother out of town? Would he know who was responsible? Surely he can have a word with them."

Lawrey shook her head. "I wouldn't want him putting himself in a difficult or dangerous situation on my behalf."

"You've put yourself in one plenty of times because of him."

Lawrey gave a sad smile. "Maybe that's true, but I'm his mother, no matter how old he gets, and it'll always be my job to protect him." She noted it was still hot inside the station. "Anyone been to fix the air yet?"

Iris grimaced. "He tried. Says he needs to get a part for it."

"Course he does. How long is that going to take?"

"Not sure. A day or two, maybe."

Lawrey huffed out a breath of frustration. "Great."

"You gonna write a report about what happened?" Iris asked.

"Yeah, I will later. First, I need a large coffee and a sit down."

Before that, she needed to pee.

She went into the restroom. Thankfully, no one else was about. She hadn't told Iris about the damage to her car, or the damage to herself. She unbuttoned her short-sleeved shirt and eased herself out of it, revealing the simple cream t-shirt bra beneath. Already, bruises from the seat belt were forming across her collarbone and down over one breast.

"Dammit," she muttered.

She turned to get a look at her back, where the bruising didn't seem as bad.

She didn't think anything was broken, no cracked ribs or collarbone. She suspected she'd have a nasty case of whiplash for the next week or so, but she'd have to take some Advil and get on with things. She wasn't one for sitting around feeling sorry for herself, especially not when she had a potential murder case on her hands and a missing girl to find.

Moving carefully, she shrugged her shirt back on and did the buttons up. Who had been behind the wheel? She was determined to find out.

She wished she could have seen the rear of the truck, then maybe she could have picked out some bumper stickers that would have made the vehicle more easily identifiable. She wasn't going to let this slide. Was it Hella Billy driving? The size was about right. It wouldn't take too much for her to ask around and find out what he was driving these days.

Another thought occurred to her. What if the people in the truck had nothing to do with Sandtown? What if they were actually trying to run her off the road because they knew who her father was? What if they were behind the letters she'd been sent?

She shook off the idea. It wasn't likely. Far more likely that they were trying to send a message to stay out of Sandtown.

Well, the message had been heard, loud and clear, but that didn't mean she was going to take any notice of it.

She'd never been a woman who did as she was told.

Chapter Twenty-Four

"Sarge, I've just had a call that Zack Jones has been picked up not too far from here. We got a hit on his car via an ANPR camera. Uniformed police are bringing him in now."

"He was somewhere nearby?" Lawrey hadn't even made it to her desk when Annie intercepted her.

"Yep, about thirty-five miles from here."

"Well, shit. That doesn't look good for him. Any chance he had Emily with him?"

Annie shook her head. "No, sorry, Sarge. He was alone."

"Dammit," she cursed. "That doesn't mean he's not responsible, though. He could have her hidden somewhere. How long until they get here?"

"Half an hour, tops."

"Can you make sure he's taken straight to interview room one. I want to speak to him."

"Will do, Sarge."

She was still shaken by what had happened on the desert road, but she needed to pull herself together if she was going to find out exactly what Zack Jones was doing this close to Sandtown. The only reason he'd have for being here was because of Emily and Stephan. He knew something, she was sure of it, and it was her job to find out what.

Lawrey filled in the rest of the team on the development. They were all aware that not enough progress had been made on finding out the identity of the female victim, or on finding out what had happened to Emily. With the fire wiping out the majority of the evidence, and there not being any CCTV of the local area, and the locals all keeping their lips tightly sealed, it was proving to be a difficult case.

She caught Abel staring at her intently.

"What?" she asked.

"You all right, Law? You seem pale."

"Yeah, I'm fine. I had a bit of an incident driving out of Sandtown."

He frowned at her. "What kind of an incident?"

"A couple of assholes in a black Ford truck tried to drive me off the road." She paused and then said, "Actually, they did drive me off the road."

"Jesus Christ. Why didn't you call nine-one-one?"

"I knew they were only trying to scare me. Someone doesn't like me asking questions over there."

He cocked his eyebrows. "Guess it worked."

"I'm fine."

He scrubbed his hand across his mouth. "You can't just let it go, Law. That's assault with a deadly weapon. We need to open an investigation."

She shook her head. "No. I think that's what they want. We switch our focus from what happened in that trailer the night of the fire and start trying to hunt down whoever was driving the truck, and we'll be asking all the wrong questions."

"You don't know that. We might be asking all the *right* questions. If you're correct, and whoever tried to drive you off the road is trying to frighten you off going back there, then they might know something about our victims."

She considered this for a moment. "Or they have nothing to do with the trailer burning and don't like the police poking their noses around. That trailer burning down and the couple dying is hardly going to be the only crime happening in Sandtown right now."

He sighed and pressed his lips together. "I don't know, Law. You can't let this slide."

"I'm not, believe me. I'll be keeping an eye out for that truck and whoever owns it."

"Did you get a look at the driver?"

"No. The sun was reflecting off the windshield, and you know what the dust is like driving on that road. It clouded everything. There were two of them, though, and from the shape and size, I'd say they were both male."

"You should speak to Tommy," he suggested. "Wouldn't he know two big men who drove a truck like that?"

She experienced a pang of guilt at the mention of her son's name. She hadn't told anyone other than Patrick and Alyssa that Tommy had been sleeping with Emily.

"I don't want to put him in a difficult position. You know what folks can be like out there. I don't want him being the next person they try to run off the road if they think he's talking to me."

Lawrey thought for a moment and then said, "What do we know about Hella Billy?"

He blew out a breath. "I dug a bit deeper into his background. He's done time for almost every charge you can think of, barring actually taking someone's life. Drug and assault convictions, mainly."

"Why is he not behind bars?"

"Oh, he has been. He's in his fifties now but he spent most of his twenties and thirties serving time. But then he got out of the motorcycle gang he was part of, and he hasn't been charged with anything since. He cleaned himself up."

Lawrey's curiosity had been sparked. "So what changed?"

"His twelve-year-old daughter died. Got caught in the crossfire between two rival MC gangs. She bled out in his arms."

"Jesus Christ."

"Yeah, he pretty much fell apart after that. Left the gang, lost his home, ended up on the street, and was getting through each day with drugs and alcohol."

"And then he ended up in Sandtown."

"That's right."

She almost felt sorry for the guy. No one should have to go through the absolute heartbreak of losing a child. She'd thought she was going to lose Tommy on multiple occasions. Getting those calls at two in the morning because he'd got into an accident or had overdosed, and her heart seeming to freeze, her breath trapping in her lungs, her whole body and soul poised to hear the words 'your son is dead.' But then they'd tell her he was still alive, and everything rushed back, and she could function again. Until the next time.

Yes, she could feel sorry for Hella Billy for losing his daughter, but it had been his choice to live the gang life. He was the one who'd ultimately put his child's life in danger by hanging out with those kinds of people. Your child was a lot less likely to be shot to death if you were a musician, for example, or worked in insurance.

"Do we know what kind of car he drives?"

He pursed his lips. "Nothing coming up other than the RV he lives in."

She nodded. It didn't mean the black truck wasn't his, of course. Owning an unregistered vehicle was probably the least of his infractions. Unless she was completely wrong about Hella Billy's involvement. Someone else could easily have spotted her there and decided she needed a warning.

Annie caught Lawrey's attention again. "Sarge, Zack Jones is waiting in interview room one."

"Thanks, Annie." Lawrey turned to Abel. "Let's go and see if he knows what happened to Emily Clark."

• • • •

LAWREY PEERED THROUGH the small window in the door at the young man sitting in the interview room. He sat in that slouchy way some people do when they like to take up more space than necessary—legs spread, shoulders rolled back, arms hanging. He didn't appear in the slightest bit perturbed at being in a police station.

"Zack Jones?" she said as she walked in, Abel close behind. "I'm Detective Winters. This is my partner, Detective Kavanagh. Do you know why you're here?"

He gave a curt nod. "Yeah, because of Emily Clark and that asshole, Stephan."

Lawrey took a seat opposite him, and Abel remained standing, his arms folded.

"I'd like to ask you some questions, if that's all right?"

"Yeah, I'll answer whatever you want to ask."

"I appreciate your cooperation. I also need to let you know that this conversation is being recorded. Do you want a lawyer present before we get started?"

He cocked an eyebrow. "I've not been arrested, have I?"

"Not yet. You're free to leave, unless you give me reason to arrest you at some point during this interview."

"I don't have nothing to hide." He sat back, his jaw jutted. "If there's something I know that can help catch whoever the fuck killed Emily, then I'll sit here all goddamned day."

"Emily isn't dead," she announced. "At least, we hope she's not."

His eyes went round, genuine surprise in them.

"What?"

"Whatever reports you've been following got it wrong. We did find the body of a young woman in the trailer, together with the body we believe to be Stephan Porter, but she wasn't Emily."

He covered his mouth with his palm. "Jesus Christ. Where the fuck is she then?"

"That's what we're trying to figure out. Care to explain to me why you were picked up so close to Sandtown?"

He exhaled and slumped down. "Look, I've got an alert on my phone to any mention of the names Emily and Stephan used together. My phone blew up a few nights ago. Loads of local people were talking about the fire and mentioning the victims by name. Of course, it had to be them, but I wanted to come here to find out for sure."

The police had never released the victims' names, and certainly not their surnames, but there was nothing they could do to stop people mentioning them online. There would probably even be video footage of the fire somewhere online if she dug deep enough. Nothing was sacred these days. If people came across a tragedy, the first thing they'd think to do was whip their phones out of their pockets and film and post whatever was going on for Facebook or Instagram or whatever social media app was trending.

"When was the last time you saw Emily?" she asked.

"I don't know. A long time ago. We're talking months."

"Everyone we've spoken to says they were forced to run away because you were harassing them both, even after the restraining order was granted."

"That's bullshit." He shook his head.

"Excuse me if I sound cynical, Zack, but you're bound to say that, aren't you?"

He shrugged. "It's still bullshit."

She linked her fingers together on top of the table that separated them. "Where were you the night of the fire, Zack?"

"What? I'm not sure..."

"You need to get sure," she told him.

"Well, I was nowhere near here, if that's what you're asking."

"Where have you been then? You haven't been an easy man to track down. We sent local police to your last known address, and your roommates said they hadn't seen you in weeks. That sounds pretty suspicious to me. Are you telling me you weren't trying to find Emily and Stephan?"

"No, I wasn't. Fuck that. I was just traveling around. Seeing a bit of the country."

"Where have you been staying?"

"Nowhere. I sleep in my car."

"You need to think harder. Where were you the night of the fire."

"Jesus, okay, let me think." He put his head in his hands for a moment and then sat up. "I was up near Sacramento."

"Can you prove that?"

"No, but surely you can? You've got all that high-tech camera surveillance shit now. You must be able to catch me on CCTV or something." He snapped his fingers. "Wait, I paid for food using my credit card while I was up there. I ate in a bar and drank some beer while I watched some sports. Is that enough to prove I was nowhere near Sandtown?"

"It'll help," she said. "You can give me the name of that bar, too. They might have cameras that'll prove it was you using the card and not a buddy you asked to help cover your ass."

He waved his hand. "Yeah, well, go do that, then. I'm telling the truth. I didn't have nothing to do with whatever has happened to Emily."

She tossed him a notepad and a pen. "Write down the name of the bar."

He did and handed the notepad back.

Lawrey picked it up and twisted in her seat to give it to Abel. "You think you can follow this up for me?"

Abel nodded. "You going to be okay?"

He meant with the fact she'd be alone with Zack.

Lawrey turned back to Zack. "We're not going to have any problems, are we?"

"No, ma'am," he said.

Abel left the room, and Lawrey refocused on questioning Emily's ex-boyfriend.

"Why did you have an alert set up on your phone about her?"

"Honestly, I was worried. That new guy, Stephan, was up to no good. I know everyone thinks I'm a piece of shit, and they're probably right about that, but just 'cause I lost my temper a few times doesn't put me on anywhere near the kind of level he's on."

"I heard you were sending him messages, threatening ones."

"Yeah, telling him to stay away from her."

"He used it as a reason to get Emily to leave with him and not tell anyone where they were going."

Zack banged his fist down on the table. "Fuck."

Lawrey didn't respond, but she saw that flash of violence in him, most likely the same thing that had made Emily get the restraining order out on him in the first place.

"What was it you disliked so much about Stephan, other than the fact he was with your ex-girlfriend?"

A muscle ticked in his jaw. "Rumors were that he was into some sketchy shit."

"What kind of sketchy shit?"

"I dunno exactly..."

He trailed off, but Lawrey didn't prompt him. Sometimes letting someone fill in their own silences was better than her trying to twist information out of them.

Eventually, he let out a huff of air and then sat forward. "Okay, I don't know how much truth there is to this, but I heard he was into some pretty violent sex stuff."

"Like BDSM?"

"Nah, worse than that." He couldn't meet her eye. "Like really violent stuff. Stuff you can only find if you dig into the darkest corners of the dark web. I was worried he'd get Emily involved somehow. That's why I was so worried when they took off. Why I wanted to track them down. I honestly didn't expect to find him dead, though. I thought Emily would be the one who..."

"Who what?"

"Was killed."

Lawrey let this sink in. They hadn't been able to find out much about Stephan as a person. They hadn't been able to track down any next of kin, or even any friends. The only person they'd really found who seemed to know him was Hella Billy, and he hadn't said much. Were they missing something there?

She changed tactics. "Do you have any idea who the other victim might be? The woman we found instead of Emily?"

He sucked on his teeth. "No, sorry. No clue."

"Do you know where Emily might have gone? Is it possible she left willingly?"

"I have no idea."

Lawrey nodded, believing him. "You mind if you wait here until we check out your alibi?"

He threw his hands out either side of him. "If it means clearing my name from the investigation, sure thing."

Lawrey left the interview room and went back to her desk. She was starting to feel like they were never going to know what had happened to Emily.

Abel joined her. "I've got the manager of the bar sending over the CCTV footage from the evening of the fire. He doesn't remember Zack being there specifically, but he says it's a busy bar."

"Okay, thanks." Lawrey twisted her lips. "As much as I hate to say it, we're going to need to go to Sandtown again. From what I can tell, the only person who really got to know Stephan is Hella Billy. Now, rumor has it that Hella Billy has been known to chase people who stirred up trouble in Sandtown out of town by setting fire to their trailers. We've got a situation where a trailer was burned down and two people were killed, one of them being someone Hella Billy knew."

"You think he might be responsible?"

"I'm not totally sure of anything right now, but I think it's a connection we can't ignore. I don't know how believable Zack is, but he says Stephan was into some dark, sexual violence. What if he shared that information with Billy, and Billy decided he didn't like that much? Maybe he wanted to run him out of town."

"But why kill them, if that's all he wanted to do?"

"Maybe things went wrong and he felt he had no choice."

Abel's forehead crumpled. "But the girl in the trailer wasn't even Emily."

Lawrey let out a frustrated breath and covered her face with her hands. "I know. I'm not saying I have all the answers, but this may be a part of the puzzle."

"Let's get a warrant for Hella Billy's home, and for The Crowbar, see if we can find that missing bottle of denatured alcohol," Abel said. "But this time, Lawrey, you're not going alone."

Chapter Twenty-Five

"What you doing, Raye?" The voice came from behind him, and his heart sank. Why the fuck couldn't people leave him alone to work? It was all he wanted, to get some paint on canvas and lose himself for a while.

He bristled. "Just trying to get some work done, except people keep interrupting me."

"You don't want to score today?"

Raye glanced over his shoulder at the two men standing in the opening of the makeshift structure that was his studio. One of the men held up a little baggy of wraps and gave it a shake.

Raye did his best not to look at them. "You know I'm trying to stay clean."

The guy with the wraps smirked. "It won't last. You always come back with your tail between your legs."

"Speaking of legs," his friend said, "you sure you got enough of yours on show, Raye? If those shorts were any smaller, your balls would be hanging down on either side of the leg holes."

He punched his friend in the arm and laughed as though he'd said the funniest thing in the world.

His friend joined him. "Do you think Raye even still has balls? Maybe he took a knife to them and cut them off the same time he did his cock?"

Raye wanted to run away and hide, but he knew men like his. They were nothing more than a couple of bullies, and if you wanted bullies to leave you alone, then you had to stand up to them.

"I've got a cock and balls," he said, putting his shoulders back and lifting his chin, "and they're a hell of a lot bigger than anything you two are hiding in those jeans."

The friend grabbed his crotch. "You wanna compare dicks, Raye? Bet you'd like that wouldn't you?"

"What about titties, Raye?" the guy with the drugs said. "You growing any of those yet? Maybe you should give us a flash."

A shot of worry went through him, but he kept up the bravado. "You'd have to be a lot better-looking than either of you two ugly sons of bitches to get anywhere near me."

Drug Guy moved closer. "You sure about that? I'd bet we can get as close as we want."

Raye took a step back. He knocked his easel, and a small paint pot fell off the stand, red paint splattering on the floor like blood. He put up both hands in front of himself.

"I don't want any trouble. I only want to be left alone, is all."

The friend put on a babyish mimicking voice. "I want to be left alone..."

"Please," Raye said.

The two men moved closer. He glanced past them, wondering if he could make a run for it, but they were blocking the exit. Behind him was his trailer. Could he get inside and lock the door on them? He glanced over his shoulder, judging the distance. Could he make it?

Drug Guy must have guessed his intentions. "Don't even think about it. We can easily break that door down if we need to."

The atmosphere had changed. Gone from snide teasing to something darker, more dangerous. These men hated him. Hated what he was. Hated what he stood for. And being trapped in here with them was a precarious position to be in.

"Wha-what do you want from me?"

The friend curled his lip. "You been talking to the cops about some denatured alcohol going missing?"

"No! I mean, yes, but only because they already knew. What was I supposed to say?"

"Nothing," said Druggie. "Absolutely fucking nothing."

"I'm sorry. I'll keep my mouth shut from now on. I promise."

He was right beside his easel. He had no choice but to try and run. If he didn't, something bad was going to happen. He could feel it in his bones.

With his left hand, he swiped at the back of the easel and his art supplies, sending them flying in the direction of the two men. They both let out yells of annoyance and dodged out of the way.

Raye took his moment and darted around them, his sights fixed on the exit.

But he wasn't fast enough.

One of the men caught him around the waist, yanking him backward. Raye let out a howl of desperation, praying someone would hear and come to his aid. But then the man's meaty palm was over his mouth, shutting off the sound.

"Fucking asshole," Druggy hissed in his ear. "Think you can get one over on us? We'll make you pay for that."

Raye struggled and fought, but the man was too strong. He had Raye pinned against his body, and a hardness pressed into the small of Raye's back. His eyes prickled with terror. He found himself shoved toward a table and then bent over it. Druggie yanked down his shorts, while his friend held him down.

"No, get off me!" Raye cried.

"Guys like you are asking for it," Druggie spat. "This is what you really want, isn't it?"

To Raye's horror and shame, a tear rolled down his cheek. "Please, no, stop."

But they didn't stop.

Raye took himself away. He clenched his teeth and pretended he was somewhere else—*someone* else—even while he felt as though he was being impaled by a red-hot poker. This wasn't happening to him. It was happening to another version of Raye, but not him.

Druggie finished up, and his friend spoke.

"Move over. It's my turn."

Raye bounced back and forth while the man rutted inside him. He tried not to hear his grunts of pleasure or even feel the pain.

When the friend was done, they both stepped back, as though admiring their handiwork.

Raye wanted to die.

The friend unwrapped a piece of gum and flicked the wrapper to the floor. Druggie took one of the wraps from the baggy and tossed it down to where Raye was still slumped over the table.

It landed by his head, and he just lay there staring at it.

"Call that payment," Druggie said. "It's about as much as whores like you are worth."

Tears stung his eyes, but Raye found himself reaching out and covering the tiny wrap of meth with his palm, cupping it in his hand and pulling it back to him.

Chapter Twenty-Six

L awrey wanted to get out of the office.
       She winced as she picked up her purse. The bruises from the car accident were already an angry blackish purple. She could tell nothing was broken, though, and the bruises would fade quickly enough.

The more she thought about it, the more it seemed clear that Hella Billy had sent a couple of his guys after her to scare her off. The only reason he'd have to do that was if he was hiding something.

It shouldn't take long for the warrant to come in, but it would be long enough for her to grab a decent iced coffee and a sandwich. She had a favorite place right around the corner from the station that plenty of the police officers dined at. The owners always joked that they kept them in business.

She left the station and walked the couple of blocks to the diner. She pushed through the doors, relieved to be back inside a building that had their air working. The station was hotter than the Devil's armpit right now, and it was affecting everyone's mood.

She got in line to wait to be served.

Someone tapped her on the shoulder, and she turned to find Joe Martinez, the man who her sister and brother-in-law had tried to set her up with, standing directly behind her.

"Lawrey, hey," he said. "Twice in one week. This is a treat."

"Is it?"

Begrudgingly, she had to admit he was good-looking. Thick wavy hair, with a hint of gray at the temples, good shoulders, brown eyes with thick lashes. It only served to make her more suspicious of his motivations, though. Surely a guy like him would be better off hanging out in a bar picking up women ten years her junior. While she didn't think she was unattractive, she definitely felt like she was past her prime. She was also short-tempered, swore too much, rarely smiled, and was obsessed with her work.

Hardly a catch for someone like Joe Martinez.

Lawrey still felt burned out on relationships. Patrick leaving had hurt, even though she'd known the marriage had run its course. It had hurt even worse when he'd met someone new and had moved on so quickly. Other than a couple of quick flings in college, Patrick had been the only real relationship she'd had, and she had no idea how she was supposed to conduct herself with anyone else. Maybe she could put on some makeup and make an effort to laugh and smile, and tell funny stories, but eventually they'd find out who she was deep down, how she took herself too seriously and worried all the time. They'd learn how she could never be bothered to shave her legs and didn't wash her hair often enough. They'd discover how she'd prefer to heat up a TV dinner and drink a beer with her feet up than cook a nice meal.

Letting people in was dangerous. People were unpredictable, and, for the most part, all they'd ever done was hurt her.

He chuckled. "Well, it is for me. I was hoping I'd get to see you again."

"The town's pretty small, Joe. We were bound to bump into one another."

He scuffed his foot on the floor, gazing down. "Actually, I was hoping we'd be able to do more than bump into one another."

"You were?"

"I'd love it if you let me take you out for dinner one night. Maybe tomorrow?"

She winced. "I don't think it's a good idea, Joe. I'm sorry. I'm super busy with work…"

He gestured one hand out toward her. "Maybe when work's a little quieter then?"

"The thing is, it's never really quiet. Work is what I do. Being a detective isn't something I can just clock in and clock out of, you know. It's like the rest of my life has to work around that."

"That's the great thing about my job. I'm super flexible."

She eyed him curiously. It seemed like every barrier she put up, he found a way around. Why wasn't she putting him off yet? Surely he could see that she wasn't a good catch? She couldn't help it—her suspicious nature sent her alarm bells ringing.

"Your job," she said slowly. "The one as a content creator. The one you had to move to Calrock to do?"

Most people didn't enjoy being around a police officer. Even if they were as innocent as a newborn child, something about being around a cop made people feel guilty. So why was he wanting to spend time with her? Did it have to do with her past? He said he was a content creator. Was that anything like being a journalist? Was it that he really wanted to get some inside story on her father to write about?

"Why not? The rent is cheap, the weather is good—"

She snorted. "The weather is good? Are you serious?"

"Yeah. I come from up north. Newport, Maine, to be precise. Honestly, I hate the snow and the cold. This is perfect for me."

She stared at him. "I actually think you might be insane."

"Why? You live here."

"Yeah, 'cause it's my home. I've always lived here."

"But if you hated it that much, you could have moved away. I mean, what's keeping you here?"

"Family. You already met my sister and her family, of course. My mom is elderly now, and my son lives in Sandtown."

He seemed to consider this for a moment. "Okay, but your sister could look after your mom, if needed, and your son is an adult now, right? You could leave if you really wanted to."

She folded her arms. "Now I feel like you're trying to get rid of me."

He laughed, a pleasant sound. "Not at all. I'm trying to work out who the real Lawrey Winters is underneath all the barriers you put up."

"Is that right? What have you got so far?"

He put out his hand so he could count his points off on his fingers. "Hardworking, loyal, strong, sarcastic, beautiful."

He threw her with the last one, and, to her embarrassment, she found her cheeks warming. She couldn't remember the last time someone had paid her a compliment, never mind told her she was beautiful. Not that she believed him, of course, but it was nice to hear. Then she gave herself a shake. This was how men won women over, wasn't it—told them what they thought they wanted to hear?

"Nice try," she said. "I'm still not having dinner with you."

"You need to eat, don't you?"

"So? I'm quite happy eating alone."

"What about if I see you're home, and I happen to have picked up takeout?"

"You know this is bordering on harassment. Finding out if a woman is home alone, and then stalking her house."

"Does this mean you're going to arrest me?" He had that twinkle in his eye. He put both hands out to her, wrists up. "You do have handcuffs, right?"

"Would you stop it," she said, but laughter danced behind her tone.

He raised both eyebrows. "Is that a yes?"

"I like Chinese," she said, by way of an answer. "Something with chicken and noodles."

He lifted his fingers to tip a salute to his forehead. "Chicken and noodles. That I can do."

The girl behind the counter was calling to her. "Ma'am? Can I help you, ma'am."

"I have to order now."

Shaking her head, she turned to the counter and got her iced coffee and sandwich to go.

• • • •

BY THE TIME SHE GOT back to the station, the warrant had come through to search Hella Billy's properties.

She wasn't wasting any more time. "Let's put a team together and get over there."

After being run off the road, she wasn't taking any chances. She made sure she wore body armor, and she had her team around her.

Within the hour, they were all at Sandtown.

The team moved fast, swarming over The Crowbar and Hella Billy's trailer like termites, leaving nothing unturned. Though the warrant was to search for the bottle of denatured alcohol, Lawrey was also hoping they might turn up the location of Emily Clark as well. Could Hella Billy be the one holding her somewhere all this time? It was certainly possible, though it didn't explain why he'd have broken down the door to help put out the fire. She didn't understand that at all. If he'd set the fire to destroy evidence, why help put it out before that happened?

As expected, Hella Billy wasn't happy about the intrusion.

"What the fuck is this?" he yelled, gesturing at all the police officers tossing down his bar.

"We've got a warrant, Billy," she told him. "Don't do anything stupid that'll make me arrest you."

Though he was clearly seething, he took her at her word and sat at one of his bar tables, glaring at her.

The minutes passed, and Lawrey was starting to think they weren't going to find anything, but then one of the officers gave a shout from the rear of the property.

"We found something!"

"Make sure he doesn't go anywhere," she instructed one of the officers.

She went around the rear of the property. Several galvanized steel dumpsters were out the back, getting heated in the sun. The stink of rotting trash had her turning her head away. Much of it had been emptied out on the ground, but the object they'd been looking for was held in one of the officer's gloved hands.

Buried beneath all the trash from the bar was the bottle of denatured alcohol they assumed had been stolen from Raye Diante's place, and the hose he'd used to feed the accelerant into the trailer through the open window.

They took it around to the bar where Billy was waiting.

"I'm going to bet your prints are all over this bottle, Billy," Lawrey said. "I think it's time you were honest with us, don't you? Did you steal this from Raye Diante so you could set fire to Stephan and Emily's trailer?"

"No, I didn't fucking steal it."

"You had someone steal it for you then?"

From his lack of a response, she could tell she was onto something.

"Who stole the canister, Billy?"

He shook his head. "I don't know what you're talking about, and don't try to pin the deaths of those two on me either. I didn't have anything to do with that."

"You sure? The same way you didn't have anything to do with the trailer burning down?"

He pursed his lips and didn't reply. It didn't matter if he didn't talk here. They'd be taking him down to the station for questioning now anyway.

"According to people we've been talking to," she continued, "you've got a bit of a history when it comes to setting fire to trailers. You do it when you want to run people out of town. Why did you want to run Emily and Stephan out of town, Billy?"

"I didn't."

She could tell he was lying. "Listen to me. If you tell me the truth, I can help you. We can find whoever it was who actually killed them instead of you taking the fall for it. But if we don't know the truth, then we have to fill in the blanks with whatever we can. Do you understand?"

Billy's body language completely changed, his shoulders rolling in, his chin dropping. "I didn't know they were in there, I swear I didn't. That's why I broke down the door."

"So you did burn down the trailer?"

He nodded. "Yeah, that was me, but I didn't kill them. I swear I didn't. I just wanted them to leave."

"But why did you want to run them out of town?"

"The guy, Stephan, he was into some weird shit."

"What kind of weird shit?"

He glanced away. "Porn."

"Okay," she said slowly. She highly doubted someone like Hella Billy could be riled by a bit of porn. "Care to elaborate?"

"I guess you'd call it snuff porn."

That got Lawrey's attention. "You're saying he was into watching porn where the actress is murdered at the end?"

"Yeah, but not only at the end. Like, she was dead, and they...carried on."

"Fucking hell. He showed you one of those films?"

Billy glanced down and nodded. "He'd had a few drinks. I didn't get the impression he only liked watching them, you know. I think he had more of an involvement than that."

She narrowed her eyes. "What kind of involvement?"

"Like maybe he recruited the girls."

"Girls like Emily?"

"Yeah, they like them young and blonde."

Her chest tightened, and suddenly she was short of breath. Fuck. Was that what had happened to Emily? Had she been taken to be the next victim in some snuff film?

Jesus Christ.

"What happened to Emily?" she asked. "Where is she? Is she still alive?"

"I have no idea, I swear. I thought it was her inside the trailer. I don't know what happened to her."

She studied him. On that, at least, she thought he was telling the truth.

"Whose idea was it to burn down the trailer, Billy?"

His lips thinned. "No one. It was all mine."

"You sure about that?"

"Sure as I am about anything." His lips tightened. "I might have talked about it with the pastor, though."

"The pastor here in Sandtown? Pastor Saul Payne?"

Billy nodded. "He was worried about Emily. Thought it might be better if her boyfriend knew he wasn't welcome."

"We're going to need to get all this on record, Billy. This conversation is best continued down at the station."

Uniformed officers would take him. They cuffed Billy and read him his rights, and they took him to the back of the squad car.

Lawrey turned to Abel. "Do you think we're too late? To find Emily alive, I mean?"

"Honestly, I don't know."

"We're still no closer in finding out who took her, but if what Billy says is true, then it must be someone Stephan was connected to."

Lawrey agreed. "We need to be looking at exactly who Stephan's contacts are. He must have had a second phone or a laptop or something to stay in contact with whoever he's involved with. He didn't do it via smoke signals."

Abel twisted his lips. "Whoever killed him could have easily taken it. They'd have been wanting to cover their own backs, too."

"Fuck." Lawrey thought for a minute. There was no way she was going to give up. "We have to go farther back. Dig into his life in Portland, Oregon. His address, his job, what did he drive, who were his friends, where did he go to school? I want every single detail we can find on him."

"You think what Billy said about the snuff films is true? That Stephan manipulated Emily into coming here so she could be part of it?"

"It makes sense, but if that's what Stephan was into, why is Stephan dead?"

"Maybe he pissed off someone higher up the line?" Abel suggested.

"Possibly. Perhaps he didn't want to hand Emily over. Maybe her time had come and he told whoever was making the films that he'd changed his mind and they couldn't have her, so they came along, took Emily, and put the other girl in her place, and then killed Stephan."

Abel nodded. "They might have never anticipated that someone was going to burn the trailer down."

Lawrey put her hands on her hips. "No, I'm not buying that. They wanted it to burn. Why else would they try to put another girl in Emily's place? The plan wouldn't have worked if it hadn't burned."

"The plan didn't work," Abel pointed out. "The residents stepped in and stopped the fire before it could completely char the bodies, so we were able to identify them."

"Maybe it's a coincidence and Hella Billy simply got there first."

She allowed everything they'd learned to sink in.

"There's something else I need to do before we leave," she told Abel.

"No problem."

On the way out of town, they swung by Raye Diante's place.

Abel stayed in the car, while Lawrey went to call on Raye. It all seemed quiet. Normally, there would be music blaring out, or sounds of voices as Raye entertained visitors. But all was silent. Maybe he wasn't home.

"Raye?"

She peered into his studio. The place was a mess. His easel had been knocked to the ground, red paint splatted everywhere. Her eyes caught sight of a small screwed-up ball of yellow paper lying on the ground. What was going on?

"Raye? You here? Everything all right?"

She walked through the studio, toward the trailer at the back. The door stood partly open. She rapped on it with her knuckles and then poked her head inside. "Raye?"

His voice called back to her from the bedroom. "In here."

She frowned. Had she disturbed him sleeping?

She made her way through the trailer, to the bedroom, where she found him lying on his back on the bed.

"Hey, Raye," she said. "I wanted to let you know that we've arrested Hella Billy for the theft of your denatured alcohol and for burning down the trailer that night."

Raye didn't react to the news.

"You okay?" she asked.

"Sure."

She glanced to the side of his bed, where drug paraphernalia lay scattered on the floor. Her heart sank.

"What's wrong, Raye? You using again?"

"Maybe."

She let out a sigh. "Why? You were doing so well."

"It's none of your goddamned business, Detective."

"No, you're right, it's probably not, but I'm worried about you. Did something happen?"

She moved farther into the bedroom so she could get a better look at him. He'd covered himself up, dressed in long pants and a baggy shirt. Where was the wig he normally sported—though she didn't know how he could stand all that hair in this weather? It was way too hot for long sleeves, however, so he hadn't been able to hide the marks on his wrists and up his arms.

He twisted his face away. "No, nothing happened."

"What about those bruises?"

To Lawrey's trained eye, she recognized fingerprints when she saw them. But she also knew how close-lipped the residents of Sandtown were. If there was trouble happening in town, they dealt with it themselves rather than going to the cops. The problem was, when something happened to someone who didn't have anyone to turn to, it meant people got away with doing bad things.

"I fell," he replied.

His voice seemed dull, like there was no life in it.

"Do you want me to get you some help?" she offered. "Take you to the hospital?"

"I just want to be left alone."

"I don't mind—"

He interrupted her. "What part of alone don't you understand, Detective?"

She hesitated for a moment and then slid her card beneath a pot of paint on the table. "You can call me, you know. Anytime you need to. It doesn't have to be to report something. I'm here if you want to chat."

He pressed his lips together but didn't reply.

"I'm not the bad guy here, remember that, okay? I know you've probably had some uncomfortable run-ins with the police in the past, but I'm not like that."

He still wouldn't meet her eye. "I know."

Had someone hurt him because he knew something about the case? It wouldn't surprise her, but then little could in this place. Some of the people here were a law unto themselves, with no respect for the laws that actually governed their county, or the people employed to ensure the civilians abided by them.

She was reluctant to leave him, but what else could she do?

Chapter Twenty-Seven

How many days had she been in here now?

Emily didn't think she'd ever felt so sick. Her headache was like a vise clamped to her skull, pressing harder and harder.

Why hadn't they killed her already? What did they want with her? A part of her wondered if she'd be better off dead. At least then she wouldn't be going through such pain. But at the same time, she knew she wanted to live. She was only twenty-two years old. She'd barely gotten started with her life.

She needed to attempt to escape. She didn't know how she was going to do it, but she had to try.

There wasn't much in the room. She had the bare mattress on the floor, the bucket she was supposed to use as a toilet, and another that had water in it for her to drink. The paddles of the fan spun slowly overhead, barely doing anything to cool the space. It meant there was electricity here, though she didn't have any lighting. When it got dark in here, it got really dark. She could barely see her hand in front of her face. But at least it was cooler then, and she was able to sleep. Her dreams were her only escape.

Emily crawled to the door and pressed her ear to it, trying to sense if there was anyone outside. She couldn't hear much of anything at all. No voices, no music playing, not even a distant road.

Where the hell was she?

What had happened to Stephan? Those men spoke as though they'd known him. Had they? Were the people responsible for this those same ones Stephan had gotten friendly with over at the club? There had always been something about them that left her uneasy. They'd reminded her too much of her ex. She hadn't liked Stephan hanging out with them, but when she'd tried to say something, he'd gotten defensive and thrown it back at her, telling her that he was the one who should be upset, and that he'd seen how she was flirting with Tommy Winters. He kept accusing her and accusing her, until one day she broke down and decided that if she was going to get accused of something, she might as well do it. She'd regretted it right away, but she couldn't take it back.

Was this God's punishment for her being unfaithful to Stephan? It wasn't as though they were married, but she'd still done wrong.

Emily lifted her fist and hammered on the door. With no one to talk to, all she could do was shout, her lips pressed against the hot metal.

"What do you want with me? Someone tell me something. Fucking talk to me!"

Her throat burned from screaming, and her hands were bruised from hammering on the door.

They weren't going to let her out. That much was clear. If she was ever going to get out of here, she needed to take things into her own hands.

The men brought her food and water twice a day. When they did, they had no choice but to open the door. Their hands were full then, too. More often than not, they took turns coming here, so they were alone. That was her opportunity to get out of here.

She needed a distraction, something she could use so he wasn't focused on her the moment he opened the door. Maybe if she threw something to the far end of the metal box she was in, it would clang loud enough to distract him and allow her to get past?

It didn't feel like enough, though. She needed something bigger. She needed to slow him down, to hurt him.

Her gaze lit upon the metal bucket she'd been given to relieve herself in. She tried to stay well away from it when she wasn't using it. The heat, combined with her dehydrated urine, was enough to make her eyes sting.

That was it, she realized. If her eyes watered just by being near it, what would happen if she threw it right in one of their faces? It would blind them, at least long enough for her to run.

If it didn't work, what was the worst that could happen? They killed her? They were going to do that anyway. If they did, at least she'd have had the satisfaction of throwing her piss at them.

Chapter Twenty-Eight

They got back to the station where Hella Billy was processed and would be questioned at length. She would let Abel run that, together with her other detectives. She trusted them to do a good job. Her time was better spent trying to identify their Jane Doe's body. Doing so would open up a whole new line of investigation.

She filled her team in on what they'd found and made sure everyone knew what their next actions needed to be.

If Emily had been the victim of some kind of snuff-porn-making syndicate, then it made sense that the body they'd recovered from her bed had also been a victim. Lawrey thought of the number of broken bones and the indication that she'd been strangled. They'd assumed it had happened at the same time that Stephan had been killed, but what if they were wrong? Finding out an exact time of death was hard enough, but it was near impossible in bodies that had been burned. Wasn't it possible that the female victim had been killed before Stephan—hours, or possibly even a day or two—and then the body put in Emily's bed?

Lawrey wanted to get another look at the medical examiner's report for the Jane Doe. What had she missed? There had to be something that would help them identify who she was.

The DNA samples they'd taken from their Jane Doe's body hadn't had a hit. They were no closer to finding out who she was. All local misper cases that fit the profile had drawn up a blank, so they'd expanded their search. It was still a veritable needle in a haystack, though.

Lawrey opened up the medical examiner's report on her computer. The charring of the body made it difficult to be able to evaluate things like scars or tattoos. The bone fractures were all recent, so there was no medical record to compare them to. There wasn't anything noticeable about any dental work she'd had done that might give them a lead.

Sometimes people were never identified. It was sad but true. Maybe she had been a homeless girl, a drug addict, someone no one would miss. If that was the case, then they'd never find out who she was.

Lawrey was nowhere near giving up, however. She scrolled through the photographs taken by the medical examiner, pausing on each one and increasing the sizes so she was able to absorb every detail.

She got to a photograph of the torso, pictures from before the autopsy had started, creating the now stitched Y shape on her chest and abdomen. The skin was burned but not completely charred. Clothing must have given it at least some protection.

Lawrey increased the size of the photograph, zooming in on a particular area. What was that? She frowned and leaned in closer. A mark on the skin. A burn mark. A circle, with what appeared to be a shape inside it.

She zoomed out again. There was another one, about an inch farther down her chest.

She drew her forefinger back and forth across her upper lip as she thought. She knew she should recognize it, her brain searching for the answer. They looked like tiny branding marks, but who the hell would have branded her like that?

It suddenly hit her. Fuck.

She clicked onto the part of the report that went through what the victim had been wearing when they'd been brought in. Due to the fire damage, most of the clothing had gone up in flames and wasn't recognizable, but there was enough of the Jane Doe's clothing to have marked it down. She'd been wearing a blouse.

"They're from the buttons," she said to herself. "The marks are from the buttons of her shirt." They must have been metal. It was the only way they'd have left branding marks on her when they'd heated up.

She went back to the photographs, blew them up as much as possible. What were those letters? It looked like a J and a P inside a small circle, and there was something on top of them, too, but she couldn't make it out. She needed a clearer image.

She got on the phone to someone in digital forensics, Amanda Rivard.

"Hey, it's Lawrey. If I send you an image, do you think you could clean it up for me?"

"Yeah, no problem, Law. I can do that right away."

"Thanks, it is urgent."

She sent the file off and then tried to distract herself.

It didn't take long for Amanda to clean up the image and send it back. It was much clearer. She could easily tell the image on top of the letters was a crown.

Lawrey uploaded the picture and did a reverse image search, her heart thumping too fast. Was it really possible this was going to come up with anything?

She got a hit! She couldn't believe it.

The image was of the logo of a small boutique clothing store in a town in Maine.

Alarm bells sounded inside her. Didn't Joe say he was from Maine? It must be a coincidence. But did she believe in coincidences? Nevertheless, she forced herself to focus.

Did this mean their victim came from the same town where the boutique was located?

It was a long shot. The blouse might have been bought while on vacation, or it had been a present, or maybe she'd bought it secondhand from one of those online clothing apps, but at least it was something.

It was a lead.

Lawrey got on the phone to the local police department in Maine and asked to speak to the person in charge. She was put through to a Detective Blake Chesterfield.

"Hi, my name is Sergeant Lawrey Winters from the Calrock Police Department in California. I've been dealing with a case recently, and I have reason to believe it may be linked to one of yours. Can you tell me if you've had any recent cases involving a female victim, young, between the ages of eighteen and twenty-five, five feet three, about a hundred and ten pounds, blonde hair, and blue eyes. She may have gone missing recently?"

"Can I call you back?" he said. "Nothing springs to mind right away, but I'll run a search."

"Thanks, I'd appreciate that."

She ended the call, picked up a pen, and tapped it against her desk. To keep herself busy, she did her own search, checking news reports for that area, seeing if anything seemed like a match.

Like Abel had said, if the victim was homeless, it might be that no one missed her, but why would a homeless woman be wearing a shirt that was from a fairly expensive store?

Her phone rang, and she snatched it up. "Detective Winters."

"Detective, hi, it's Blake Chesterfield. You asked me to call you back about any cases that matched your victim."

"Yes, that's right. Did you find anything?"

"I mean...not really...at least nothing that could be connected to your case."

Her heart sank. Had she been completely wrong about this?

But he continued, "We did have one case a couple of months ago where the victim matches your description, but she's not missing. She died in a fire in her apartment. The victim's name was Heather Heath. She was nineteen years old."

Lawrey's ears perked up. Another fire victim? "Are you one hundred percent sure that was her?"

"I'm not sure what you mean."

"I mean, was the identification on the body definitely her? Were you able to get a DNA sample to ID her?"

He paused as, she assumed, he checked the files. "No, it doesn't look as though that was possible. The body was too badly charred. She died in her own bed, though, in her own apartment. We think it was caused by an electrical fault with a cell phone charger. Fire started in her bed, so we think she may have had the phone under her pillow or something like that. There was no reason to think the body wasn't hers."

"But there's a chance that it isn't?"

"Why are you asking?" He sounded perturbed.

No one liked to be told they'd got something wrong.

Lawrey took a breath. "The reason I'm contacting you is that the body of someone I believe might be Heather Heath has been found in a trailer in Sandtown, California."

Silence buzzed down the line.

"I'm not sure I understand," Detective Chesterfield said eventually.

"I don't know who the victim was in the bed who you identified as being Heather, but I don't think it was her. A few nights ago, we were called out to a fire where two people were found deceased. Initially, we believed the female victim to be another woman, Emily Clark, but since then we've discovered it wasn't her."

"But why would you think it's Heather?"

She explained what she'd learned.

"That's a pretty tenuous link, Detective."

She took a breath. "It's not only the shirt. It's the way she died, too. I believe someone staged the fire to hide the fact the woman in the bed wasn't Heather Heath. They did the same thing in Sandtown, except the town's residents stepped in and kept the fire under control until the fire department was able to get there. It meant the bodies weren't so badly burned they couldn't be identified."

"Are you sure about your theory?" he asked.

"Not yet, but it won't be hard to confirm it. Are you able to get a DNA sample of your victim from anywhere? Maybe a family member so we can compare to the sample taken from our victim here."

"Yes, of course." He hesitated again. "But if it comes back that your victim is actually Heather, then who the hell was it in her bed that night?"

"I have no idea, but I do believe we might be looking at a pattern of events here. We also believed our victim was someone else initially."

"Jesus Christ."

She pushed on. "I don't believe this is a one-off. If there's a pattern, then it's something that can be traced. From what we know of the victims so far, they're both blonde with blue eyes, Caucasian, and between the ages of nineteen and twenty-two. They're also small in stature. Heather was only five feet three, Emily is five feet four. Both weighed less than one hundred and twenty pounds."

"Smaller size made them easier to manhandle," he said.

"That was my thinking, too. If people think these girls are dead, it means no one is looking for them. Someone got them out of their beds, possibly, though they might have been taken from a different location. We do have witnesses saying they saw Emily and her boyfriend, Stephan, entering their trailer several hours before the fire. There's a possibility Emily left after that, maybe with someone else, but we don't have any witnesses to prove that. Right now, we're working on the theory that someone broke into their trailer via a window, killed Stephan and snatched Emily, and then replaced Emily with Heather Heath's body."

"Without anyone seeing them?" His tone was doubtful.

"Their trailer is situated on the outskirts of town. It's remote out here. The only thing on the other side of them is miles of desert. Also, you don't know the residents of Sandtown. For the most part, there's an unspoken code that they mind their own business. Unless something like a fire happens, or someone is getting hurt who doesn't deserve it, they tend to stay out of things."

"So someone could have snatched Emily without anyone seeing anything?"

"That's what we believe, yes. Sandtown is also suspicious of anything to do with authority, and we don't have things like everyone owning security cameras or anything like that to fall back on. Even the businesses out there don't have security cameras. They're mistrustful of anything like that, including the cops. No one wants to talk or be seen talking to the police. It doesn't make our job any easier."

"That can't be easy." He paused and then said, "So where do we go from here? I'll need to reopen Heather Heath's case. I'm not sure we're ever going to find out the real identity of the body in her bed. It was too badly damaged to get DNA from. We don't have anything we can use to trace her real identity."

"Maybe not, but we do know the killer's MO. How many young white women, most likely with long blonde hair, have been killed in a fire over the past six months, maybe even more? Who the fuck knows how long this has been going on. How many victims we might be looking at."

"I'll do whatever I can to help," he said.

"Thank you, I'd like us to work together on this, if possible. Find out if any of our suspects has a connection to either Newport, Maine, or Portland, Oregon, where the victims are from. You're going to need to talk to Heather's family, see if she ever mentioned Sandtown or the names of the other victims."

He blew a breath down the line. "This is going to be hard on the family, them finding out Heather's been alive all this time, only for them to learn she's been killed again."

"I understand, but we need to know what's going on. I don't think it's only these two girls. Something tells me this has been going on some time. God only knows how many victims are out there."

"But where has Heather been all this time? What have they been doing with her?"

It never got any easier to tell people bad news, even when they were part of the police force. "Her body was found to have signs of serious sexual assault. Vaginal and anal rape. Plus, there were traces of semen in her throat. We haven't matched the DNA from that yet—again the fire damage was too bad. She had several bone fractures, including the hyoid bone, which indicates she was strangled. I'll send the full report over to you, but I'm afraid it doesn't make for pleasant reading. There's a possibility she was taken to be a victim in a snuff movie."

"My God. And you think whoever did that to her now has your victim, Emily Clark?"

She clutched the phone tighter. "That's the theory I'm working on right now, yes."

"The poor girl."

"I hope to find her before she has to go through the same thing as Heather, and however many girls came before her."

Lawrey hoped she was going to make good on her promise and wasn't already too late. How did she even know that Emily was still alive, that she hadn't already been beaten and raped and murdered? The only thing she was relying on was that whoever had taken Heather had kept her alive for a couple of months before they'd killed her. The fact was, though, she had no proof that they'd do the same thing again. If Emily put up a fight or tried to escape, the kidnapper might feel they had no choice but to kill her sooner.

Chapter Twenty-Nine

A bel stood in the surveillance room, watching the interview happening with Hella Billy remotely.

His phone rang, and his daughter's name appeared on screen. She didn't normally call him when he was at work, so his heart immediately jumped.

He swiped to answer. "Everything okay, Suze?"

It was instantly clear from the way her voice was thick with tears that it wasn't.

"It's Mom. She's not doing so good. She started breathing really strangely, all slow and rattling, and she didn't want to wake up. I called the doctor out, and he says she has fluid on her lungs and that she's nearing the end." Suze broke down, and when she was able to speak again, her voice was tight and high-pitched. "I need you to come home, Dad. I can't do this on my own."

"Of course, sweetheart. I'll be right there. You're doing great, okay?"

He could hear from the way she was speaking that she had her hand clutched to her mouth, trying her best not to completely lose it over the phone. His heart broke for her. Yes, he was about to lose his wife, but she was losing her mother.

He ended the call and left the surveillance room to find Lawrey. He found her at her desk, having got off the phone.

He walked over, a weight heavy in his stomach.

"Sorry to interrupt, Law, but I just had a call from Suze. Marlene's taken a turn for the worse. I know this isn't good timing, what with the case, but it doesn't look like she has much longer."

Lawrey's eyes went round with worry. "Oh my God, Abel. I'm so sorry. Of course you must go."

"Are you sure you can manage without me?"

"Yes. Don't even think about it. Go be with your family."

She got up and put her arms around his neck and hugged him. "And I'm so sorry."

Now he felt close to tears. They constricted his throat with a painful knot that made it hard for him to speak or even breathe. He still couldn't picture a world that didn't have Marlene in it. Though this moment had been coming for a long time, there was still a part of him that had felt it would never really happen.

Not wanting to leave Suze alone to cope for a moment longer than he had to, he grabbed his belongings and jogged out to the car. As he left, he sensed people shooting him sympathetic smiles and glances. Word got around quickly, and everyone knew about Marlene's prognosis.

He drove back to the house as fast as he dared. The whole time, that sick sense of dread in his gut stayed with him. He told himself he needed to be strong for his family now, but deep down what he wanted was to get far away from here and pretend like nothing bad was happening.

Their lives were about to be shattered, and Marlene...poor Marlene. Was she scared? He wished he'd asked her now, but maybe he'd been afraid of the answer. If she'd said yes, what would he have done? There wasn't a single word in the world that he could have used to ease her fear.

Abel pulled up outside the house, took a couple of breaths to calm himself down before entering.

Suze hurried out to greet him.

"Dad—" she managed and burst into tears.

For one horrible moment, he thought he was too late.

"Is-is she?" It was all he could say.

He reached out and pulled his daughter into a hug, trying to comfort them both.

Suze swiped at her face. "No, she's still with us."

Relief drenched him. He couldn't have handled that.

He released her. "Oh, thank God. Let's get inside then."

She nodded and followed him into the relative cool of the house.

"I've called Grace," Suze said, "but I don't know if she's going to make it in time. I should have called her sooner. She should have had the chance to say goodbye."

"Shh, it's okay," he tried to soothe her. "She still might make it in time."

"She's going to blame me if she doesn't. You know what she's like."

"No, it's my fault. I was the one who told you not to call her. I didn't want to worry her. This is all on me."

He went into Marlene's bedroom and paused in the doorway. His heart broke to see her like this. The sound of her struggling breath filled the room. Her eyes were closed.

He sat by the bed and took her hand in his. It was so frail now, her fingers like matchsticks, the skin so thin it barely covered the thick blue and purple veins beneath.

"I'm here, darling," he told her. "And Suze is here, too, and Grace is on her way. Hold on a little longer. We all love you."

He wanted to tell her she was safe, that she'd be okay, but how could he? She was dying, right before his eyes.

Suze took a seat on the other side of the bed. "Is there anything we can do?"

"No, sweetheart. We have to let things take their course."

That acceptance finally settled inside him. It had taken a long time to arrive. He lowered his head so he could press his forehead to the back of her hand. His eyes burned with tears.

On the other side of the bed, Suze started to cry again.

"Why don't you go and make some iced tea," he said. "I could do with a glass. It might be a while yet."

It was better that she have something to do.

Suze nodded and got to her feet and left the room.

Abel got up and slid onto the edge of the bed. He hadn't slept in this bed for months, but it still felt like his. He moved closer, so he was able to fit his body around Marlene's shape, and then he wrapped his arm around her waist and pressed his nose to her bony shoulder. The rise and fall of her chest, that rattling breath, all served to remind him that she wasn't gone yet.

These final minutes and hours might be all he had left.

Chapter Thirty

At twenty past eight that evening, when Lawrey was on the sofa, lost in thought, she got the message to say that Marlene had passed, surrounded by her family.

Lawrey pressed her knuckles to her mouth, her vision blurring. Her instinct was to get up and go straight over there, but the family probably wanted a little privacy right now.

She sent a reply back saying how sorry she was, and to let her know if there was anything she could do to help, and then decided she needed a distraction.

She contacted Eddie to ask for Joe's number and then sent a second message, this time to Joe, asking him if he'd been near any takeout restaurants recently.

He replied back within a minute. "Funnily enough, I appear to be heading to one now."

He'd seemed pleased to hear from her, and she tried not to feel guilty that she was luring him in under false pretenses. That Heather Heath was from Maine as well, niggled at her, and she preferred to think about work than the loss of her partner's wife. She doubted her questioning was going to go down too well, but if she decided she needed to bring him down to the station, she was pretty sure whatever their burgeoning friendship had been becoming would be over anyway.

Within the hour, her doorbell rang, and she answered it. Joe stood on the front doorstep, a brown paper bag clutched to his chest, and a wide smile on his face. Of course, he knew nothing about Marlene, and for that she was grateful. She felt as though if anyone showed her even a hint of kindness or compassion, she would lose it.

"Smells good," she said, suddenly aware she hadn't made the slightest bit of effort with her appearance. She hadn't so much as brushed her hair and still wore the slouchy gray sweatpants she'd been hanging out on the couch in.

If he minded, he didn't let it show. "Hope you're hungry."

Her stomach gurgled.

"I am, actually." She stepped back to let him through. "Come on in."

He brushed past her. "Kitchen through here?"

"Yep," she said. "Keep on going."

She followed him into the kitchen, where he'd already set the takeout food down on the counter. He immediately started opening cupboard doors, searching for plates. She liked when a person made themselves at home and didn't stand on any formalities. It almost seemed a shame that she was going to fuck this up from the start.

"Can I get you a beer?" she asked.

"Sounds good."

She opened the refrigerator and took out a couple of bottles. She cracked open the tops, while Joe set about dishing the food up onto the plates he'd found. He'd remembered her request for chicken and noodles. They carried the plates into the snug to eat on the couch.

"Sorry this isn't very glam," she said.

"No worries. It's exactly how I like to spend my evenings."

He lifted his beer bottle, and she did the same, so they clinked the necks together in a toast.

They dug into the meal, but Lawrey struggled to even taste it.

"Is everything okay?" he asked her, lines appearing between his brows.

She forced a smile. "Yeah. Long day, that's all."

"Still no closer to finding out what happened at that trailer fire in Sandtown?"

Instantly, her hackles rose. Was he trying to mine her for information? She decided to flip the tables on him.

Trying to make herself appear more casual, she put the plate of food on the coffee table, picked up her beer, and tucked her feet under her body.

"Explain to me again why you came to Calrock."

His eyes narrowed a fraction. "Didn't I tell you already?"

"Humor me."

"It's for work."

"You're planning on doing some kind of social media thing on Sandtown?" she checked.

"That's right. It's a fascinating place. I was thinking that a YouTube channel would work well."

"You know no one is going to speak to you. They appreciate their privacy."

He shrugged. "You never know. It's always worth a shot."

"Have you spent much time there, then?"

"Not yet."

"You weren't up there the night of the fire?" She was aware she'd fallen into a kind of interrogation, but she was too pissed with life to care. Maybe it was because she was hurting and she wanted someone else to hurt, too.

He jerked back. "No. Why?"

"Do you know this girl?" She opened a photograph of Heather Heath on her phone, one Detective Chesterfield had sent her.

He frowned down at it. "No. Should I?"

She swiped the screen to open up a picture of Emily next. "How about this one?"

"That's the girl who was killed in Sandtown, isn't it? Why are you asking me about them, Law?"

She swiped back to the first girl again, so he could see it. "Her name is Heather Heath. You sure that doesn't mean anything to you?"

He sat back, his expression changing, hardening, shutting down on her. "Tell me why you're asking me this?"

"She's from Maine."

He gave a small laugh, but there was no humor in it. "So are a million other people."

"Yeah, but they haven't all shown up here with a girl from a similar area who's then turned up dead."

He lifted his hand in a stop sign. "Hang on a minute. I never showed up here with a girl. I have no idea who she is. Are you suggesting I brought her here, killed her, and then burned up her body in a trailer, and then what...kidnapped the other girl?"

"Honestly, I'm not sure right now."

He set his beer down on the table. "Jesus Christ, Lawrey. You're allowed to be nice to someone every now and then. Not everyone is a goddamned serial killer."

"In my job, I don't have room for being nice, or being polite, especially not if I see a connection between that particular person and a crime I'm investigating."

He shook his head. "So what? I'm guilty now in your mind, is that it? You have no proof I even knew this girl."

"You're right, I don't, because if I did, I'd already have had a warrant out for your arrest. Where were you the night of the fire?"

"At home. Watching the television."

"Alone?"

"Yeah, alone."

"Did anyone see you? Do you have any home security to prove that?"

He stood from the couch. "I don't need to listen to this bullshit. If you want that kind of proof, arrest me or get a search warrant. And if you ever want to get over yourself, Lawrey, get in touch, but until then, stay the hell away from me."

Joe stormed from the house, slamming the door behind him.

Frustratingly, her chin wobbled. Had she gone too far? Did she really think Joe was capable of doing those things? How could she? They barely knew each other. But then hadn't her parents been married for years before her mother had found out the truth about the man she'd married and had children with? That Joe had said a couple of nice things to her didn't mean he was suddenly clear from her suspecting him. Had he got defensive because he was guilty?

Her personal relationships didn't matter. What mattered was finding out who'd killed those girls—and finding Emily.

Chapter Thirty-One

Night had fallen, and it was growing closer to the time when they normally brought her food.

Emily held the bucket of piss in her hands and braced herself. She shook all over from the nerves, her teeth chattering so she was sure she'd be heard.

Footsteps grew closer, a jangling of keys. Her arm muscles trembled, partly from the adrenaline, partly from fatigue. After days spent locked in here, with only the tiniest amount of food and drink, she was weakened.

Please, God, she prayed, *let me get out of here, and I'll live the rest of my life like a nun, I promise I will.*

She wanted him to hurry up, so she could get this over with, but also hoped he'd turn around and walk away. She'd never liked confrontation, which was why men like her ex-boyfriend got away with walking all over her. She always found it easier to go along with whatever they wanted, but then they got used to always getting their own way, and, if she ever did try to make her voice heard, they rebelled against it.

Was he on his own? If there were two of them, she wouldn't stand a chance. She could throw the urine in his eyes, half blind him, maybe even hit him with the bucket, but if the second man was there, too, he'd grab her and throw her back inside.

A rattle. The key in the lock.

She bunched every muscle, her breath trapped in her chest. She didn't think she'd ever been so alert, not even when she'd been worried about Zack stalking her, listening out for him breaking into her house. Deep down, had she truly believed Zack would hurt her? At the time, she'd have said yes, but now she'd been faced with these men, she wasn't so sure. She had no doubt that they would kill her if they wanted to. Zack had wanted to control her, but had he ever really wanted her dead? She didn't think so.

The door cracked open and creaked on its hinges. She pressed her shoulder to the wall, trying to make herself invisible.

She sensed him standing there, peering inside. He needed to enter the room fully, so she could throw the bucket and its contents, and then slip past him. If he wasn't inside, his body would block the doorway and she'd never get by. The lack of light was to her advantage.

But he didn't move. He must have realized something was wrong, perhaps that he couldn't see the shape of her on the mattress, but didn't quite know what.

Another step, she willed him. *Just one more step.*

"I brought you something to ea—"

He was about to crane his neck, looking for her. If he did that, he'd spot her.

With a shriek of rage and fear, she threw the bucket filled with her urine directly at his head. She let go of the bucket so it hit him as well.

He let out a roar of anger and lifted his hands to cover his face, the bag of food he'd been holding dropping to the floor. "You fucking bitch!"

Why was it men thought they were allowed to do whatever they wanted, but the moment a woman tried to stand up for themselves, *they* were the bitch?

As she'd hoped, he kept his eyes shut, wiping at his face to clear them.

Emily darted past, barely evading his clawing hands. She hadn't recognized the man who'd received the face full of her piss, but he was older, she guessed at least in his fifties, maybe even early sixties. Who was he? What did he want from her? She didn't have long, only a matter of seconds, but she ran out and paused.

Where was she? Was she still in Sandtown? The building was directly behind her, but in front of her she could only see desert which was quickly swallowed by darkness.

She stood with her feet rooted to the spot, frozen in her indecision. Which way should she go? Was it suicide to run out into the desert? It was cooler right now, but the moment the sun came up, she wouldn't last long. In her weakened state and with no water or shelter, she'd never make it.

It felt incredible to breathe fresh air again.

As her eyes adjusted, she spotted a truck parked some distance away. It was far enough that she hadn't heard the engine. Would there be keys in the ignition? She'd be incredibly lucky if they were, but didn't she deserve a little luck?

Did the presence of the truck mean that her captors didn't live anywhere nearby? Were they having to travel out here to give her food and water?

She ran for the truck, sprinting as fast as she could, her arms pumping, the air heaving in and out of her lungs.

Sharp stones stabbed the bottoms of her bare feet, but she did her best to ignore the pain, though it wasn't easy. Movement and noise came from behind her, and she knew he was coming after her now, was right on her tail. She wasn't going to make it to the truck.

Her bare toes slammed into something impossibly hard, and she felt bone snap like parched twigs. A scream of agony burst from her throat, her eyes flooding with tears, and she dropped to the dusty ground. She'd broken at least one of her toes, if not more. The pain was excruciating, fire spreading up her lower leg.

Emily let out a sob of frustration. She couldn't run now, not with her foot like this. Already, her toes had turned purple and were starting to swell.

Rough hands grabbed her upper arms and hauled her back to her feet. Sensing this was her final chance, she filled her lungs with air and screamed as loudly as she could.

One hand let go of her arm and clamped over her mouth. "Shut up, you fucking slut."

If he wanted her to be quiet, did that mean someone was around who might hear her? She'd been banging on the door and screaming for days, and no one had come, but perhaps out in the open her voice would carry farther.

Not that it even mattered. She'd had her chance to escape, and she'd failed.

Chapter Thirty-Two

The atmosphere in the office the following morning was subdued.

Abel was noticeably absent, and Lawrey's heart broke for her partner. Every time she thought of Marlene, and of Abel and his two daughters, she found herself on the verge of tears.

The station did a collection, bought him a card and flowers, and everyone offered to make lasagnas and casseroles, though she doubted he'd feel anything like eating. It all felt so useless and shallow, and she wished she could do more.

Marlene and Abel had been together their whole lives. She couldn't imagine the sort of pain he must be going through. Even so, she couldn't help but think how they'd been blessed to have had each other in their lives all this time.

Despite all this, she had a case she couldn't simply give up on because there had been a tragedy.

"Sarge, the DNA results have come back," Annie informed her. "The girl in the trailer was definitely Heather Heath."

"Thanks, Annie."

She wondered if Detective Chesterfield had learned about the results yet. With the revelation that their Jane Doe was Heather Heath, it also created another question. Who was the body they'd thought to be Heather?

Lawrey called her team together.

"I'm aware that we are one man down, as Abel needs to be with his family today, but that doesn't mean we can take our foot off the pedal. If anything, we need to work harder than ever to make up for it, okay?" Nodding heads responded. "I believe we're looking at a pattern of killing, and if there's a pattern, we need to find it. We need to narrow down any young women, let's say below the age of twenty-five, most likely white, blonde hair, and blue eyes, who were killed in a fire over the past couple of years."

"That could be a lot of people," Lieutenant Monroe said from the back. He'd sat in on the briefing. "Thousands of people die in house fires every year. Last year, it was almost four thousand. Potentially, only a handful of cases out of those might be connected to our investigation."

"Yes, it could," she agreed, "and we're going to comb through every single one of them. If a positive DNA test confirmed the victim's identity, then we can scrub them from the list, but if a positive ID was not able to be confirmed, then we need to dig deeper into whether it was the right victim."

"How could the killer be sure the cops wouldn't be able to figure out the victim wasn't who they thought?" Annie asked.

"My guess is that they didn't. They relied on the fire being enough to make it impossible to ID them. We know an accelerant was used in the Sandtown trailer fire. Maybe the accelerant used in the Heather Heath case was missed for some reason. It's another thing we can use to narrow down the cases, the presence of something that burns fast and at a hot temperature to make sure the bodies are destroyed.

as much as possible, making it impossible to retrieve DNA samples."

She looked around the room. "Does anyone have any questions?" No one spoke up. "Good, then you know what you need to be doing."

Lawrey got on the phone to speak to the Maine detective. "I assume you saw the results?" she said. "It is Heather Heath's body we discovered down here."

"Thank you for following that up. It's caused more questions than answers from our end, though."

"I know, but believe me, we've got a lot of questions, too. We've still got a missing girl on our hands, and my worry is that if we don't find her soon, she's going to end up being another scorched girl."

"Does the missing girl have anything to do with Maine? Any connections at all?"

"Not that we've found so far, but that doesn't mean we're not missing something. There has to be a connection somewhere."

"Agreed," he said. "I'm going to have the difficult job of speaking to Heather's family. I'll see what I can find out."

"Appreciate that," she replied. "I'll send you over everything we have so far, including the names of everyone we have connected with Emily, see if anyone rings a bell for them." She thought back to the previous night and added, "And add the name Joe Martinez to the list, will you?"

"Will do."

Lawrey ended the call. She got lost in her work, happy to have something to focus on rather than the loss of Abel's wife.

Her phone rang, her sister's name appearing on the screen. Shit. Had Joe spoken to them? Or was she calling because of Marlene?

Lawrey swiped the phone to answer. "Hey," she said.

Maddie's voice chirped down the line. "Happy birthday."

"What?"

"It's your birthday," Maddie said. "Don't tell me you forgot?"

She glanced at the calendar. Fuck. So it was. She was forty-six years old today.

"I forgot," she admitted.

"Don't forget that we're having drinks at Tipsy's tonight. You're turning forty-six, that's something that should be celebrated."

"I don't think so, Mads. We lost Marlene yesterday. How can I possibly go out tonight? It feels wrong."

"Rubbish. I bet Marlene would have given anything to see another birthday, to be surrounded by her family. Growing older is a privilege not everyone gets to experience, and you shouldn't take it for granted. You never know, it might be the last one you get."

"Jeez, thanks, Maddie. Is that supposed to make me feel better?"

"You know what I'm saying."

Lawrey let out a breath. "Yeah, I guess I do."

"So, we're having a party then?"

"Not a party," she said sternly. "Just a few drinks down at Tipsy's. Friends and family only."

"Do you want me to invite Joe?"

"No. He won't want to come. Trust me on that."

She had the feeling her sister would invite him anyway, even without her permission. She wasn't sure how she felt about that. Did she want to see him again? It didn't even matter because he wouldn't want to see her.

Besides, the whole thing felt like too much of an effort. She didn't want to have to take someone else's feelings into consideration or worry about what the future might hold. She had enough issues in her life already. But there was still that little nagging feeling inside her that told her she didn't want to spend the rest of her life alone.

She wasn't alone, not really. She had her sister, and niece and nephew, and Tommy, of course. She knew her mom wouldn't be around forever, but for the moment she didn't look like she was going anywhere. Those were all different kinds of relationships, though. A different kind of intimacy. It wasn't like having that one person who was there for you, no matter what.

"Okay," Maddie said, "but we'll definitely see you at Tipsy's at eight?"

"Sure, why not?"

"And happy birthday again."

"Thanks."

She ended the call. Was it strange to forget her own birthday? She'd been so caught up in everyone else recently, she hadn't given her own life a second thought.

Lawrey worked through lunch, eating at her desk.

Mid-afternoon, a commotion came at the door, and she glanced up to find her partner standing there, his colleagues surrounding him to offer their condolences.

She got to her feet to join them.

"You don't need to be at work, you know, Abel. You should be with your family."

"I have been. I think they're sick of me by now too."

"I'm sure that's not true."

He shrugged, as though the weight of the world pressed down on him. "We all need a bit of space to process what's happened."

"Are you processing it?" she checked. "Or are you trying to use work as a distraction?"

"If it's a distraction, it's one I'm in need of, Law. I can't just sit around the house, noticing how she's not there anymore. It'll drive me crazy."

"Okay," she relented. "I understand. We could definitely make use of you here. We've got a lot of case files we're going over."

"Good. Put me to work."

Lawrey hesitated. "Also, Maddie wants to have drinks for me at Tipsy's tonight at eight. I told her no, because it feels in bad form after..."

He shook his head. "Shit, Law. I'm sorry I forgot your birthday."

She gave a small laugh. "Don't worry about it. I forgot my birthday. I know you have far bigger things going on right now."

"Yeah, but you should have those drinks. Marlene would have wanted it. You know she'd have been the first one at the bar buying a round."

She found her eyes prickling again and sniffed. "Yeah, she would."

He squeezed her arm, and she felt bad he was the one comforting her rather than the other way around.

"That's settled then," he said, "and we'll raise a glass to Marlene, too. Now, how about we both get some work done."

"Deal," she said.

While the rest of her team were working on finding a pattern in the murders, Lawrey focused her attention on trying to work out what might have happened to Emily. If she was taken sometime between the fight that one of the residents had witnessed and the breakout of the fire, that gave them about a four-hour window in which she was snatched. Unless, of course, Lawrey was wrong about that, and Emily went willingly. If she did, it meant she knew her abductor.

That would explain why no one heard or saw anything. She could have simply slipped away with someone. With no traffic cameras along the stretches of road leading in and out of Sandtown, they didn't even have a vehicle they could trace.

The window that had been left open for the fuel to be poured through must have also been the route of entry as well. It faced the desert, which again must have been the reason no one saw anything. If someone had a vehicle, they could have driven to that side of the trailer, snatched Emily and left Heather's body in her bed, and killed Stephan, ready for Hella Billy to come along later to set fire to the trailer.

In the formal interviews with Hella Billy, he insisted that he'd only been planning on scaring Stephan out of town. He'd looked through the window and hadn't seen anyone, so he'd thought the place was empty. Had a sheet been placed over the top of the bodies, so they weren't easy to spot? There had been a sheet burned up in the fire, but they hadn't thought anything of it. It wasn't as though a sheet on a bed was something to be suspicious of. Maybe the heat warmed the air beneath it and caused it to billow off the bodies before it caught fire? If that was the case, Hella Billy was telling the truth—about that part, at least—though she still thought it was more than a coincidence that he happened to set fire to a trailer containing two bodies.

"Lawrey?"

She lifted her head at her partner's voice.

"I think I might have a hit on another girl."

Adrenaline spiked through her. "Tell me."

"She's twenty-year-old Lizzy McAllister. Died in a fire started in her car outside of Baltimore, Maryland, three months ago. Looks like there was an accident. She veered off a road and hit a tree when she was driving back from a party. No one saw it happen. The fire was put down to faulty wiring, combined with leaking gas from the accident. Like with the previous fires, the body was so badly burned that they couldn't make a positive ID with a DNA sample. By the time anyone even noticed the vehicle, it was literally only a shell."

He pushed some printed photographs onto the desk in front of her. The image was barely recognizable as being that of a vehicle. It was a burned-out husk. She turned her attention to the images of the body. Like the car, they were barely recognizable. The fire had caused her limbs to amputate, so all they were left with was a torso and the vague shape of a head. It was completely charred black. No wonder they weren't able to ID her.

Abel had one more photograph to show her.

"This is Lizzy before the fire."

Lawrey found herself staring down at the picture. "She could be sisters with either Emily or Heather."

"That's what I thought."

"Shit." Lawrey let out a sigh. She put her elbows on the table and dug her hands in her hair, her fingers pressing into her scalp. "Let me get this right in my mind. If we're correct about this, then the body found in Heather's bed was most likely Lizzy's. So if that was Lizzy's body, then whose body was burned in the car?"

"No idea, but if we keep investigating, I'm sure we'll find out."

"This must have started somewhere. When they took the very first girl, they wouldn't have had a body to replace her with. She must have been a missing person."

"Young, blonde, white, pretty...they're the kind of victim the press likes to get people worked up over. Maybe that first case drew a lot of unwanted attention, to the point where they thought they were going to get caught, so to prevent that happening again, they came up with a plan to make it seem like they'd died in an accident involving a fire, instead of them going missing."

That made sense to Lawrey. "The previous girl's body was put in their place."

"Exactly. So we need to also be looking for a missing girl, not just ones lost in a fire that weren't able to be ID'd. If we find her, she'll be ground zero, the person we can use to draw the dots between all the others."

Lawrey didn't want to think about how many others there might be, how many dots there might be on their map.

"What's tying the victims together?" she wondered. "They're all from different parts of the country. Is there any possibility they know the same person, or went to the same school and then moved? What about social media? Is there something they were all a part of that got them noticed by the killer?"

"We're going to need to put some requests in with the girls' families," Abel said. "It's not going to be easy for them to hear. It's bad enough that they thought their daughters and sisters died in a tragic accident, but this is something else entirely."

"It's possible the girls were all killed in the making of a snuff film."

The families were going to ask questions of themselves, blame themselves for not knowing the bodies of who they thought to be their loved ones weren't actually them at all. They were going to wonder why they didn't instinctively sense their daughter or sister was still alive, even after they'd believed them to have died in a fire. Maybe it wasn't logical to most, but grief doesn't always make sense. For these families, they were about to have their pain burst back open, and then they'd have to cope with even more. It didn't seem fair—hell, it *wasn't* fair. But the people responsible for the killings didn't care about that. They didn't care how many lives they destroyed in their quest to get what they wanted.

Lawrey got up from her desk to place another pin in the map to pinpoint the new location of the possible victim.

It was a scatter graph. As far as Lawrey could tell, nothing connected them.

One victim was from a big city, while Sandtown was almost as small as you could get.

But someone was seeing them, and they were staying in the area long enough for them to plan their abduction, and to rape and murder the girl who'd take their place.

Chapter Thirty-Three

A bel got back from work and stood outside his fron door, his keys in his hand.

He lost track of how long he'd been standing there for His heart hurt—physically ached—as though someone had taken it from his chest, stabbed it viciously, and then stuffed it back in again.

To walk into an empty house, knowing Marlene would never be there again, was all too much. From the way his daughters had both let him know that they wouldn't be home either, he knew they felt the same way.

A crash came from inside.

His stomach lurched. What the fuck was that? Someone was inside the house.

Crazily, the first thing he thought was that it was Marlene's ghost. That she was angry about being dead and was still in there in some kind of poltergeist form. But he shook the thought off as quickly as it had entered his head He wasn't the sort of man who gave much time to things like ghosts, but when a person had just lost the one they loved most in the world, it was hard not to speculate on what happened when they moved on.

Another sound came from inside the property, a thud, as though someone had knocked something over.

That got Abel moving.

He should call nine-one-one, but he didn't have time to think it through. Anger that someone should be in his house when he'd only just lost his wife took over all thought. This should have been a place to be respected. She'd died here. They were sullying her memory.

He slammed open the door.

Movement came from the back of the house. He caught a glimpse of a man outside the room that had been Marlene's bedroom for her final months. He was tall and lean, male, Abel guessed, though the figure had a black hood pulled up over their head, despite the heat. He held a canvas bag tight to his body. The sleeve of the black hoody was pushed up, revealing a narrow wrist with a leather bracelet wrapped around it.

Abel drew his weapon. In the mood he was in, he'd shoot the motherfucker there and then.

"Police! Freeze."

But the man was already gone, darting away. The tinkle of fresh glass falling, followed by the catch of a door, came from the rear of the house. Abel realized the intruder had gone out the back.

He broke into a run. Adrenaline coursed through his veins, his heart beating so hard it knocked against the inside of his rib cage. He'd be the first to admit he wasn't in the best of shape, and the past few months had taken their toll on him. Not to mention he'd barely slept recently. He got the impression whoever was in his house was young, and they most likely would be able to outrun him within seconds, but that didn't stop Abel trying.

He slammed out of the back door, into his yard. He turned his head, trying to spot which direction the burglar had gone. He spotted a figure in the distance, leaping over a fence. Fuck. If they had a vehicle nearby, they'd be gone within seconds. Even so, Abel did what he could and took off after him. Maybe he'd get a look at the vehicle, take down the license plate. He wanted to get the son of a bitch.

Forgetting he was fifty and overweight, he broke into a run. In less than a minute, a band had formed around his chest, his throat had almost closed over, so his breath whistled through a pipe, and his calf muscles threatened to cramp.

"Shit. Fuck. Jesus Christ."

Giving up, Abel came to a stop, folded in half, his hands on his thighs. The sun beat on the back of his head where his bald patch had recently started to form. He told himself the heat was the reason he was unable to run, but the truth was, he was seriously out of shape.

How the fuck was he supposed to worry about something like staying in shape while his wife had been dying?

Abel slowly made his way back to the house to inspect the damage.

Someone had broken one of the small panes of glass in the backdoor and then reached through to unlock it and let themselves in. Why the hell would they do that? He didn't have much to steal. From a quick glance around, it didn't look as though anything had been taken either. Had he disturbed the burglar before they'd gotten the chance to scout the house?

Then he remembered how he'd first seen them outside Marlene's room. Had they been in there?

With his chest feeling tight—from emotion this time, not the running—he entered the bedroom. The adjoining bathroom door stood open, and through the gap, he could see the medicine cabinet above the sink. It was also open, several bottles having fallen out into the sink below.

"Dammit."

Abel moved in for a closer inspection, but he already knew what he'd find.

All of Marlene's opiates were missing.

He should have kept them locked up, really, but he'd become apathetic.

Grief and anger solidified into a ball of darkness inside him.

Maybe he'd have been better going with her. He could have taken the morphine and slapped on the fentanyl patches, so at least some shitty little drug addict wouldn't have gotten their hands on them, and curled up in bed beside Marlene and waited for the opiates to slow his heart and breathing down to the point where he drifted away.

He wouldn't do that to his daughters, though. They might be adults, but they'd just lost their mom and they still needed him.

Instead, he got on the phone to Lawrey.

"You okay, Abel?"

She sounded concerned. Understandably considering, though she didn't yet know about the burglary.

"No. When I got home, some fucker was in my house. They stole all of Marlene's drugs, the fentanyl and morphine."

His voice cracked, and he realized he was on the verge of tears. It felt so wrong that someone would do such a thing. It must have been someone who knew she had died, and that she'd died of cancer, recently, so there would be drugs in the property that he hadn't had the chance to clear out yet.

That someone would take advantage of such a terrible situation made him want to break down and rage against the world, all at the same time.

"Oh, shit. Don't touch anything. I'll be there in ten."

"Thanks, Law."

"No need to thank me. Hold tight."

Abel took a seat on the porch, in what had once been Marlene's favorite spot, and waited. He was so lost in thought and grief that Lawrey was there before he knew it.

She pulled up to his house, a response car right behind her.

"We'll treat this like any other crime scene, Abel, and right now, you're the victim, so I'm going to need you to let us do our job. Have you got any CCTV anywhere?"

"No, I never bothered."

She put her hand on his arm. "Don't worry about it. Did you get a look at them at all?"

"Yeah, I did, but I didn't see his face."

"His?" She lifted her eyebrows. "It was definitely a him?"

"Yes. He was tall, over six feet, and a slim build. Caucasian. Young, I think."

"How do you know he was young if you didn't see his face?"

"Something about the way he moved. Let's call it gut instinct."

"You get hair color, anything like that?" she asked.

He sucked on his teeth and shook his head. "No, sorry. He was wearing a black hoodie, though, which he had hiding his face, and jeans and sneakers."

"A black hoodie in this heat? We won't need to catch him. He'll collapse from heat exhaustion before long."

He was grateful to her for trying to make him smile.

She carried on. "Is there anything else you can remember about him? Did he say anything?"

"No, not a word."

"We'll keep an eye out on the streets over the next few days and weeks. I expect the thief will attempt to sell it, unless they stole it to take themselves."

"If they end up taking all that, they'll most likely show up dead before anything else."

"True." She placed her hand on his arm. "You don't have to come tonight, okay. I totally understand if you don't."

"Honestly, Law, I'm happy to have an excuse to get out of the house."

She gave him a hug. "Okay. I'll see you later then."

L awrey didn't much feel like celebrating.

She didn't like birthdays at the best of times, bu with it being so close to Marlene's death, plus knowing Emil Clark still hadn't been found, it felt almost like she wa dancing on their graves.

Not that she knew for sure if Emily was dead, but wit each day that passed where they hadn't found her, th chances of them getting a positive outcome decreased.

It was only because Abel had insisted it would be wha Marlene would have wanted that she didn't cancel th gathering. Maddie had gone to the effort of stringing banner and hanging some balloons, hiding the photograph that lined the walls from when Calrock had only just bee settled almost two hundred years ago. They reminded he of snapshots from an old Western movie. Though the tow was far from big now, it was still amazing how much it ha changed.

The atmosphere in the bar was heavy with th knowledge that one of them was missing, however. Lawre found herself greeting people with repressed smiles, huggin them in a way that conveyed sympathy rather tha celebration.

Everyone she loved had shown up, and she was gratefu for that. They weren't the only ones in the bar that evening Though Maddie had arranged for the party to happen at th bar, she'd only booked out one corner of the space, not th whole thing.

Even Tommy had bothered coming over from Sandtown, and he wished her a happy birthday and apologized for not bringing a present or card. She told him it didn't matter, that his company meant far more than anything he could buy.

Lawrey couldn't shake her self-consciousness, so she drank too fast to try to relax. Were people wondering why she hadn't cancelled? She hated the sense that she was being judged and wished she could have worn a badge that read 'It was what Marlene would have wanted.'

"No Joe then?" Maddie said as she approached with a drink.

"No. I didn't think he'd want to come. He actually brought over a takeout last night, and I may have interrogated him."

"You did what?"

Lawrey cringed. "I may have implied that he had something to do with the murders."

Maddie widened her eyes at her. "Oh my God, Lawrey."

She shrank inside herself. "I do regret it now."

"You know, you're never going to get laid again if you accuse all your dates of murder."

Lawrey covered her face with her hands. "I know. I'm a nightmare, aren't I?"

"Absolute total nightmare."

She caught her sister's eye, recognized the mirth there, the way she was pinching her lips together, trying not to laugh. Like when they'd been kids, once she'd seen Maddie was trying not to laugh, she felt the same laughter bubbling up inside her as well. Within seconds, it burst from them both, and Lawrey found herself howling, rocking in her seat and wiping tears from her eyes.

"I think I might have to accept that I'm going to be single forever," she said when she finally pulled herself together.

Maddie swiped at her eyes. "Maybe that's for the best."

"You're probably right." She tried not to laugh again and failed.

Lawrey glanced across the bar, hoping no one had been watching, and spotted Francis Knight, Carol Hayes' granddaughter, sitting at a table in the bar with her husband. They were sharing a pitcher of beer and some nachos.

"Give me a sec," she told Maddie.

She left the others and walked over to their table. Francis must have spotted her coming as she turned toward her with a smile.

"Oh, hi, Detective Winters. How are you?"

"I'm good. How's things with you?"

"Really well." Francis looked to the man across the table. "You remember my husband, Jude?"

"Sure." Lawrey offered him a nod. "You're back in town now?"

"Not for too long, unfortunately," he said. "Got to go where the work is."

Francis covered her husband's hand with hers. "It's not ideal, but we're managing, aren't we?"

"What is it you're doing now?" Lawrey asked, mainly to be polite.

Francis answered for him. "Jude is a seasonal worker at different warehouses. There aren't many opportunities around here. My father set the job up," Francis said. "He's doing great. Going to be a supervisor before we know it."

"Where have you come back from?" Lawrey asked.

He shifted in his seat. "Washington State."

His wife frowned at him. "I thought you were in Oregon."

He cleared his throat. "It's right on the border. The warehouse is near Portland, but officially it's located in Washington State."

The name of the place hit her in the solar plexus. That was where Emily Clark and Stephan Porter came from. Portland, Oregon.

She wanted to think it was a coincidence. People traveled for work all the time.

"That's a long way to go for work," she said. "You fly up there?"

"Nah, I take the RV. That way I've got somewhere to live at the same time. Wouldn't be worth it if I had to pay for lodging as well. The company pays toward the campsite fees too."

"You wouldn't ever consider going along?" she asked Francis.

"God no, I love my job here. Teaching is what I do. Besides, I think we both like our space. I couldn't imagine us living on top of one another in the RV."

They both laughed.

Someone must have said something funny in a group behind them, because a swell of laughter rose into the air. Someone smashed a glass, and everyone cheered. Even the music suddenly seemed louder. She found she had to raise her voice to be heard, and the young couple leaned across the table toward her.

"How long were you there for?" Lawrey asked. Her heart was beating too hard, her senses on high alert.

"A few months. That's pretty normal. It's all seasonal, so I move around a lot."

"Where were you before that?"

He took a drink of his beer. "This is starting to feel like an interrogation, Detective," he said.

His tone was jokey, but she could tell there was a warning in his words. He didn't want her to keep asking questions. Why was that?

"Did you know that young couple killed over at Sandtown were from Portland, Oregon?"

"Nope. I didn't know that." He took another swig of his beer. "Why would I? It's a big place. It's not as though we all know each other."

Francis glanced between them, catching the tension in the air. Lines appeared between her brows. "What's this about, Law?"

"Just interested, that's all." She tried to relax her shoulders. "Must be a freeing kind of life, being on the road all the time, seeing the country and meeting new people."

Francis squeezed her husband's hand. "Yeah, though it's not going to be forever, is it, sweetheart? We'd like to start a family some day, and then you're going to need to be home more."

"Yeah, that's right."

"I wanted to ask how your grandmother was doing," Lawrey said, changing the subject, but pinning this new knowledge at the back of her mind like a lepidopterist would pin a butterfly on a piece of board. "Did she tell you she had a bit of a fright the other day? Thought there was someone on her property, and they'd got in through the window."

Francis relaxed at the switch of topic. "Yes, she did tell me about that. I do worry about her, being on the outskirts of town without any direct neighbors. I've tried to convince her to move into town a little more."

"She wouldn't do that, would she?" Jude twisted toward his wife.

"No. It's her family home, and she's not going anywhere. She can be a stubborn old goat when she wants to be."

Lawrey found herself laughing. "I did notice that."

Francis offered a smile. "Thank you for watching out for her."

"Of course. It's my job."

Francis shrugged. "From what she says, you came before you'd even clocked in."

"Not sure this is a job you can actually clock in and out of."

"Well, I hope you have now," Francis said with a grin, nodding at the beer bottle in Lawrey's hand.

"Oh, yeah, it's my birthday." She felt embarrassed admitting it but wasn't even sure why.

"Happy birthday to you. And I'm sorry to hear about Marlene. She's going to be missed."

Immediately, Lawrey's eyes prickled with tears, and a painful lump tightened her throat. "Yes, she is."

She should have gone to see Marlene while she still had the time. Why hadn't she? She'd been frightened of seeing her like that, of being shocked and not knowing what to say. She'd been scared Marlene would see the fear in her eyes, and it would have made them both feel worse. Now her regret sat heavy on her chest, and there was nothing she could do to change things.

A shout came from behind them. "Hey, Law, you abandoned your own party or what?"

She lifted her beer bottle. "Guess I'd better get back to it."

"And thanks again for taking care of Grandma," Franci said.

Lawrey shot Jude one final glance, then turned from the table and headed back to the booth. The conversation niggled at her. It wasn't only that Jude had been in Portland; it was the way he'd tried to make it look as though he'd been someplace else, and then he'd gotten defensive when she'd tried to probe deeper. She knew speaking to cops sometimes made people automatically feel guilty, but sometimes it was simply because they *were* guilty.

She wasn't going to interrupt the rest of the party to start questioning him, but more than anything, she wanted to ask him where he was the night of the fire.

"You okay, Law?" Abel asked. "You seem distracted."

"Oh, it's nothing... At least, it's probably nothing. I'll fill you in on it tomorrow."

"Tomorrow is Saturday."

"Shit, so it is."

She glanced back over at the table the young couple were occupying. If Jude was off work now, until his next trip, then he would most likely be home. It wouldn't hurt to drop in there tomorrow, maybe under the pretense of something else, poke around a little. She made a mental note to run a background check on him as well. He'd never done anything around town to end up on her radar, but maybe that was simply because he didn't live here most of the time. In a place like Calrock, rumors tended to get around.

There had never been any rumors of Francis, the local elementary school teacher, suffering any violence at home, or anything like that. From the outside, the two of them appeared to have a good marriage, even if they weren't together that often. Lawrey held back a smile. Maybe that *was* the secret to a good marriage. Stay apart long enough that you don't drive each other up the wall and you're always pleased to see each other again.

Now the thought had entered her head, she couldn't focus on anything else. She kept sneaking glances over at Jude Knight, wondering if there was any possibility he was involved. She wanted to get to her laptop and search the locations of the warehouses. Maybe she was completely wrong about this, but she couldn't let it go, especially when their leads were practically nothing.

Could the warehouses be the locations where the girls were being kept before they were raped and murdered?

No, there would be too many people around. It was too big of an operation to take a risk like that.

"Lawrey? Earth to Lawrey."

She realized her sister had been speaking to her. "Sorry? What?"

"I was saying that Noah got picked for the soccer team next week. He's not on the bench for once."

Lawrey did her best to feign interest. "Oh, right. That's great."

"Think you can swing round to watch him? I'm sure he'd love to see you there."

She dodged the question. "Actually, I think I'm going to take off. I've got a headache brewing."

"You can't leave now. It's still early. This is your party, remember?"

"Yeah, the party I was strong-armed into having. And it's just at the bar, isn't it? It's not like it's anything special."

Maddie stared at her in disbelief. "Jeez, thanks, Law. Glad you appreciate me going to the effort to gather some of your friends together to celebrate."

Lawrey winced. She hadn't meant to hurt Maddie's feelings. "Sorry, Mads. I didn't mean it like that. I was trying to say that you're here with everyone, and you don't really need me here as well. I'm not good company."

"You're not good company when you're clearly thinking about a case and not listening to a word anyone else is saying."

Her guilt was quickly replaced with irritation. "Sorry, but I've got four people dead—possibly more—and a young woman still missing. Excuse me if I'm not focusing more on your kid's soccer practice."

Maddie ground her teeth. "You're unbelievable. I'm sorry the rest of our lives aren't more important than yours."

Lawrey knew she had to leave. She couldn't get into a full-blown fight with her sister in front of everyone.

She did the rounds to say goodbye, pleading a headache and apologizing, but thanking everyone for coming. She spotted Abel and Tommy standing together. They had their heads close. She couldn't read their body language, but whatever they were talking about seemed intense.

Tommy saw her coming and stepped back from Abel.

"Everything all right?" she asked.

Abel nodded. "Of course. Just catching up."

She accepted him at his word. "I need to go now. Something's come up. I'll give you a call in the morning, okay?"

He frowned. "You think you're onto something?"

She glanced over at the table where Francis and Jude had been sitting, only to find it empty. "It might be nothing, but it's worth following up."

"Sure. Let me know if there's anything I can do."

"I should be the one saying that to you," she said.

He gave her a sad smile.

She leaned in and gave him a brief but tight hug. She did the same to Tommy and then left the bar.

• • • •

THE FIRST THING SHE did when she got back was open up her laptop and do a search on where the company Jude worked for had warehouses located, and compared them to the locations of the bodies, possible victims, of the killer.

They had a lot of locations more than thirty and scattered all over.

She already knew of the one near Portland, where Emily and Stephan were from, but there was also one outside of Baltimore, Maryland, where Lizzie McAllister's body had been found. Quickly, she scanned the map for a location near Newport, Maine.

Sure enough, there was a warehouse situated nearby.

Each of them matched with one of the places a young, blonde, female victim had been found burned beyond all identification

The only place that broke the pattern was Sandtown. Why was that? What had happened? Had something gone wrong, maybe someone didn't want to play ball, and they'd been forced to take action? Her mind was spinning. There was a location outside of Portland, Oregon, where Emily was from, except she didn't *actually* go missing from there. Nobody took her place. Stephan convinced her to run, blaming it on the ex-boyfriend threatening her, but had they actually run for a different reason?

She shook her head at herself. But then why come here? If there was a possibility Jude was connected, and Stephan was trying to protect Emily from her fate, why bring her closer to someone who was involved?

Unless Stephan didn't know.

Or he did know, and Lawrey was completely wrong on this, and Stephan wasn't trying to protect Emily at all. He'd actually brought her here because someone had been watching too closely in Portland. Someone who might notice something was wrong right away.

Could that someone have been Zack?

She didn't think he was involved, but maybe he had been stalking Emily, in part because he was worried about what Stephan's intentions were, and Stephan had decided hat Zack could cause them problems and so had whisked Emily away?

But why had Stephan chosen Sandtown to bring her to? What was the connection?

She was determined to find out.

Chapter Thirty-Four

As soon as the hour was early enough—or late enough—to not feel too intrusive, Lawrey got dressed and drove over to the Knight household.

She rang the doorbell and waited for someone to answer.

Francis did, still dressed in her robe, and her hair knotted on top of her head. She squinted in the bright morning sunlight at the sight of Lawrey standing there.

"Good morning, Francis," Lawrey said, her voice a tad too bright. "I'm sorry to disturb you on the weekend. I wondered if Jude was home so I could have a word?"

Francis drew her eyebrows together, her lower lip pouting slightly. "Sure, Lawrey, but can I ask what this is about?"

"It's just something the two of you said last night about the warehouses and how he moved around a lot. I'm not saying he's connected at all, but I checked out some of the locations, and they tie into one of my cases."

"The one involving the young couple from Sandtown?" she asked.

"Yes, though they weren't from Sandtown. They'd only been there a couple of months. They were from Portland, Oregon."

"Lots of people are from Portland, Law. Millions of them, in fact."

She shrugged. "I know, but right now I've got to follow whatever leads I can, no matter how small. I want to talk that's all. He's not in trouble or anything."

"I think he's getting out of the shower." Francis leaned back into the house and called up the stairs to him.

Within a minute, Jude came down, his sandy hair almost brown when it was wet. "Twice in as many days, Detective. What can I do for you?"

"You mind if I come in?" she said.

"Sure. You want a coffee, Law?" Francis offered.

"Sounds good, thanks."

She followed the two of them into the kitchen and sat at the table when Jude did.

"You got me thinking last night when you mentioned about the job you do. The case I'm investigating has possible victims right across the country, and I've been killing myself trying to figure out what could possibly link them. It seemed so random to have victims all hundreds, some even thousands, of miles apart. But these things are never random. There's always something that connects the dots, if you like."

"So what did you want to know from me?" he asked.

Francis set mugs of hot coffee down in front of them both and then sat opposite, nursing her own drink. She was clearly concerned.

"I'm wondering if someone connected to the warehouses is responsible. Maybe another traveler, someone else who lives out of their RV, who might also have a connection to Sandtown that we're not aware of yet. How many people would you say live that way?"

"I don't know," he replied. "Probably thousands. But not everyone works full time, like I do. Plenty do part-time shifts. Lots of people take on the job but then can't keep up and decide it's not for them."

"I see."

If they were looking for one person out of a possible thousand, that didn't help narrow things down much. But this was also someone who had a connection with Sandtown.

Someone like Jude.

"Where were you the night of the fire, Jude?" she asked.

"I don't know. Here, I guess."

"Can anyone else confirm that?"

"I can," Francis interrupted. "He was here with me, all night."

Jude narrowed his eyes at Lawrey. "Why are you asking that? I thought I wasn't a suspect."

"You're not. They're standard questions. Did you know either of the victims, Emily Clark and Stephan Porter?"

"No."

"Are you sure?" She found a photograph of the couple on her phone and placed it in front of him.

"No, I already told you I didn't."

"We don't know them," Francis insisted, "and Jude was here the night of the fire. And anyway, why on earth would Jude want to hurt two people he didn't even know? It doesn't make sense."

None of this case was making much sense to her.

"When you were working away, did you ever hear people talking about making porn movies?"

Francis paled. "What kind of question is that!"

"A relevant one." She turned back to Jude. "Well, did you? In particular, violent ones?"

"No, I didn't. Jesus. Violent porn movies? This is hardly polite conversation for a sunny Saturday morning."

Lawrey shrugged. "Sorry, just doing my job."

Francis and Jude exchanged a glance, and Francis reached out and took her husband's hand.

There wasn't much more Lawrey could say, so she rose to standing, leaving her coffee untouched.

"Thank you both for your time. If there's anything else you think of, will you give me a call?"

She dropped her business card on the table. Despite what they'd said, she couldn't shake the feeling that there was more going on than they were letting on.

"I'll see you out," Francis said.

Lawrey allowed herself to be guided out of the house, and she went back to her car.

She needed to get an inventory of exactly where Jude had worked over the past twelve months. Something in her gut told her that they'd match up with the locations the burned bodies had been found.

It might be a Saturday, but Lawrey still went into the station. There was too much to do to warrant a day off.

The first thing she did was contact the company Jude worked for to get a roster of exactly where he'd worked and when. It didn't take long for the company to provide it, but, when it came through, her stomach sank.

He wasn't at the locations at the same time as the bodies had been burned. It couldn't be him. In the case of Lizzy

McAllister, he was over a thousand miles away when her body was found.

Dammit. Maybe she should have done that before she went around to his place. She'd been so sure, though. What was she missing?

She also requested a list of their employees who had connections with Sandtown or the local area but was told they had thousands of people on their books and it would take some time for them to compile one.

That was fine. She'd be waiting, she told them.

By mid-morning, Abel joined her.

"Hey," she said. "I didn't think you'd be in today."

"I've been over at the funeral place, making arrangements for next week. Thought I'd swing by here and see if you needed any help. I don't much like being home by myself."

"What about Suze and Grace?"

"I don't think they like being there either, especially not after the break-in yesterday. It's not easy being hit by memories everywhere you turn."

"I understand."

She filled him in on what she'd been doing.

"Jude's got a clean record anyway," Abel said. "What made you think it might be him?"

"I don't know. He seemed shifty when I was asking him about it. Like he was hiding something."

"Police make some people nervous."

"Yeah, but then there was the connection with Portland, Oregon, and the way he tried to lie about it."

"It wasn't a lie. The site where he was staying was in Washington State."

"Okay, but it felt like a misdirection." She tapped her pen against her teeth. "I think I want to speak to the parents of the other girls who were killed, find out if either of them mentioned being around the warehouse or hanging out with people who worked there, or who lived the RV life. Can you take Lizzie McAllister's parents and I'll speak to Heather's?"

"No problem, Law."

Lawrey took a moment to look up the phone numbers from their files and then placed a call to Heather Heath's parents. She got hold of Heather's mother, introduced herself, and offered her condolences, and then got straight down to questioning.

"This might sound like a strange question, but was Heather ever involved with anyone from the warehouse situated on the Washington State border? Did she ever work there herself? Was there anyone she mentioned, perhaps a seasonal worker who liked to travel?"

"No one in particular. She did used to hang out with some people who lived in their RVs, though. RV nomads, she used to call them. I think she liked the idea of the freedom. All that traveling, meeting new people. It seemed dangerous to me, though, especially as a young woman traveling on her own. She insisted that lots of women lived that kind of life. She said there was even a community for church and that everyone watched out for each other."

Lawrey sat straighter. "Heather was religious?"

"Oh, yes. We've always been churchgoers. Honestly, I think it's one of the only things that's gotten us through all

of this. We've had our faith to hold on to, and knowing tha
Heather was with God gave us such comfort." Thick tear
filled her voice. "Except, all that time when I told mysel
Heather was with God, she wasn't, was she? She was with
some monster who snatched her and burned some othe
poor girl's body in her bed. She was actually alive, and in he
own version of Hell. Believing she was with God was a lie."

"I'm so sorry, Mrs. Heath."

There was nothing else Lawrey could say to offer th
poor woman any comfort. Often, family members believed
their loved one to still be alive, even after it was clear they'
been killed, especially when a body wasn't found to drill i
home to them. But in this case, things had been the othe
way around, and they'd grieved over a body who wasn't th
person they thought.

"Would you excuse me, Mrs. Heath? Something ha
come up."

"Yes, of course,"

"And I really am very sorry for your loss."

She ended the call and glanced over at Abel's desk. H
was still on the phone, so she scribbled down a note an
carried it over. She stuck it right under his nose to make sur
he saw it.

Was Lizzy religious?

He asked the question to Lizzy's family and then nodde
at Lawrey, his eyes wide.

Maybe she was wrong about this, but hadn't Pastor Sau
Payne, the pastor who was working out of Sandtown, sai
that he moved around a lot? He might not have
connection to the warehouses, but then maybe she'd bee

wrong about that. They did have thirty locations, after all. That covered a fair part of the country.

The moment Abel ended the call, she was already waiting, keys in hand.

"Heather Heath's mother said she was religious, that she was part of the church community. When I was in Sandtown, Pastor Saul Payne said he'd moved around a lot. I think we need to find out exactly where he was before he came to Sandtown."

Abel frowned. "You think he might have had something to do with this?"

"I think I missed something, and I'm kicking myself for not following this up sooner," she said. "But why did a pastor convince an older biker to burn down the trailer of a young couple?"

Chapter Thirty-Five

The sun was blazing by the time they reached the small wooden chapel on the outskirts of Sandtown.

Lawrey didn't even know if they'd find the pastor there. He might have run off again.

But they found him at the front of the church, praying. If he had anything to do with these young girls' deaths, she thought he'd have to do a hell of a lot more than pray.

"Detectives," he said, when he heard them enter and turned around to greet them. "What can I do for you?" He got to his feet and brushed down the front of his clothes.

"We have a few more questions for you, if that's all right?" Lawrey said, though she intended to ask the questions, whether he liked it or not.

"Of course." He gestured for them to take a seat in the pews. "Whatever I can do to help."

Lawrey took a seat beside the pastor, and Abel sat in the pew in front.

"You've been moving around a lot over this past year or so," Lawrey commented.

"That's right. I go where I'm needed."

Where had she heard that before?

"Can I show you something?"

"Sure."

She pushed a photograph of the map with markers on it in front of him. "Each of these locations have had girls killed and their bodies burned. I highly suspect that if I request your bank or phone records, I'll discover that you've been in the same places around the same time."

His whole body went rigid, and the color drained from his face. "I didn't kill those girls."

"No? Can you prove that? Because right now, it's not looking good."

"Isn't it your job to prove that I *did* kill them? Because I already told you, I have an alibi for the night Emily was killed. A strong alibi. I was at Bible study with lots of other people. I already told you that."

"Here's the thing, though. Emily wasn't killed, was she? She was taken and the body of another girl put in her place."

"I don't know anything about that."

"That's where I think you're lying to me. Tell me why you were in the same areas as these poor women who ended up raped and murdered and their bodies burned. There's no point in denying it now, Saul. You know we're going to get proof."

"I wasn't in any of those places when those girls were killed or even taken. I'd moved on by then."

She paused, cocked her head. "How do you know that?"

He stuttered. "Wh-what?"

"How do you know you'd moved on by then? I haven't given you the times or dates of their deaths."

His pale face suddenly flushed with color. "Well...I...uhhh."

"Don't bullshit me, Saul. I can smell it a mile off. If you're right that you weren't in the areas at the time these girls went missing or were burned, then you can't be charged with kidnapping, or raping or murdering them, can you?"

"I haven't done that to anyone!" he cried. "I wouldn't."

She believed herself to be a good judge of character, and honestly, she'd have said he didn't have it in him. But he was involved, she was sure of that.

"Why did you tell Hella Billy to burn down the trailer?"

"What? I didn't."

She ran her tongue over her teeth. "You want to come with me to find out why he's lying then?"

The skinny man blanched. "No, no. We don't need to do that. Okay, I might have mentioned something to Billy, but I didn't think he'd do it while someone was still inside. I just wanted to get Stephan out of Sandtown. I thought they'd help get Emily away from him, like they had before."

"Why did you want Stephan out of the way?"

Stephan was into some messed-up stuff." He almost wailed the words. "He'd gotten into this terrible snuff pornography because of his brother."

"His brother?" Lawrey remembered that they'd learned Stephan had a half-brother, but they hadn't been able to track him down. "Who is Stephan's brother?"

"I don't know."

She slammed her hand down on the pew in front of them, and he jumped.

"Don't fucking lie to me. You knew those girls, didn't you? You knew the previous victims. You got close to them, the same way you got close to Emily. Tell me why."

He broke down. "I never wanted to do it. You have to understand that. I wouldn't rape or murder anyone. I-I don't even like girls that way."

"So tell me," she said, softening her tone. "I can't help you if you keep lying to me, Saul. But if you help me catch whoever did this, then I'll put a good word in with the judge."

"Everyone will know."

She shook her head. "I can't help that."

"No, I don't mean about the girls. I mean everyone will find out about what I am."

"I don't understand."

"He has a video of me." Saul covered his face with his hands. "With a young man. Only he wasn't a young man. He was a boy. But I didn't know that at the time, I swear I didn't. He told me that it's what everyone expects of someone like me. A pastor abusing boys. But it wasn't like that, I promise. The boy told me he was eighteen, and I believed him. I mean, he did seem young, I'll admit that, but what reason did he have to lie?"

"Someone filmed the two of you together? How? Where?"

"In an alleyway outside a club in San Francisco." He sniffed and swiped at his cheeks. "The video footage...it doesn't exactly make me appear...gentle."

"You're saying you were rough with this young man?"

"He asked me to be like that. He said it was his kink. But you can see how this would make me look? All the blackmailer wanted was a favor, that was it, and when he told me what it was, it didn't seem like that big of a deal."

"What was the favor?" she asked.

"He wanted me to find girls. Young, blonde, blue-eyed. Not too tall, not too short. He definitely had a type that he wanted to know about, and that's all he asked, for me to befriend them and find out a bit about them. Nothing more. I didn't do anything wrong."

Lawrey wasn't so sure about that. "Were these girls being picked to be the victim of these snuff movies?"

He threw up both hands. "I don't know anything about that."

"Oh, come on. Don't give me that. You told Hella Bill that you thought Stephan was into stuff like that, and you had his trailer burned. What did you think was going to happen to those girls after you pointed at them?"

"I don't know. I didn't want to think about it."

"Well, you're going to have to fucking think about it. Girls are dead. You're supposed to be a man of God, but instead you allowed this to happen right under your nose. No, you didn't just allow it, you enabled it, all to save your own reputation."

He broke down, his shoulders shaking. "I'm sorry. I'm so sorry."

It was too late for him to be sorry. Three girls, that they knew of so far, had been kidnapped and raped and possibly murdered, and their deaths filmed to give perverse satisfaction to whoever was willing to pay to watch it happen. Their bodies were then burned so badly they were unidentifiable.

"Who is 'he', Saul? Who took the video? Who's been blackmailing you with it. Is it Jude Knight?"

He frowned and sat back. "Jude? No, I don't know anyone called Jude."

"Who then?

"His name is Gordon Hayes."

The name hit her like a punch. "Francis's father?"

"I don't know who Francis is either."

She remembered how Francis had told her that her father had gotten Jude the job at the warehouse. Why hadn't she considered him?

Shit.

Her thoughts went to when Carol Hayes had told her how Gordon had been around more than normal now he was back in town. How he'd checked out the noises she'd been hearing.

Her heart lurched. Was that the cause of the noises Carol Hayes had been hearing? Was Gordon holding a girl captive on Carol's property?

She turned to her partner. "Abel, I think I know where Emily might be."

She could be wrong, but with Saul's statement, it seemed to her that there was little other explanation.

Chapter Thirty-Six

S he drove back to Calrock with Abel in the passenger seat and Pastor Payne in cuffs in the back. She wasn't completely sure what they'd charge him with yet—conspiracy to kidnap, perhaps?

Abel was on the phone, putting together a team to search Carol Haye's property and getting things in motion to get a search warrant. It was the weekend, so things tended to take longer, but if there was any possibility Emily Clark was still alive somewhere on that property, they didn't have a moment to waste.

At the station, she handed Pastor Payne—who was still crying—over to be processed.

They also needed a warrant for Gordon Hayes' arrest.

It had rocked her. Was he really behind this? She'd met him on a number of occasions, and he had always seemed like an amenable kind of guy. She never thought he'd be into something so sordid.

Did he have a connection to Sandtown other than his mother? The place had been a good setting to dispose of a couple of bodies. Perhaps he'd thought that people would have been less likely to ask questions about a couple of Sanders. But if that was the case, what was Stephan's involvement in all of this?

The whole thing felt too big to be down to only one man

Lawrey got her hands on a map of Carol Hayes' property

She hadn't realized how big it was, how far out the boundaries extended. Right out into the desert. They were going to need to cover all of it in the search for Emily.

The warrant came through, and Lawrey set her team in motion.

It didn't take long for the convoy of vehicles to drive to the Hayes' property.

Carol's eyes went round at the sight of all the armed police on her doorstep.

"Where's Gordon?" Law asked her.

"What's going on?" She strained her neck to peer around Lawrey at her colleagues.

"Please, Carol, we need to know where Gordon is. Has he been round here today?"

They'd already sent armed officers around to Gordon's home address, but there had been no sign of him there. They'd search the place, too, to make sure he wasn't keeping Emily there. He was married, though, so unless his wife was also in on things, or else he was very good at hiding a grown woman in his own home, it would be unlikely he'd have kept her there.

She clutched her hand to the collar of her blouse. "I don't know. I haven't seen him. Is he all right? Has something happened?"

Lawrey hated that this poor lady was going to find out exactly what sort of man her son was. She empathized. While Tommy had never done anything as terrible as Gordon Hayes, he'd still broken her heart time and time again.

"I'm sorry, Carol, but we have a warrant to search these premises, including all your outbuildings and the house and the land."

Carol's chin trembled. "A warrant? Why?"

She didn't have to explain any of this to Carol, but she felt she owed it to her. Poor Carol hadn't done anything wrong, or at least they didn't think she had. There was the possibility that she knew exactly who and what her son was, however, and was helping to cover things up for him.

"A young woman is missing. We have reason to believe she's being held here."

"What? No, that's not possible. I would have known if there was a young woman here."

Carol stepped back as police swept across her home. The majority of their efforts were on the outbuildings.

"We need the external properties all searched. When was the last time you went out to the outbuildings, Carol?"

"I'm not sure. I don't go out there. My mobility isn't so good. I'm worried about falling."

"How about you take a seat, and I'll get one of my officers to make you an iced tea. We'll try to be out of your hair in no time."

She wasn't sure if that was strictly true, but it was the best she could do. If Carol's home proved to be a crime scene, then Carol would be asked to leave it completely while they got forensics in.

She told her team to be respectful of Carol's belongings and then let them get on with their job. As much as Carol's distress bothered her, finding Emily alive was more important.

maiden name? They didn't necessarily have to keep the same names."

"It's a possibility. We need to find proof. But if that is the case, then what's their connection to Gordon Hayes?"

"I wish I could tell you."

A rush of blood pumped through her veins, an urge that they needed to move.

"I don't think Emily is being kept here," she announced, getting everyone's attention. "We need to go back to Sandtown."

Chapter Thirty-Seven

I t was hot. So hot.

No one had brought Emily any water or food since she'd tried to escape. She didn't even have the bucket to pee in anymore. Not that she needed to pee. Her blood was like sludge in her veins. Her head pounded.

By far, the worst pain radiated from her foot, however. It was swollen to twice its usual size and was literally black and blue. A couple of her toes stuck out at a strange angle, and she didn't dare touch them.

She didn't even know why they bothered to keep the door locked anymore. It wasn't as though she was going anywhere. She'd seen on her small excursion that there was no one nearby to help, nowhere to run to, and it wasn't as though she was going to be doing much running. Even if she hadn't managed to smash up her foot on a boulder, she didn't think she had it in her to move. Lifting her head off the floor took every ounce of strength she had left.

She was going to die in here. It wasn't even a question anymore.

If only she hadn't left her father the way she had. He hadn't deserved that. Why had she let Stephan convince her it was the right thing to do? She'd never regretted anything so badly.

She wanted to cry, but she was too dehydrated to form tears.

Above the hum of the generator, another sound met her ears.

Was that an engine? Was he coming back for her? They'd never driven the truck so close to the building before.

Emily willed herself to die faster.

Better that than she ended up in the hands of those men.

Chapter Thirty-Eight

Leaving a couple of officers in place at the outbuilding where the makeshift film studio had been assembled, she pulled her team back together to inform them of the change in location. She really hoped she was right about this one and that they weren't too late. If Gordon had a head start on them, he'd be there already, and they had no idea where Landon Hawkins was.

"We need to put out a BOLO for Landon Hawkins. I believe he's involved in the kidnapping of Emily Clark, and the murders of Heather Heath, Lizzy McAllister, and possibly Stephan Porter, too."

Lawrey had got one of her team back in the office to run a check on the name Landon Hawkins, and it had been revealing. An obituary for Stephan's mother revealed both Landon's name, and that of her ex-husband, Gordon Hayes.

It turned out the making of snuff porn movies was a real fucked-up family affair.

"We have our connection," she told Abel. "Landon Hawkins is Gordon's son from a previous marriage, a marriage to Stephan Porter's mother, Lily Hawkins. She took the name Porter when she married Stephan's father."

Abel's eyebrows shot up. "Holy shit."

Did Francis even know about her half-brother? It was going to break her heart when she found out what her father had been up to.

"Where does he live?" Abel asked.

"Landon owns a plot of land about a mile east of Sandtown. It's not even residential, but from what I can tell, there's a structure on the property."

"You think that's where Emily is?"

"Yeah, I do. We need a warrant ASAP, but I'm not waiting around for it. We need to get this team there right now. If there's any chance either Gordon or Landon know we're on to them, they might be going there right now to dispose of Emily. You know what they say about no body, no crime? If that's the way they're thinking, with there being so little physical evidence in the other murders, they might drive her into the middle of the desert and leave her there."

"Is it possible Gordon spotted us all heading to his mother's place?"

Lawrey thinned her lips. "Yeah, it's definitely possible."

"You don't think Carol would have warned him that police are looking for him?"

She shook her head. "We've had officers with her the whole time. I don't think she'd have the chance."

As soon as she'd briefed the team, she jumped in her car, with Abel in the passenger seat. She pulled out of Carol's property and headed for the desert road linking Calrock with Sandtown—the same road she'd been driven off.

She thought of the black truck. Had it belonged to Landon? She'd assumed Hella Billy was behind all of that, but if Landon had come into work and spotted her questioning Billy, he might have decided to take things into his own hands to warn her off.

As crazy as it sounded, she was at least relieved to know that it hadn't belonged to someone who was linked to her

father and his abuse. Criminals she could catch, but secre
victims were something else altogether.

The police convoy drove fast. They kept their sirens of
not wanting to alert anyone to their arrival.

They reached Landon's property. An outbuilding, muc
like the one at Carol's place, only smaller, sat on the dust
red land. Heat shimmered off the corrugated iron roof. I
that was where they'd been keeping Emily, Lawrey feared fo
what sort of condition the girl would be in, assuming she wa
even still alive.

The door stood ajar, and Lawrey's hope of finding th
girl unharmed faded. If they'd left the door open, didn't tha
mean they were too late?

Police jumped out and ran toward the building, weapon
drawn to cover themselves and each other.

Lawrey climbed out of the car, too, but in her gut, sh
already knew they wouldn't find anyone. The air was hot, s
hot it seemed to scorch the inside of her lungs every time sh
inhaled.

This wasn't good. This really wasn't good.

One of her officers checked inside and then gave a shou
"It's clear. There's no one in here." He paused and then adde
"But it looks like there has been."

She wanted to scream. It was too late. They'd lost her.

With her hands knotted in her hair, she turned a slo
circle, taking in the vast expanse of desert and the blue sk
decorated with wisps of white cloud.

In the distance, a dust cloud signaled a vehicle drivir
out into the wasteland.

Her heart lurched.

"Over there!" she shouted, already spinning on her heels and running back to her car.

Abel was already standing beside the passenger door. He followed her line of sight and then spun back toward the car and got inside.

Fuck. Were they too late?

Had they already killed Emily and were now disposing of the body?

Around her, her colleagues did the same. If it was the same black truck that had run her off the road, then it was built for off-roading. Would they be able to catch up?

One thing the driver of the truck didn't have, that Lawrey and her team did, was experience of high-speed chases. Plus they outnumbered them, five vehicles to one.

Lawrey stamped her foot down on the accelerator, desperate to pick up speed. The wheels spun on the loose ground but then caught, and with a screech, they were moving.

Six vehicles all raced across the desert, dust billowing behind them.

Her heart pounded. Where would this end?

Lawrey drove as fast as she dared. Beside her, Abel had drawn his weapon, waiting for an opportunity to take one of the sons of bitches down.

She was gaining on the truck. They bumped and bounced and rocked across the uneven terrain.

"They're not going to stop," Abel said. "We're going to need to make them."

She understood what he was saying. With no roads out here, it wasn't as though they could try to cut them off or barricade the way. The truck would be able to swerve around them. The only way to stop them was by making the truck as immobile as possible.

"Do whatever you have to," she said.

"You're going to need to get me closer."

Lawrey jammed her foot down harder. She leaned forward, curled over the steering wheel as though that could somehow make them go faster. Whatever she was doing was working, as they gained ground.

Abel slid down the window and aimed his weapon.

Shooting a moving target wasn't easy.

He squeezed off a shot but missed. "Fuck," he cursed.

"Keep trying."

He repeated the attempt, and this time hit one of the truck's back tires. The vehicle went into a skid. Lawrey's heart all but crawled into her throat. What if the truck rolled and Emily was still alive, but the accident killed her? Lawrey would never forgive herself.

But it didn't roll. The back end swung from side to side as the driver tried to keep control.

One of the men leaned out of the passenger window with a rifle and fired shots back at them. Lawrey ducked as much as possible while still keeping an eye on the road, but the shots went wide.

Fuck.

The truck's back tire was completely flat, flapping around, so they were driving on the metal rim. Their speed slowed, and she knew they'd get them now. They were outnumbered.

She desperately tried to see if Emily was with them. She prayed the girl was still alive.

The truck slowed and then stopped.

Both the driver and passenger doors opened, and the men jumped out. They tried to cover themselves, firing back at the police, but trying to run and shoot wasn't an easy thing to do.

Where did they even think they were running to? Under the hot sun, and with no shade or water, they'd quickly die out here.

A part of Lawrey thought they didn't deserve anything better.

Gordon Hayes was older and slower, and his son quickly left him behind.

"Police!" the officer closest to him shouted. "Drop the gun and get on your knees."

Realizing he had no choice, and that if he didn't stop, he was most likely going to end up with a bullet inside him, Gordon finally slowed. He lifted both hands in the air and let go of the gun. One of the armed officers picked up the weapon, and then Gordon was pushed face-first into the hot desert sand to be cuffed.

One of her colleagues shot Landon in the leg. He let out a cry and fell to the ground. Police were on him in an instant, swarming over him. They kicked his gun out of reach and pinned him to the ground, wrenching his hands behind his back.

Seeing her colleagues were dealing with the men, Lawrey threw herself out of the car and ran for the truck. If Emily was in there and was still alive, she hadn't made any attempt to make a run for it. The idea that they were too late sickened her. Was she about to find Emily's body?

Lawrey reached the vehicle. Both the driver and passenger doors stood open, but this was a four-door truck and had second-row seating.

She yanked open the rear door closest to her and gave a cry of relief.

The girl lay on the backseat, her arms and legs bound, a piece of tape across her mouth. Her eyes were wide and wild with terror, her face filthy, tearstains streaked in the dirt.

"Emily, I'm with the police. You're safe now."

Lawrey climbed into the truck with her and carefully removed the tape from her mouth and then worked on the bindings of her arms and legs. The girl cried, her whole body shaking, until Lawrey had finally freed her.

"It's okay," Lawrey said. "I've got you. I've got you."

The girl clutched at Lawrey, sobbing against her chest.

Lawrey caught sight of the girl's black and swollen foot. "We need to get a medic over here!"

"My dad," Emily sobbed. "I want my dad."

"He's staying in town. We'll get him to meet us at the hospital, okay? He's going to be so happy to know you're safe."

"I'm so sorry," she managed. "I'm so sorry I ran away. I should never have left without telling him where I was going."

"It's okay. Don't worry about that now." Lawrey smoothed Emily's dirty hair with her hand, trying to offer her some comfort.

The girl gazed up at her with bloodshot, tear-filled eyes. "What about Stephan? What happened to Stephan? Is he all right? I can't remember what happened."

Lawrey's stomach knotted. So Emily had no idea what Stephan had been planning with his half-brother and Gordon Hayes. She still cared about the bastard.

"I'm sorry, Emily," Lawrey said and explained everything.

Chapter Thirty-Nine

Lawrey pulled on the floral summer dress and tried not to grimace at her reflection.

It wasn't the sort of thing she normally wore—especially not to a funeral—but Abel and his daughters had insisted that no one wore black. They wanted the event to be a celebration of Marlene's life, not a time for sorrow.

While Lawrey appreciated the sentiment, she didn't think it was going to be as easy as that. How could they not be sad when they'd lost someone as wonderful as Marlene had been?

Everyone was going to be there. The whole town wanted to be involved, and Abel had felt the more people, the better. It wasn't what Lawrey would have done, but she kept her mouth shut and let him do what he thought was best. Seeing the number of people whose lives Marlene had touched gave him comfort. He'd even invited Tommy over from Sandtown, and Tommy had promised he'd come.

Despite the brevity of the day, Lawrey still found her thoughts going back over the case. A week had passed since they'd rescued Emily and arrested Gordon Hayes and Landon Hawkins, but it wasn't over yet.

Gordon Hayes had remained tight-lipped about the possibility of there being any more victims, but Lawrey was certain the three they'd identified weren't all. Now they knew that Gordon had been the person responsible for kidnapping the girls and setting things in play, they were able to use his locations to narrow down the cases they suspected as being his.

His son, Landon, had been the one responsible for the movie aspect of the crime. They'd unearthed some of the films and discovered Landon was also the person who starred in them, together with whichever poor girl had been taken. It was he who'd ultimately murdered the girl in the end. The movies they'd found on his laptop had made for horrific viewing.

The pastor lured the girls in, built their confidence, learned what was needed about them, and Gordon was the one who took them to be filmed being raped and murdered by his son.

Landon folded quickly enough. He hadn't been happy about Gordon killing Stephan, his half-brother. Stephan had been threatening to go to the police if they laid a hand on Emily. Gordon hadn't thought it was worth risking the business to keep him around and had been worried Stephan was going to take off with Emily again. He believed Stephan would have dragged the two of them down with him, and letting him live hadn't been worth that risk.

Emily went back home with her father.

It was going to take many hours with a therapist to work through what she'd experienced. The shock of finding out about Stephan's involvement had done a number on the girl's ability to trust anyone. Her father had offered to sell the house and the business and move anywhere they wanted to get a fresh start. All he wanted was for his daughter to be safe.

Lawrey had gone to see Raye Diante a few days after everything had gone down. He still wasn't speaking, but he'd seemed relieved to hear that Landon was most likely going to be spending the rest of his life behind bars. Lawrey didn't know the full truth of what had happened, and she wasn't sure she ever would, but she'd noticed Raye had been wearing a wig again and that he was starting a new painting.

Lawrey traveled to the church on her own. Abel and his daughters were standing outside the main entrance, greeting people as they arrived. Not everyone was able to fit inside the church for the service, but those closest to Marlene were there.

Her sister, together with Eddie, and Lawrey's niece, Cara, and her nephew, Noah, sat with Lawrey's mom. Lawrey gave them all hugs and kisses.

"Any sign of Tommy?" she asked.

Maddie shook her head. "No, sorry, Law. Not yet."

They settled in for the service, and there wasn't a dry eye in the house. Beautiful hymns were sung, and both Marlene's daughters spoke about their love for their mother.

As the service ended, the heavy wooden church door opened, and Lawrey glanced back to see Tommy slip inside. She caught his eye, and he gave her a half-smile. She was glad he'd come. She hadn't seen him since her birthday, and her instincts told her that something wasn't quite right with him, but she didn't know what.

She tried to tell herself that he was an adult now and was allowed to have his own privacy. Just because he had problems didn't mean that she needed to be involved. It wasn't that easy, however, letting go.

After the service, everyone went to the nearby park for the wake. Anyone who wanted to come had to bring a potluck, placing it on a trestle table, to be shared among the community Marlene had loved so much. It was a beautiful day, and quickly Lawrey realized Abel had been right. There was an atmosphere of a summer cookout instead of a wake.

It was exactly what Marlene would have wanted.

News of the way Lawrey had helped save the young woman from Sandtown had also got around the community fast. As much as commiserations about Marlene, she found people were coming up and telling her what a great job she'd done. No one could believe something so terrible had been happening right under their noses. Even Mitch Pearce begrudgingly came up to her to shake her hand.

Lawrey helped herself to a drink and then looked around for her son.

He wouldn't normally be seen dead at big events in town, but she guessed this one was different. Tommy had known Marlene pretty much his whole life, so it was understandable that he'd want to pay his respects.

She spotted him, standing beneath a tree with Abel. Something about his body language sent her heart twisting. The furtive way he was hunched over. It reminded her of the evening of her birthday in the bar. She'd been too distracted then by the case to give it any more thought, but she wasn't now.

Lawrey made her way over to them. "Hey, you two. What's going on?"

Tommy had his sulky face on, his foot scuffing the dirt. "Nothing."

She looked to her partner. "Abel?"

"It's nothing, Law."

"Doesn't seem like nothing to me, and I hate when people are keeping secrets from me. You want to tell me what's going on between the two of you?"

Abel shot Tommy a look, tight-lipped, his nostrils flared. "Go on, Tommy."

"You said you wouldn't say anything."

"If you brought it back. You only brought back a fraction."

Her confusion deepened. "What are you both talking about? Brought what back?"

"It's better coming from you, Tommy," Abel said.

Lawrey folded her arms across her chest. She jutted out her hip, already bracing herself for what was to come. Hadn't she been here numerous times before? Tommy had screwed up again, and this time it had to do with Abel. She was protective of Abel right now. Normally, it was Tommy she felt that way about, but Abel had suffered enough. It was her responsibility to protect him from her son.

"Tell me, Tommy. Right now."

He wouldn't meet her eye. "I stole Marlene's leftover meds."

Her jaw dropped. "You did what?"

"I broke into the house and took the morphine and the fentanyl. Abel came home early and caught me, or at least he recognized me."

"I recognized his bracelet," Abel said, nodding at the leather cuff around Tommy's wrist. "I didn't at the time, but then I saw him that night of your birthday."

"Jesus Christ, Tommy. That was you?"

She couldn't believe her own son was responsible for the break-in. Actually—yes, she could. This was exactly the sort of shit she should expect from him.

"And you didn't arrest him the night of my birthday?" he asked Abel. "Because you should have."

"I told him if he brought it all back, then I wouldn't say anything. He promised he would, but he's only returned half of it."

Tommy stared at the ground. "I'd already sold some, what was I supposed to do? It's not like I could get it back."

Lawrey ground her teeth. "Sold some? Or taken some?"

He shrugged one shoulder. "Half and half."

"For fuck's sake." She shook her head and glanced away, not even wanting to look at him. How could he have done that, right after they'd lost Marlene, too? The kid had no fucking morals. What had she done to make him that way? Or was it more nature than nurture? Was he too much like his grandfather—not that the two of them had ever met?

She'd always believed in reform, but what if she was wrong? Maybe Tommy would never change because it was simply how he was made up. It was in his genes. And if it was part of his genetics, didn't that mean it was part of hers, too?

She turned back to him. "Come on, Tommy. Get in the car."

"What? Why?"

"I'm arresting you for burglary and possession of class A narcotics with intent to supply."

"You can't be fucking serious?"

"Law—" Abel started, but she put her hand out to sto[p] him.

"Don't, Abel. He's not getting away with this shi[t] Maybe I looked away a few too many times. God knows, I'v[e] done something wrong."

They were drawing attention, people glancing ove[r] nudging their friends and family members and nodding i[n] her direction.

Patrick noticed something was happening and made h[is] way over. "Lawrey? Tommy? What's going on?"

"I'm taking him down to the station. He broke int[o] Abel's and stole Marlene's leftover opiates."

"He did what?"

"Maybe we were too soft on him growing up? I don[t] fucking know. But enough is enough. If you have to spen[d] the rest of your life in prison, then so be it."

He wouldn't be spending the rest of his life in priso[n] With the charges against him, combined with his previo[us] record, he'd probably get a sentence of at least a few years.

"Then I'll deny it. You've got no proof. Just two co[ps] trying to set me up."

She rolled her eyes. "Sure. Like anyone is going to belie[ve] that."

Abel placed a hand on her shoulder. "You don't have t[o] do this, Law. It can stay between us."

"You're wrong, Abel. I *do* have to. Come on, Tommy."

As she marched her son toward her car, she sense[d] people watching. She peered through the crowd and caug[ht] someone's eye.

Joe Martinez lifted his hand in a half wave and offered her what appeared to be a smile of sympathy. Did that mean she was forgiven? She realized she'd screwed up badly when it came to Joe, but then didn't she seem to screw up everywhere?

No. She reminded herself of the moment when Emily had fallen into her father's arms, the tears they'd all shared. She didn't screw up everything. There were some things she got right.

Nothing was forever.

This difficult moment, just like so many that had come before her, would pass. They'd all suffered. Abel had lost his wife. She was having to arrest her son. Emily would learn how to cope with what she'd been through.

A moment in a storm didn't mean the sun wasn't waiting for them all on the other side.

One day, Tommy would forgive her. Maybe he'd even thank her for this moment.

In the meantime, she would hold fast and focus on what she believed to be right.

Acknowledgements

Thank you, as always, to my editor Emmy Ellis, and to my proofreaders, Jessica Fraser from Finishing by Fraser, Tammy Payne from Book Nook Nuts, and to Jacqueline Beard for always being that much needed final set of eyes. I promise I will get the next books in the post very soon.

Final thanks to you, the reader, for giving this new series a try. I hope you enjoyed it.

Until next time!

MK Farrar

About the Author

M K Farrar had penned more than twenty novels of psychological noir and crime fiction. A British author, she lives in the countryside with her three children and a menagerie of rescue pets.

When she's not writing—which isn't often—she balances out all the murder with baking and binge-watching shows on Netflix.

She can also be emailed at mk@mkfarrar.com. She loves to hear from readers!

• • • •

Get a free book when you sign up to M K Farrar's newsletter
mkfarrar.com

• • • •

Order signed books and exclusive e-Book bundles and audiobook bundles direct from
https://mkfarrarstore.myshopify.com/

Also by the Author

DI Erica Swift Thriller
The Eye Thief
The Silent One
The Artisan
The Child Catcher
The Body Dealer[1]
The Mimic
The Gathering Man
The Only Witness
The Foundling

• • • •

Detective Ryan Chase Thriller
Kill Chase
Chase Down
Paper Chase
Chase the Dead

• • • •

Crime After Crime
Watching Over Me
Down to Sleep
If I Should Die

• • • •

Standalone Psychological Thrillers

1. https://www.amazon.co.uk/gp/product/B08L6XN1X1/